THE SKULLFACE CHRONICLES
The Unwritten Diary of a Zombie

Dorothy Davies

THE SKULLFACE CHRONICLES
The Unwritten Diary of a Zombie

GRAVESTONE PRESS

A GRAVESTONE PRESS PAPERBACK

ISBN: 978 1 78695 528 9

Gravestone Press
is an imprint of
Fiction4All
www.fiction4all.com

This Edition
Published 2021

Dedication

This book is dedicated, with great affection, to Richard Laymon, who has been a great influence on my horror writing. I also want to mention Mary Shelley whose seminal story 'Frankenstein' is at the very heart of this book. My anti-hero is her wretch, with a few modifications. I hope she would have approved.

The book is also dedicated to Terry Wakelin, rock and anchor as always and to friends who supported me through the writing and put up with the nonsense I bombarded them as I worked. I especially want to mention Ken L Jones and Kevin L Jones, both fine horror writers from Yucaipa, California, who read the book as it progressed and told me to keep going and Todd Ocvirk, film director from Los Angeles, who encouraged me as well. Thank you, thank you; thank you.

Author's Foreword

All the places named in this unwritten diary are real. The businesses are real and so is the County Press. I have been everywhere on the island Skullface went, I know where he rested, where he walked, what windows he gazed into, what shops he frequented. I am fortunate that I don't get the same disbelieving looks he did… not all the time, anyway.

The people, on the whole, are not real. Occasionally we allowed a living person to slip by us; we felt it added verisimilitude to the story to include genuine walking talking working people but mostly the characters are figments of our imagination.

As far as we are aware, Rob Da Bank has never hosted a Zombie Convention at Robin Hill. It might be that, after reading this book, he will decide to have 'zombie' as his fancy dress theme for a Bestival one year… if he does, we just might go.

The Skullface Chronicles

The Unwritten Diary of a Zombie

(Not everyone who comes alive again has mush for a brain...)

On Waking

This earth bound space is very small, not sure how I got into it but here I am. Really, I can't move, can't stretch my arms and legs and my head seems fixed.

How long have I slept?

Slept? Underground? Idiot, what a stupid thought. I have to be dead, surely. Oh, what… I thought I was alone, but the creature who shares the space with me stares through myopic eyes, no doubt trying to work out what I am and why I'm there. I have no answers… In an effort to divert my thoughts; I try working on an escape plan but that – excuse the pun – escapes me.

There are two problems.

The first is, the creature appears to be a mole and I am partly in his chamber.

The second is; I certainly seem to be dead, if my rotting flesh is anything to go by. I can smell it. You never forget the smell of rotting flesh, says he with no experience of such a thing, so how the hell do I know?

Why ask me? I don't know. But then again, how do I know I am rotting?

Well, perhaps the bits falling off as I try to move might provide a clue.

Am I talking to myself, or to you, oh mole? He stares at me as if petrified. Probably is. Not every day you go to your chamber and find a face staring back at you, is it?

A shocking thought has occurred to me. The mole has interfered with my eternal rest! Even in the pitch black of this subterranean home I can see his agitation and he surely senses mine.

I'm not staying here. I want out! I want to drag this body, rotting or otherwise, outside into the air. I want to feel sun, see shade; see people…

Oh. Another shocking thought. They won't want to see me. Foolish creature, why had I not thought of that?

Because, oh foolish creature, you are fresh woken from sleep – or death - by a mole, of all things. You cannot think rationally.

Yet.

But you will. Oh yes, you will…

Meantime, whilst you learn to think rationally for once, meditate on why you should be bothered by your eternal rest being disturbed. What does it matter? Is there a reason you should be bothered?

Oh yes, I want –

Say it.

What do I want? Why have I woken up? What has disturbed me? Something pounding in what passes for a brain…

The word, the concept, the thought of -

Revenge.

Ha! She thought I would be forever buried, for sure! And here I am, awake – just, functioning – just, thinking – probably… the last thing she will ever believe is that I'll come back, stand on the doorstep and demand she let me in. What I will do then is anyone's guess. A lot depends on how rotted I am, if you see what I mean.

Some of me has decomposed: I can't remember my name. Or where I lived. Or where she lives. Or what happened to me. Why am I assuming she killed me?

Now you're being stupid. Why else would you be in some underground space, no coffin, no nice satin to surround you, no head on a pillow… I despair at just how stupid and confused you are. And you want to get out there, in the real world?

Are you ready for that?

No. what I am ready for is food. I hunger, a deep burning hurting clawing hunger.

The mole is no more.

I managed to move an arm, at great risk to the walls of the tunnel I appear to be in, moved and in his shock and petrification, he stood still, foolish animal. Is there such a word as petrification? Probably not, but it fits exactly the way he stood, wide eyed and rigid, as I reached for him.

And now the bones are crushed and splintered, the skin cast aside, the blood, rich and thick, is in my veins. I need energy and sustenance to push myself out of this mole hole. Time for the invisible to become visible, time to emerge into the world.

Do I have the gall to expose myself to the living? It would be fun to try and touch them, see them run… but first I have to get out.

Logic says I am too large for a mole hole. He must have burrowed into my grave.

Poor innocent creature. But the law of nature is the strong will survive. And we are top of the food chain. Even if we are dead. Or I am, anyway. I am, aren't I?

You ought to know. You're the one moving about. Is there breath and pulse and all?

No.

Enough! I have to get out. I am awake and need to be free of this earthly coffin. Not much fun, no satin, no mementoes buried with me. Not only that, it isn't good enough, not by a very long way is it good enough. More to add to my revenge. If I get there. Wherever 'there' is.

I retrieved the skin. I might need a mask.

I don't know why; don't even begin to ask me why. I want a mask. Would you deny me that small thing? After all, here I am, dead and buried and asking nothing of the world but the sticky gory untanned skin of a foolish helpless mole. No, it is not too much to ask.

Look, I'm making moves to get out.

Need to dig.

I can't dig with one hand. Don't want to let go of the moleskin. I can't find my pockets, if I have any. Did she bury me dressed? Or did she take all my clothes to the local Oxfam shop and pretend I'd left home, or something?

How come I can remember her, even her name – or can I? when I can't remember other things, like –

I can't remember.

I wish I knew how long I've been dead. I mean, how much of me is rotted, how much clings to my bones, how much strength I have, can I stand? Walk? Reach out and touch? I might need to hold on…

The person who put me in the grave has the answers. He may think himself invisible, no, impenetrable, no… Forget it. Too much else to think about.

Hold on a minute. Just a minute. He?

He who was shagging she. Him. The blond hunk with the pecs and the abs and the whatever-you-call-it stomach. Him. Damn it to hell, what's his name?

I want revenge!

I'll wish him gallstones, that'll do for now.

My revenge will come later. Time to plan. Ha!

Internal Dialogue

Madam, I come!

Hold on just a moment. Stop it! I just said that! Or something very like that anyway. Damn thoughts invading my mind.

Dead = grave = quiet = what? Eternal life? Ghost existence? But I think, I know I move, earth falls in, so; if I'm one of the living dead, surely I should be grunting and snarling and seeking human brains to eat.

Hold on just a moment – again.

Listen, Skullface, stop it with the repetition. No one wants a repetitive wind up creature, even if it is a zombie.

Rationalise. Realise. Zombies are not supposed to think, allegedly. Here I am, thinking. What went wrong?

Ha! You always were different, Skullface. Always the odd one out. I can remember that much at least.

Shut up chirping, birds! I can't think with all your inane chatter going on. The sun's probably out, go catch a worm or something.

Think. Who am I? Logically…

Oooooooookkkkaaaaayyyyyyy – I have thought. I am an anomaly, a zombie who thinks. Whoo hoo. Madam will be shocked when I get there! Good. I am pretty damn sure she had something to do with my being underground.

Wish I could remember. Her and him, they must have done it together. Got tired of me after all this time, wanted me out of the way. So… when I get out of here I will check my skull, see if they hit me over the head. Seems a bit brutal but then he is, all that bodybuilding stuff, he could do it, no problem. I'm not as big as him. I wasn't as big as him. I am not/was not –

Skullface, shut up.

What jabbed me then? Hold it… a bone! A large bone! I have a tool now… it's not one of mine, I did a quick check. Mine are intact. It's the flesh which isn't. That's soggy and soft and gives with a squishy feel.

Who needs flesh anyway? Let's rid ourselves of it, prance around in our bones instead.

The birds, irritating as they are, invite me out. I'm ready to go.

Hello, world…

But not yet.

It's slow progress.

What's worse is, I've no idea how far underground I am.

Back to that logic thing, Skullface. Use your – as far as I can tell – unbattered head, why don't you? You can't be that far underground; they didn't hire a digger to create a grave, did they? A spade and some muscle is all they had. So keep going, it can't be far.

I hate people who are right all the time.

Crawling, crawling, see me go. Time to get hustling out of here before my bones get weary and decide I have to stop. It's hard work, the damned earth is worse than a coal seam to get through, having only a bone to dig with.

The thought that the world awaits is enough to keep me going, though.

Pause for – breath? Do I then breathe? How strange! How very odd, how nonsensical… I think it's my imagination, I think myself alive when I know well I'm dead.

What etiquette is there for a clapped out zombie, I wonder…

And then I ask, am I indeed a clapped out zombie and if I am, what is one of them? Oh inelegant English, zombie or not, you can do better than that.

I would suggest, Skullface, you stop bitching and wondering and thinking and get digging. Now!

I will, I will…

Could I stitch my flesh back together? Seams down my face and body? Frankenstein and all?

And while I think nonsensical thoughts, the better to dig without being weary, I ask, what etiquette is there for meeting living beings when you are half rotted and half bone…

Hey look, I see daylight! Hallelujah!

How long have I been underground?

Too long, it seems…

Out! Really, really out! Standing up straight, see me stand! See me looking and wondering where the hell I am. And remembering I have a mole's skin in my pocket should I need a mask. Remind me of that, would you? Thanks.

Now tell me, what do I look like? And tell me, how long have I been underground and what is the ratio of decomposition to time spent buried… questions no one is around to answer.

Ha! Skullface, what are the chances of someone being stood right here with enough expertise to work out that ratio: burial x decomposition. I can tell you one ratio that it is: zero/zero.

Point taken. Don't you just hate know-alls?

OK, with no one to tell me what I look like; let me tell you what the world looks like.

Overbright. Everything wears a crown of light that hurts. Colours that shriek. Noises that bang on the ears. Wind that blows the dangling bits which have not fallen off me – yet.

Tears. I realize what I am. Who will want to know me?

Tears. There is still moisture in the body, then. Surprised me, that has. Oh, I smell. The earth is not sterile. It's full of bacteria and crawly things and growing things and decomposing things. Me among them.

I need a bath.

The sound of running water attracts me, puts the idea in my head.

Really? It normally has the opposite effect, Skullface, sends you rushing to the bathroom. You know that.

I wish I didn't argue with myself.

Water. River. Look, see it run, clean and fresh and clear and inviting. I can dump what clothes I still possess right here and walk in and lie down… and let the water run over me and…

Ah, the wonderful feeling.

Hey, I still feel!

No you don't. It's all in your mind. All nerve endings are dead, gone, corrupted, decomposed; out of commission. Gone.

Stop it. You're depressing me. Oh hell and damnation! I'm losing essential components. Look at that! An essential bit of me is floating away downriver! Ah, such sadness, lost forever… worse than that; my crowning achievement is now denied me. I wanted to use it… I wouldn't have impregnated anyone; she accused me of being sterile and was no doubt right. But then again, did anyone test me? They can't now. My chances of fathering a child are gone forever.

It's my fault for wanting that bath. The stream looked inviting and it was easier than breaking into a house and borrowing the bath. The bits of flesh I lost might have clogged up the drain.

Stop thinking about it. That girl you dated back when, the one who went off with the chimney sweep, the one who… she never got pregnant, did she? Ah, but did you ask if she was on the Pill? You were pretty damn naïve those days, Skullface!

Too late to worry about it now. Move on…

If I stand around – dare not jump; might lose more bits – I will dry, surely. If not, oh well, damp clothes. I was told by the other side of my brain, which continues to lecture and argue with me, that I have no feeling anyway. So, does damp matter?

Well, yes, the clothes will be out of shape.

Skullface, what clothes? A rotting shirt and a creased pair of pants? We will conveniently, quietly, treat the undergarments as if they do not exist. Not in their current state anyway. 'Nuff said, right?

Right. For once I agree.

Discoveries

Skullface, we just found out something that is of tremendous benefit to all zombiekind. If you stub your toe it doesn't hurt. From which you could conclude that to hit anything against anything, root, tree, wall, person, will have the same effect. That is, you won't feel it and it won't go nasty on you.

Nothing living, you see, apart from my desire to incite panic and mayhem by walking about and pretending to be alive. Now where did that desire come from? I only want to take revenge on one – no, two – people, not humankind as a whole.

Or do I?

Actually I quite like that idea, the inciting of panic and mayhem. It started a thread of thought that, if I follow it to its logical conclusion, could mean us zombies taking over the world. There are enough of us; after all, no matter which way you look at it, there are more people dead than alive. Because, humans have a habit of dying. Dropping down dead, all colour gone from their faces, all breath gone from their lungs, all…

Shut up, Skullface. You're boring me. So, zombies take over the world, fine, but what would we do with it?

Well, change it, reform it, bring in laws that stop people writing about us in derogatory terms, depicting us as thoughtless, mindless, brain dead individuals in films and books and…

Take all the fun out of horror stories. Right. I can see that happening, Skullface, can't you? I mean, what would the horror writers do then?

Find some other subjects? Or is that too obvious an answer, oh ye who will not let that part of my mind rest? Give it up, you, whoever you are. I wish I could remember your name.

You could find one, Skullface; you can call yourself anything you like. Nameless will do for now.

Well, you see, with all this arguing going on… I am becoming quite attached to the name Skullface. I think I might go with that.

Then you will confuse yourself with which part of your mind is telling you what. Find a name, one you can live with.

One foot in front of the other, moving on… our ambition will be fulfilled, you just wait and see. I will think as I walk… Perceval, how will that do for a name? Sounds elegant, medieval, chivalrous –

And stupid. Try plain old Tom.

I think it's time I stopped thinking.

Way to go, the first living person has run screaming after one look at me. One down, how many to go? Perhaps he thought I was a walking monster or something. Surely I'm not that bad-looking, am I?

I need a mirror. Yes, but that might incite panic in me and that would never do.

What I want to know is; why has no one come in response to his screams? Do they think him insane, perhaps? What's their problem? You see how careful I am in not asking what is his problem?

I know what it is, a hunk of once-living person is tramping his way across this relatively open space and it must look horrendous. Straight out of a horror film. Hey, I could go auction myself –

Audition, Skullface? No one would pay a bent penny for you. Not the way you are now.

What am I now? Dead, for sure, but living, for sure, why else do I walk, think, hunger… oh the hunger; it sits like a craven creature in my guts and screams for fulfillment. I'm busy ignoring it.

My flesh seems to unravel like a pulled thread destroys a garment. I think of myself as whole and then a bit falls off. I lost a little finger a short time ago. Very upsetting. But then, who needs it? Bones are clean and strong and… why don't I believe what I'm saying?

Because although what you're saying is true, it isn't what you want to hear, is it? You want to think yourself a whole living person, instead of a half living one. Am I right or am I right?

Shut up. I don't want to think that route.

I do want to know, though, what happened to the gold ring I had on the finger I lost a short time ago. It was nice; I was incredibly fond of it. Did she strip me of all jewellery, or did he? I mean, I see no signet ring, no watch, no – now, come on, I haven't looked for that particular ring, have I? Could I do that, right out here in the open? Definitely not! Wait for dark. Then see what you can find out, Skullface. But I lay odds, any odds you care to name, she had that one too.

Of course she did. She no longer had a need to tether me with it. Oh the hours, the hours…

Forget it. That's long gone, by the feel of things.

I'm hoarding good thoughts. I'm collecting images half seen, the shadow people; the hunters, those with guns who would bring me down. I am, after all, the biggest oddity some of them have ever seen or will ever see in their pathetic lifetimes. The thoughts twist like clinging vines in my over active mind. I'm hoping they'll obscure the upset and give me the positive, the fact no one's yet stopped me or challenged me as I walk, steady, trying not to lose anything, through what appears to be a recreation area – why is it deserted?

Because the rain is about to fall and there it goes, the heavens open, the torrent crashes as if God is venting his anger on us. He can go right ahead. I've nothing to save, no flesh, no clothes worth worrying about.

Hey Skullface, look, a mirror! Well, a shard anyway. Take a look at your clock, then, poor half-baked zombie, see why they run.

So, I looked and… is it so bad? A bit – lopsided perhaps, that eye could do with pushing back into place but on the whole… better than I thought. Might not need the mole mask. Might throw that away. It's beginning to decompose –faster than I am, actually.

Walk on. Leave the mirror behind, who needs it? I don't. I can see what I need to know from the faces of those I meet, or will meet.

YOu know something? I don't think there are any hunters out there after all. They would have shot me by now. Shot or Tasered or something. No one would leave a monster walking around like me, terrorizing the neighbourhood. The guy with the screams couldn't have made himself sensible enough to talk to anyone about me.

'Yes, sir, of course, sir, a zombie, yes, well, I'll send a patrol car out with a couple of officers to see what we can find. Thank you for reporting it.'

And the paper is filed – in the bin. After all, there are enough strange people walking around not to worry about another one. I could be coming from or going to a fancy dress party, one with a horror theme, right?

So the shadow people…

Skullface, are you losing your mind? Are you seeing things that aren't there?

I wouldn't be surprised. I'm losing most everything else. One bit at a time.

Full Tweed Jacket

Forgive the twisted humour; I couldn't resist it. Sometimes I believe – ha! I should know! that there is a God. Look what was left hanging from a branch. Look what He's given me, a jacket! Not one I would have been seen dead in but what the hell… Look, it's tweed, with that double vent at the back. Classy. Saves some of the bits falling off. Perhaps.

Hey, what did I say about the repetitions, Skullface? Give over with the 'look' word, would you?

The town clock is chiming – what? Damn, lost track of the dongs. Can't be that late, but is it too late to call on Madam? I'm tired; all that exertion. I need to work out what to say when I get there. I want to appear sane.

Insane thoughts. Yes.

It's dawn.

A night leaning against an oak has done wonders for my vitality. Not. No one bothered me; perhaps they think 'what's another eccentric in the park', that is, if people think. I do. It continues to puzzle me. I don't fit the accepted definition of a zombie. But then, history is never entirely accurate, is it? I like being the odd one out, the zombie anomaly. There are worse things to be – a politician, for example, or a banker. I think I said before I am an anomaly as a zombie, but a zombie anomaly works better. Getting poetic in my advanced decay.

Skullface, let's get moving. All this chat won't get him - and her - dead and gone, will it?

Not yet. I don't want to move on just yet. Do you know how long it's been since I saw the dawn? A lifetime. Nothing more or less than a lifetime.

Did me some thinking, you see. Like it or not, I'm going to share the thoughts with you. Heaven knows I have to talk to someone and if there was a guardian angel, he took off for heaven the moment someone – they - stole my life from me, right? I wonder if he got sent back to see me through these final days? Interesting thought. Not one I had during the dark hours, though, I must admit.

I did this:

What's good about being dead: what's bad about being dead?

Bad is – no more sunsets. No more fine food, I miss fillet steak with big fat chips and all. Which reminds me, I really am hungry. No kidding.

No movies, no TV, no books. No fashionable clothes, no music, no car. No freedom to travel. Goodbye Paris, Madrid, New York and all.

No warmth of a home; no snowfall and gorgeous winter days. No summers of colour and light. No autumns of gold and brown, no spring brightness and bunnies.

There's loads more but let's not get morbid here.

Let's go good instead.

Good is – no employer to please. No bills to pay. No insurance and car tax and petrol and stuff like that. Good is, as far as I know, no indigestion. But then I need to eat to find that out for sure. Eat something more substantial than a mole. No church, no priest person to preach at me what I can and can't do. I crossed over and came back; he has no jurisdiction over me anymore.

Hey, look at that long word, Skullface! Congratulations!

And, let's get serious, no threats, no menace, no pain, no hatred and no violence.

I can live without that. For sure.

One final thought which will surely strike deep passionate chords with anyone who reads this unwritten diary – NO DENTIST!!!!!

Does that sound good or does that sound good? Right, I'm all cheered up now.

Ha! Where's my head been all this time? It's autumn, I'm covered in leaves! Now, does that give me an idea of how long I've been buried and communing with the earth? About six months, I guess. In which case, I lay odds the man with the scream was told I was a Halloween character. Right?

Who would you bet with and, more important, what would you bet with…

Shut up. It's just an expression, nothing more.

Hey, walk straight, Skullface, don't want to draw attention to yourself with an eccentric walk. As if that matters right now the way you look, but still… History is full of 'accidents' like that, people who were stopped before they could do what they wanted to do. And we know well what you want to do, don't we?

"Hey!"

Who the hell's that? Looks like a gnome, little bald man with glasses and round body. Only needs a pointy hat and fishing rod and hey presto, a living gnome for your garden pond. Madam would love him. If I could make him rigid and lifeless, of course. Let me work on that…

"Hey!"

Now that is one irritating person. He has that tone in his voice that says, "I am important and you will take notice of me."

No, I won't. But I will be polite. And stop. And wait. And think food…

"You, what are you doing in that jacket?"

I can't speak. Damn.

"My friend lost that a few days ago, now give it back!"

My stomach is shrieking loud enough for him to hear, for sure it is.

"I said…"

One moment he's a bossy irritating individual… the next he's meat. For me. Blood covered meat at that. More important is the fact he cannot speak without a face. He has no face. He has gone silent. I have fed.

It was easy. Open mouth wide, bite into forehead, pull. Hard. Blood sprays in all directions – including my jacket but what the hell, it's tweed, who's going to notice a few bloodstains? Looks like part of the weave. Well, I can kid myself, can't I?

And do it so quick he didn't realize it was coming. No chance to fight me, no chance to say goodbye, or 'let me confess my manifold sins and wickedness,' no nothing. Wish it was that easy for all of us.

I feel better now.

But I could feel even better, so I will eat some more. A leg, perhaps, or the fat-as-butter belly, or – no, I'm not going there. I'm not that hungry.

What? A certain part of the body is what I'm avoiding; not refusing to eat the flesh. That's rich and good and with luck, if I nibble here and there the powers that be will put it down to a wild animal. Or two.

Do you realize, Skullface, and I am being serious here, even more than you were a few minutes ago, that you are captive to the need in you?

Yes. Nothing much I can do about it. The need for flesh is but a small part of the jigsaw that I am, even with pieces missing and all.

Got to say it's pretty tasteless. A pimento or two would help. Anyone know where I can get some, without attracting too much attention to myself?

Thought not.

Another thought, Skullface, hey, am I full of them, or what? You'd best get the hell out of here before someone sees you. Get away from the body, go hide, go rest, do something but leave the scene of the crime sharpish, as fast as your rotting body can go.

Or should that be rotten body? No matter. I will go. Look at me going.

The trees provide cover, do they not? Oh listen, just in time. I will be gone– I have to hide. The screams, the pointing, the yelling, the sirens, they didn't take long, did they?

I'm back at the stream where I washed my essential bit away. I'll cross over here, on this log, whoops, steady as I go, into the trees... no, these won't shelter me. Look at them, all twig thin trunks and no leaves. I need to get past them and on into the darkness. Watch me go... that's better. That's safer. Now, here's a nice little place to hunch down, conserve some energy, think some thoughts.

Like what?

Like remorse. I didn't expect that. It didn't happen –let's not go there. The remorse is now. A life snuffed out. A home left unlived in. Maybe a pet looking for their master. Food rotting in the cupboard, milk turning sour in the fridge. A TV unwatched and unloved. I have no problem with that but the pet and the food is bothering me.

Why?

Not sure how much of my stomach is left, not tried to find out – oh and I wanted to know if she took the ring... she has.

Where was I? Wanted to find out how much stomach was left as I suddenly had the feeling half of it had dropped out.

Because...

I have a home unlived in. I had a pet that would be looking for his master. I left food rotting in the cupboard and milk turning sour in the fridge –or I think I did. Or did I eat all the food before this happened? Or did she clear it all out and take the cat to some home or other and appropriate the unwatched TV for herself? She insisted I had one but I couldn't be asked to watch the thing. Inane chatter, biased news and endless documentaries that told me nothing.

So I'm feeling sorry for myself. Not much I can do about it, is there?

One step at a time.

Damn those sirens and lights and people and fuss and bother. I can still hear

them. 'Tis only a body, after all. A mere gnome. No great loss to the world. See, I can overcome the remorse, for sure.

Or can I?

Skullface, make up your mind! What do you want to talk about, pets, homes and uneaten food or the fact you really don't care you just killed someone?

Both.

I don't care; he irritated me. Irritants should not be allowed to live. I wonder how many others he's annoyed during his life. They will never know he is no longer capable of irritating them again. Ever.

I do care; it brought back things I wanted to forget, along with my name, her name and why I'm where I am.

Truthfully, underneath both of those was the hunger, the clawing craving ravening beast called hunger. I had to eat. He was there. I was hungry. He was irritating. Now give this zombie a break, right? I didn't touch his brain – if he had one.

I've realized that, on top of leaving my living essence in the earth, I've also left my humanity there. I can't grieve for the life I just took. It seemed natural to me, necessary, which makes me no more than a wild animal. And, if they get the chance they will shoot me down as if I was one. That would mean I would not get my moment of pure satisfaction before whatever is sustaining me, whatever form of life this is that causes a rotting body and useless brain to keep moving, stops whatever it's doing and lets me drop back to the earth where I began this escapade, adventure, mission, whatever.

The hunger is temporarily sated and the ravening creature is quiet. I can move on. I have to move on. I want to get back to Madam before I am nothing but bones. There's a reason for this, a zombie will scare her more than a skeleton.

But either will do, come to think on it. As long as she's scared out of her pathetic feminine nasty evil wits. If she stopped breathing because of it, bonus! If she doesn't stop breathing because of it, that can be arranged.

I think it would be an advantage if I could talk. I need to practice. I need quiet for that and it isn't quiet here with that lot going on, sirens and all.

And I am wondering why they haven't found me. Are they not looking in the right place?

Time to get going. They are surely there now in force (Ha!) and will start searching soon. I must go. Move on. Away from here.

Quickly.

Clarification. Edification. Elucidation

Whatever.

Skullface, give over with the whatevers, please.

I'm going out of what mind I have left. My imagination took over. I read too many crime novels when living, that state of being I no longer fully remember.

Ha! Even that's a lie. I saw a part of too many crime TV programmes when alive. Now it's the truth. And - there are no police, no sirens; no searches going on. No one has yet found the body that I know of anyway. I saw no police, I heard no sirens. The truth is, I expected to hear such things because that's what happens in films and drama, a body is created, a life snuffed out and the police and all sorts, armed with DO NOT CROSS CRIME SCENE type tape arrive in five minutes and cordon off the area. I expected it and my fevered half-baked zombie brain created it.

I also thought I was in a park, because when I came out of the earth the light was so bright, the shock was so great that the mere clearing I was in looked as big as an area of parkland. And no, I'm not lying.

I recognize this place. I'm in what is surely Firestone Copse, a densely wooded area with clearings created for walkers, birds, animals and other such creatures. Not sure if the bylaws include zombies, but they sure as hell do now.

Where did that come from? What am I, a walking tourist information leaflet? I know what bloody Firestone Copse is! Oh brain, are you so much mush now I have to tell myself where I am in such excruciating detail?

No.

But I did.

Apologies, zombie anomaly. I will refrain from tourist information claptrap in the future.

If I can.

I did hear the town clock, though, chiming across the landscape from its tower in Ryde, which is just down the road. On a clear day you can hear for miles and miles and miles.

I also lied. Again.

Lying to yourself is Not Good, Skullface! Not at all.

I didn't find the tweed jacket hanging on a tree. I took it from the still warm body of the walker who was in the wrong place at the wrong time.

First kill. Needful. A stranger going on a hike somewhere, well, he found somewhere, didn't he?

You want to know? I don't know it all, I shut it down. I remember –leaping onto his back, twisting his head round, going for the throat, remembering somehow to avoid the jet of blood, drinking fast of the remainder, needing the blood, needing the blood not the meat, just to make me fit enough to walk. I remember tearing his face off, too, because I could, not because I needed to.

I remember –feeling the earth spinning like I was going to pass out just before he came into view. I remember a scream when he saw me…

And now I know why no one came when he screamed. They didn't hear him and he didn't get away to report it.

Oh hell. That means, with the gnome as well, there are two bodies in the copse now.

Pretty damn stupid, Skullface. Why don't you care?

Don't know. Let me go on. I need to sort this…

The gnome didn't demand the return of the jacket; that was my invented reason for tearing the face from him.

Incidentally, whilst I am dwelling on such thoughts… zombiekind, if you wish to strip the face from someone, go for the throat first, rip it out, drink the blood, then with both hands, tear the face off. It works. It has for me, twice.

Enough! I justified the second killing by inventing dialogue. He didn't stand a chance, that gnome who crossed my path. He was fat, oozing with blood and sustenance. It was like a kid standing in front of the cake section in the supermarket, only I got to reach out and take where the kid has a plastic shield to contend with. Perhaps I should have one, too.

Whatever, I have time to get out of here and I am getting.

Which way? Which safe way? And where am I going, anyway…

Anywhere out of here!

Start walking, Skullface! And practice. Talk to the birds.

I will, I will. Can I walk and talk…

"Hey, crow!"

Whoo hoo, need some practice, that came out as a cackle almost as bad as the sound the crow utters and they're bad enough. That one who was on about 'nevermore' – no; that was a raven.

What's the difference?

One's bigger than the other. I think.

Do I?

Try again. "Nevermore." That sounded better. "Nevermore." Oh come on, I'm not a raven.

But it will do for now. I have to say something! "Nevermore." Getting better by the minute. As is the walking, look, nearly in a straight line now.

Hey, what's this? An abandoned pick up or someone having a quick **** in the trees? Are the keys… no, too much to ask and, anyway, I don't know if I've got the strength to drive. Hmm, interesting. Nice looking coat and hat on the passenger seat. I could do with those, cover up a lot of falling off bits, for sure. Is the door...

It is.

Well, I was wrong about the 'nice' coat, but it's worn enough to look like me, if you see what I mean. And the hat fits, there's a bonus, bit of a battered trilby but it'll do. Wonder why he took it off? It's cold out here. Guess he wasn't cold in the car. Wish I could drive; it would make life simpler, but then again, no keys – stop being stupid. Now look at me, every bit the man about town, or would be if I had half decent shoes. These are mud covered and scuffed, but it's muddy and scuffy out here so… perhaps no one will notice.

Quick, move on before Mr. 'I needed a quick ****' gets back.

And get off the road, Skullface, it might take longer to walk but no one will see you as easily as if you're strolling down the road wearing the guy's clothes. Right?

Hell and damnation, you're right. Again.

Adventures

The road is smooth, black, like liquid licorice, like oil spread even but without the colours. It's enticing, it's leading somewhere and I can't walk on it. Because… the damn cars keep coming and I don't want to be seen. Or so I am told by the over-active other side of my mind. Trouble is, it's right and I know it but oh I don't want to tramp the mud and broken bits of branch and whatever's died in the grass and whatever's been left in the grass and I want out of this piece of forest, whatever it is. Copse. How big is a copse when it's left to seed itself and grow as it wishes? Uncontrolled nature, what a nightmare.

Hey, what's this?

Crinkle crisp paper. In the pocket. The inside pocket. It crinkled and crisped and shouted 'look at me!' and I have and –

It's a ticket. No, two tickets. No good to me, there's only one of me, even if the other half of my mind doesn't agree with that. Two tickets for…

I don't believe this.

I truly seriously do not believe this.

I refuse to believe this.

But the ticket says it is real.

A zombie convention at Robin Hill.

When?

Well, whenever the 24th October is.

Skullface, what are you on about?

I don't know what the damn date is! I haven't bought a newspaper today, all right? You're so damn smart, tell me what the date is and I'll tell you if the zombie convention is happening around now!

No! Stop. Think. Bang the brain cells into submission.

The guy was heading in the general direction of Robin Hill. He had tatty scuffy old clothes in the car. He had tickets for the zombie convention in his pocket. Now, logic, supreme and overwhelming as it is at times, is saying:

It has to be either yesterday or today, because he was sure as hell heading for the convention. Right?

And so, if I keep walking, I might even there and what fun that would be…

And if I keep out of sight, he won't get his coat, his hat and his tickets back.

Excuse me, Skullface, scuffy?

So I am inventing a language. Any complaints?

No, just commenting.

That's fine. Now let's get going, shall we?

Sunshine, shadow, sunshine, shadow. And a dark, dark shadow following me that has nothing to do with me, doesn't look like me, feel like me, act like me. It walks on the road, for a start, which I can't do. Not allowed to do.

It's looking at me, it's looking into me. I don't like it.

I don't believe in entities.

But then, I didn't believe in the afterlife either. I have to now or it means I am disbelieving my very existence.

I don't like it.

"Scat, go! Run away! Leave me be!"

Oh, it worked! The shadow has run away. Surprised me, that did.

Skullface, you would frighten anything, even a shadow. Have you seen yourself lately?

Well, not since I looked in that bit of mirror you found for me. Wish I still had it, I'd like to see if my eye is coming out any more than it was then, it seemed a bit loose to me at the time.

And the problem is…?

This zombie convention. Got to be real people dressed up, right? No, stupid! Not real people: live people, living breathing people who remember their names, where they lived and some idea of what they did/do for a living. None of which I can remember.

And the problem is…?

I thought you didn't like repetition. The problem is, as you asked so nicely, I want to look something like a real person to mix with the real persons. What I don't want is you to ask why I want to mix with the real persons. It's just a sick joke on my part. So, if this damn eye is coming out too much, I have to push it back. If it isn't, it's best left alone.

Ha! For once you're making sense.

And right ahead of us is the Briddlesford Road. Turn left for Robin Hill; turn right for East Cowes, Ryde and all points east of the island. If I can remember that, how come I can't remember who I am, where I lived, what I did to earn a living and what the bloody hell the names of Him and Her are?

Oh.

I didn't earn a living… you can't earn a living tethered to a pipe in a basement rigid with bars and door and food thrust in from time to time and a reeking bucket and – In the name of God and all that is holy, I feel sick.

Ok. Sit down for a few minutes. Here, on these leaves, Skullface, not in the puddle!

Oh for goodness's sake… all right, missed it but the leaves are damp.

So? So were your clothes after the bath, however long ago that was.

I remember.

The basement, the cold, the lousy food, the damp bed, the tether from That Ring to the pipe. I remember…

And I don't want to.

I will go and enjoy myself instead.

Remorse? Forget it. Until someone knows what I've been through and what I need to make up for… anything goes. If it means eating a once alive person, then that's what I'll do. The wonderful thing is… they can't try me for murder, can they? I mean, who's going to put a rotting lump of flesh in the dock?

Exactly.

And I just realized what that black shadow was.

My conscience.

I sent it away. I no longer have one.

Well, I no longer have a life, do I? So… what good's a conscience to me?

Exactly.

All right, I'll stop with the repetition before I get moaned at again. I want this diary to be half readable, if you know what I mean.

Or it would be, if I could write it down and leave it for the world to read.

On my feet. Moving on.

I hope we can cadge a lift. Robin Hill's a bit of a trek from here for us weary zombie anomalies.

"Hey, want a lift?"

Walk over to the pickup; let them take a good look before they decide I'm fit company. He looks rough, must be a wig, no one has hair that bad. Apart from me, of course.

"Wow, man; that is some makeup you got on there! Did it take long to put it on? You look... authentic. Want a lift? You're on your way to Robin Hill, right?"

"Yes." Waving tickets at them.

"That's fine. Yes, get in the back if you can. Want a hand?"

Don't ask me that...

I think I lost a pound or so of flesh off my legs clambering in but I'm aboard and we're shifting and hey, that sun's hellish hot on a trilby and tweed jacket but I daren't take it off. Any of it. I think bits of me might go with it. I'm still musing on the offer of a hand. And wondering how I can feel heat when I'm dead.

Skullface, stop it. Concentrate on being normal.

Look at this lot trudging along the road, green faces, grey faces, rotted clothing, toes sticking out of shoes, at least my feet are still confined in something, even if the something is muddied and scuffed, or muddy and scuffy, if I revert to my new language.

Do they look authentic, though?

Dare not say. I leave that to the others who will see me walking around this convention. I am laughing myself sick inside, it's so ridiculous, so surreal, so…

Plain stupid is what it is. For sure. Bit like this diary. Plain stupid. None of it makes sense because there are huge gaps in the memory. I mean, I now remember the basement but I didn't always live there, did I? I remember going out, school, parties, shopping, girls… yes, I remember all that. So, when did the basement thing happen and why? Did she hate me that much? Was I so awful?

Questions, questions.

Answers, please, on a postcard addressed to The Only Real Zombie At The Zombie Conference, Robin Hill, Newport, Isle of Wight. I'll pick them up from the gate when I get there.

When I get there, I need to take care of something. The hunger has started up again and it won't rest. I could go looking for a burger bar but there seems to be no money in this jacket, he had the wallet and change in his pants, for sure, and I really don't think a burger would suffice…

Unless they sold it to me with raw meat. And I don't think they'd do that, not with all this environmental health rubbish that goes on. It isn't good enough. I mean, for goodness' sake, world, a zombie needs to eat blood red raw meat! Don't you know that?

Hunger, quieten for a moment, let this zombie anomaly get to the convention and size up the food on legs, right?

Shock horror, Skullface, you're making sense! Which reminds me, they'll ask you for a name. How about Nevermore?

Go0d enough for me.

Good enough for now.

The landfill tip's busy, now, why didn't she and he think of smuggling me in there? I would have been buried under tons of rubbish, household, garden, you name it and I would never have burrowed my way out, would I? Bad mistake –

I almost had her name then.

Bad mistake, Madam, as you insisted I referred to you, no pesky myopic moles there to wake me from my eternal otherwise undisturbed sleep.

And we are there.

"Here we go, mate, you OK to get out?"

"For sure."

"I'm Greyface, by the way."

"Nevermore."

"Good name! See you around the site."

"Thank you."

"Welcome. Let's go, shall we?"

He's off with his mates, Greyface & Co, with the ampersand, of course, and here are the others, loads of them, shambling in, painted green grey black brown white and blood streaked and wearing the rottenest clothes, far worse than mine.

The guy – not a zombie lookalike - checks the one ticket I hand over, nods, hands it back, clocks my face and says, "great makeup, Nipper!"

"Thanks."

I'm in and the stomach is shrieking its agony at me. Wait, wait, we only just arrived.

Talking's coming easier, it's probably due to the lack of anyone to talk to, other than beetles, worms and other underground sneaky little bastards out to eat all that someone idiotic woman and her lover had unceremoniously and illegally dumped in a shallow grave.

The place is jammed. Heaving. More zombies than a George Romano film and that's saying something. What's with all this zombie stuff anyway?

What's this… oh, a load of Goths here as well. Of course. Couldn't keep the creepy black clothed ones out of this.

Stall of makeup, theatrical stuff, of course.

"Hey, mister, great makeup, looks natural!"

"Thank you. It is."

"Ha ha! Great joke to go with the great makeup! Got any tips for me? I thought I was good."

"No, really, it's real."

"Yeah, right. OK, keep your secret; I would if I were as good at it as you are, Mr-"

"Nevermore."

"Mr. Moore."

Move on. You don't have money, Skullface, don't linger too long. He didn't believe you, others might.

And then there's the feeding issue… it's urgent.

"…two bodies in the Copse, throats torn out! It was on Isle of Wight Radio before I came out…"

Ah, at last the recalcitrant police are on the case as it were. I need to find out more. Or just ignore it. Like we said earlier, what can they do to me? If they find me.

Let's imagine that I am in the police station and they want to question me about the murders. And I pull off a finger, one at a time and put them on the table…

Sometimes, Skullface, I admire your thinking.

And the rest of the time?

It's pretty damn stupid.

Hey, now she's nice.

In what way? Nice to talk to, nice to eat?

Both.

No, don't go killing the nice ones, Skullface, kill and eat the duff ones, the overweight ones, the couldn't-care-less about themselves ones, the ugly, the nasty, the impossible.

Oh, all right, go talk to the 'nice to look at' one. Might as well make your meal attractive. That gnome wasn't much to look at, even if he did taste all right. In the end. When you're starving, any meat is good.

Getting rid of this coat, the jacket will do. It might be Autumn but it's hellishly hot here today, all these people, I suppose.

What would you rather do, Skullface, hide in the trees or among a bunch of people who look just like you, only not as good?

The coat is rid. If anyone wants it, there it is, right by that stall, hey, you over there, want a coat? Check it out by the jewellery stall here, the one with the skulls and crossbones and sabres and all sorts of other horrendous things. I can't be doing with skulls. Got enough problems with the one I have. It keeps sparking things I don't want to think about – like memories. They are flaring up like the jagged lights migraine sufferers say they have. I don't want them. Not any of them. I want to be me, zombie anomaly, forgetting all that went before, until I get to the doorstep and then I want –

"Hi, I'm Lilith. Who are you?"

"Nevermore."

"Like it! Have you been here before?"

"No, my first time."

"Love your makeup, how did you do it so realistically?"

"It's real."

"Sure, of course it is. Come and meet the gang."

So it seems if you want someone and you think about them, they walk up to you and introduce themselves. Good one. Except that now she's there, I couldn't consider killing her, not for a moment, even though the hunger is a clawing craven screaming animal right now, determined to be satisfied. It has to be satisfied. But not with this one, not with Lilith, she of the dark eyes and pouting mouth and elfin face and too many extensions, I think that's what they're called, tugging the hair in all directions and streaked with colours never thought of in nature and the black eyeliner and the black lipstick and the black nails and the smile that is devastating, exactly like-

"This is Geronimo, here's Perseus, over there is Axe, this is Delilah – everyone, meet Nevermore."

"Hey, good one!"

"Good to meet you, man!"

"I like the look of you…"

Confused and surrounded and terrified they'll touch. They don't. They stand back and look – as confused as I feel.

"How'd you do the makeup so well, Nev?"

Nev? Already they're carving up my beautiful name!

"It's real."

"Sure it is. OK, if you want to keep it secret…" They look disappointed.

"No, seriously, it's real. I'm a zombie."

"Of course you are. This place is full of them. Where did you emerge?"

"Firestone Copse."

They fall about laughing, like I made the best joke of the day. Perhaps I did, who knows? But I tell the truth and they think I jest.

Skullface, you need to eat.

Stomach, shut up. You think I don't know that?

I can't remember their names already but it doesn't matter. I don't really want to talk. I want to walk away from them, find someone isolated, take them somewhere isolated and eat them. What could be simpler?

"Nev, did you hear about the two bodies found in Firestone Copse?"

"I thought I heard someone mention it."

"The police think it was some kind of cannibal."

"Not a wild animal, then."

"No. Bite marks, said to be human."

"Scary to think someone's out there doing that."

"Hey, let's go, people!" Lilith is jumping up and down with excitement. "The Last of the Living are about to start their gig! Come on, Nevermore!"

What the hell is The Last Of The Living? How did I know she said it with capital letters? We move off, we cross endless grass and walk past endless people doing nothing at all – would someone explain a convention to me? Do you really stand around talking inanities at one another and then go home, thinking you've had a great time?

Oh my God.

The Last Of The Living are Goths turning into zombies. Their music sends sharp prongs into me, pieces of me will fall off if I stand here too long, cut by the sheer agony in their instruments, the agony of being battered and bashed into non-existence by people with no comprehension of notes or rhythms or anything. Crash bash bang thump boom boom boom. I feel ill. I need to get away.

The group is too concerned with itself, Skullface, start sliding away. Slow, careful, step by step back and back and back and walk away.

Relief.

From the intense nosiness of that group and the raucous noise of that group, if I can honour them with such a name.

The rest are riff-raff.

I'm hungry.

"Like your makeup, friend."

"Thank you." The fat one I saw earlier, the one I dismissed at the time.

"Are you not a music fan?" Somewhat coy, this one, trying to be coy, anyway but – she's more experienced than she's letting on.

"I like music. I don't like that."

Peals of laughter but no one is turning to look.

You're in with a chance here, Skullface.

"You are-?"

"Nevermore."

"Like it! I'm Glory Girl."

Really?

Be polite, Skullface: you get one chance at this and only one. And she is as unlike – you know who – as you could get. No chance of being squeamish now, is there?

Hungry.

Oh so hungry.

Even if it was her…

No, I wouldn't.

But you dismissed your conscience, Skullface, remember?

I did. I remember. I sent the black shadow away. The one walking on the road when I was trogging through the grass. The one nobody saw but me.

And?

I felt better for a little while. Now I don't. Now I don't want to do anything I shouldn't.

Stop flannelling, Skullface, you mean you don't want to kill, right?

Right.

But you have to if you are to survive and get your revenge and not just find a new grave to tumble into and rot away. Right?

Right.

Dilemma.

Of course. But you throw these at me.

"Glory Girl, what a wonderful name."

"Not as good as Nevermore, that's inspired. Shall we walk a ways?"

"Yes, away from the crowd. We can talk better."

This is –almost normal. Hey, I could get used to this! Normal is a long, long way in my past.

How old am I?

I don't know.

Glory Girl doesn't seem to mind. Glory Girl knows her way around. These grounds are beautiful. How come I've never been here to see it?

Or have I?

Can't remember. What I know is, the colours are bright, the sun is too bright in my eyes, even with this hat, this Glory Girl is going to be tasty and she is nothing like the one –

"You all right, Nevermore?"

"Why?"

"You're walking very slowly."

"Bit weary, is all."

"Right. Let's find somewhere quiet to sit, shall we?"

"Yes, please."

Yes please…

The noise is going away; the 'music' is going away the noise of so many people all talking at once is going away. We are far enough out of reach for no one to hear.

Damn it, there is no point in waiting.

It takes one bite and she is pumping the richness into the ground and into my mouth and into my veins and into my stomach and I can feel life returning full on full on full on oh I am so sorry, Glory Girl. You didn't know this day was your last, your meeting with destiny in the form of the zombie you didn't recognize as being a real one among the fakes.

I am so sorry.

But I'm so hungry and you're fat and the fat is young and rich and luscious and better than anything any chef ever cooked. No one has meat like this; forget your horse and pig and lamb and mutton and venison. This is it; this is the real real real real meat.

And I am sated.

And I can sit here for a while and watch the body grow cold and see how it changes, so I know how I changed before she put me in the earth she and he and whoever else they conned into helping them or did they?

Remember.

Remember the basement and the cold and the bars and the stinking bucket and the cold food. Never hot, never tasty. Cold nasty food.

Until the day the young one came down into the basement. The young one full of life and bursting with rich blood and –

No, Skullface, don't go there.

Not yet anyway.

There will be time enough for that.

The one thing you do not need right now is to walk in the past, is to think on that time, to think of what you lost and how you got out.

But I do.

No you don't.

Please.

Skullface, listen to me! You're sitting by a dead body and there's blood pouring down your face. You can't feel it because you can't feel. Mop it up, dry it and let's get the effing hell out of here. Two bodies already discovered with bite marks and you're idling by the third with bite marks. Will you be sensible and get the effing hell out of here! Now!

Go!

I will.

My hair is falling out.

Everyone's hair falls out.

Not in clumps, it doesn't.

No, it doesn't, does it… keep the damn hat on. Maybe no one will notice.

I did.

It's your hair, that's why.

How much blood is there round my face?

Not a lot, you cleaned most of it off. Your teeth are a bit blood stained but it looks – authentic.

It is authentic.

"Excuse me, Mr. More, isn't it?"

Who are you, I wonder? And where did you come from? You weren't there a moment ago, or was that me, not concentrating?

"Well, not really, it's Nevermore."

"Oh, I see, very funny. Ha ha! Can you give me a moment, Nevermore?"

"Sure."

"It's like this..."

He walks oddly, listing to one side, like his foot hurts, like something doesn't fit right. Will I end up like that if my foot falls off?

Skullface, concentrate, this could be important!

To a zombie?

Who knows?

"... we've been looking at everyone..."

"Could I ask who 'we' are?"

"Oh sorry, of course, the committee who organized this zombie convention. We decided that we should give a prize to the best zombie we see."

"Have you chosen one, then?"

"Yes, of course. You!"

"Me?"

"Nevermore, you have the best makeup of any zombie here, the best attitude, the best way of walking, you are the perfect zombie! I don't know how you do it but you do."

"Well, thank you!"

"Would you come over to the stage so we can announce the winner? We didn't want a fancy dress parade type thing; we've been quietly walking round observing the zombies who've come today. There's some fine specimens here but none reach your standard."

"All right."

Shuffle through the crowd, watch no one knocks anything off... whoops, nearly. Did the coat... yes it did, it's vanished, definitely rid. No problems there then. The problem is coping with this, but a prize? Best zombie? I can't say no.

You never could, Skullface, always been one of your problems.

That damn black shadow's back. I thought I got rid of it. That means my conscience is back. That's worrying.

Mind, Skullface, easy up the steps now, don't want anything falling off right now. You're supposed to be living.

Yes, I know.

"May I have your attention, please!"

Whoo, caught me by surprise, so loud!

"Ladies and gentlemen, Goths, vampires, werewolves and zombies all, listen up! Before Death Threat come on stage to entertain you, we wish to announce the winner of the best looking zombie competition. Here he is, Nevermore!"

The applause and cheers are as loud as the megaphone/microphone/racket going on behind me. I suppose that's another group setting up to play yet more hideous raucous music. Death Threat indeed!

A push. I guess I have to parade up and down, so I do. More cheers, more applause, more reason I need to get the hell out of here as soon as this is over.

"The prize is £50. Here you go, Nevermore, thank you for coming!"

"It's been a great pleasure. Some fine people here."

Wild applause. Hurts my ears. There's Lilith and Delilah and what was his name? Axe, down there at the front. Hope they didn't know Glory Girl.

Back down among the Goths and zombies and vampires and all. If you didn't know better you'd think you woke up in a nightmare, Skullface.

No, the nightmare is about to begin. I hear the first discordant chords of a discordant guitar or is it an inept and arrogant musician, says me using the word loosely… it is. The crowd loves them. Hear the roar. I can't wait to be gone.

Even if it does mean walking with that damn shadow again.

Memories come a-walking

Look, Arreton Manor. Always meant to go in there, never did. Lost my chance now, gates are locked, says private, says nevermore visitors, you done lost your chance.

Here, I get through here. I want to sit, I want to think. I want to wonder.

Damn branches! Did I lose any bits of me? No, but the jacket don't look good.

Did it ever, Skullface? Why did you think the guy dumped it?

Good point.

This will do. No one can see me here.

And?

Wish I had gone to visit the Manor, got ghosts and all, so they say.

A zombie would not have added to the attraction, you know.

Really? I mean, I could have been a star for a few days, until this lot falls from me. And, the bones might have gone on walking around.

No, recipe for heart attacks, that.

I can't see straight. Those flash things going off, all those pictures they took of me. They'll end up in the County Press, won't they? And she'll see them, won't she, and she'll realize the game is up, won't she, cos she won't be able to go to the police and say 'that's a dead man walking about and you've gotta stop him' as she would in her elegant speechifying. Cos they'd say 'and, Madam, how do you know he's dead?' and she can't say 'cos I did away with him and buried him in Firestone Copse not six months back and he's got out and is walking about and I want you to stop him before he comes looking for me.'

No. End of story for her. Can't do. She won't do, but she'll know I'm out.

Or she will do, when the pics hit the streets. Hope it terrifies her.

**NEVERMORE WINS
BEST MADE UP ZOMBIE
PRIZE AT ZOMBIE CONVENTION!**

Headline news, for sure.

Yes, but that's not the reason you're sitting here brooding at the end of a beautiful Autumn day, Skullface. And have you noticed the black shadow standing there?

Yes.

Time to give some real thought to the why; the when and the how.

And what led up to it.

Holes and all.

Back When

When did it start?

Farther back than I can recall, for sure. Seems to me it was always that way, always the bleak walls, the bars, the TV, the bucket and the bed.

Oooookkkkaaaaaayyyy, what. The bleak walls. What were they?

Breezeblock. Lifeless. Faceless. Like my thoughts at times. Both those words.

The floor, what was it?

Solid cement. Damn cold all year round. Cold enough to burn through socks and whatever I wrapped around my feet. Hey, where did these shoes come from then? I never had shoes! Not ever! From 'him', no doubt.

So ask yourself why, Skullface, why put shoes on you? They need not, they could have buried you buck naked and no one would have cared.

You are right again. I hate it when you're right.

Hard luck. One of us has to be.

I think …

Do you?

Sometimes.

Like when you kill someone and sit alongside them and drool and dribble blood and think your thoughts?

That was a mistake.

For sure it was, Skullface, for sure it was.

Where was I? Oh yes, thinking. She put clothes on me to transport me there. It would look better. I mean, I could have been drunk and being carried by two people, couldn't I? Am I right or am I right?

Conceding that's possible, yes.

So, forget the shoes. Back to the basement. We did the walls, we did the floor. Ceiling, more blocks. Solid blocks.

The TV bothers me.

Me too. I never thought of it before. Huge flat screen thing set into the wall with no way to turn the damn thing off. Tried to smash it once, everything bounced off the reinforced screen in front of it. The screen that stopped me turning it off, ripping the wires out, whatever I could do to silence it.

Why was it there, Skullface? Think!

To show me a world I would never see again. To torture me with glimpses of freedom, of people having a good life, of people moving around, of people…

Why the effing hell didn't that c- creature have a handkerchief or tissue in his effing pockets then?

Did he know a zombie anomaly would sit here wearing it whilst sobbing his heart out, Skullface?

No.

Well then, stop criticizing the poor c- creature. Move on. TV is done. Bucket?

Dis- to degrade me.

For sure. Bed?

Lumpy.

Warm?

No. Never warm. Blankets too thin and the pillow too small.

Heat in the basement?

Hot air through vents.

Specially designed for –

Captivity. Cruel, denied-everything captivity.

And?

And?

Was it always that way?

No. Once I walked in the sunshine. Once I walked in the rain. Once I ran in the snow and made snow angels and laughed. Once I fell in a river and laughed at the coolness. Once I laid in grass and felt its coolness. Once I held someone in my arms and laughed at her softness.

And?

And what? The shadow speaks. Damn it, shadow! I don't need these thoughts!

But you do, oh Nevermore, you do. To understand where you are, why you are and what you must do.

For what?

Redemption.

Not revenge?

Yes, revenge too but for redemption. I ask but once – this captivity; was it deserved?

(If there was a heart it would be beating faster by now...)

Yes.

Damn you to hell's deepest core, shadow! Damn you for making me see it and think it and feel it! If I had a beating heart still, I would rip it out and throw it at you!

Ah, zombie anomaly, remember. Remember the softness, who was it?

Grandmother.

And she loved you?

She did. As grandmothers do. No fault finding. Just love.

And she said to you…

"Oh my child, remember this: sometimes memories walk a little hard."

(If there was a heart it would be beating faster by now…)

Yes. I hurt. Damn memories. All wearing steel capped boots, for sure.

Sleep, oh zombie anomaly, tomorrow is another day, tomorrow is another mountain to climb. Another cliff face to ascend. Another kill to make. Not here, for there will be too many questions if you cluster them on this forsaken island. Not here, for there must be no link between you and the torn up bodies. No link between Nevermore and the dead.

No.

Sleep, then, Nevermore, sleep.

I will, I will, stop the talk… stop the memories from walk.

And sleep comes… walk and talk and smile and the faces smile back and the blood surges and the thoughts recede under its neap tide and want to be normal again and live again and am and will and am loved and am treasured and am free and am…

Waking in a field and am covered with ants and worms and things and birds are pecking and – damn it to hell, want out of this!

And am waking in a field and surrounded by police with guns and tasers and loudhailers and they demand my body on a plate, no a gurney, no a trolley, no a stretcher, no and…

Wake in a field half consumed by an urban fox who need not raid the bins this night and a badger with claws like something out of a horror story and am/am not like something out of a horror story and

Wake as an asteroid hurtles toward earth, toward the very field where the body is laid and am sick and tired of all this and

Want to wake.

Come, Skullface, 'tis time you were up and moving.

I am not rested.

For sure, did you expect to be? A zombie has no need of sleep but you dozed and you saw and you wished you hadn't and the memories? Were there any?

None.

Then you were fortunate for I was sure there would be something in there to upset and you say none but you have tears again.

Foolish zombie I am for sure.

Yes. Now let's go.

Where?

Portsmouth. You can hide out there for a while and oh the rich pickings of the healthy young students, full to bursting with blood and fats and goodness for the taking.

Portsmouth?

You have money, yes? You won the damn best made up zombie competition, right?

Right.

Then you have money for the fare. Until the day comes when the County Press plasters your unattractive face across its non-news laden pages, you can get away with moving around. Let's make the most of it.

God, I hate it when you're right all the damn time!

Of course there were memories. Did that black thing think I would tell it so? Did it really think I would confess to such things? Foolish shadow. Why didn't it stay gone when I sent it away?

Consciences never go away, do they? Remember that Jiminy Cricket creature, ever the conscience of Pinocchio? Never went away. Mine won't. What's the effing good of being dead if you can't escape your own conscience? Like I can't escape this bloody field – let me out of here! There, at risk of tearing a few more shreds from the full tweed jacket, I am through.

And the road awaits. The road to Kite Hill and Fishbourne and the ferry. It's one hell of a walk. Perhaps someone nice will give this oh so charming and not really smelly zombie a lift. You never know.

Meantime… it's cold. Colder than it was. I need more clothes. I never thought a zombie could feel cold. But yesterday I felt hot. And the hat is not stopping the hair falling out. I liked my hair, all long and wavy and highlighted with sort of chestnut-browny bits that I quite liked. But then again, I quite liked it when She came and cut it all off and left it with curly bits round my face. Bit girly but let's face it, be honest and all that crap stuff, I was pretty and it added to the look.

Not like now, clumps and lumps falling out and the flesh along with it. Good job I've got this crappy old hat to wear. It hides a lot even if it isn't doing much in the way of holding it on or in or –

Shut up, Skullface. Concentrate. It's a hell of a walk from here to the ferry.

I know, I done said that, didn't I?

Do I look like a man in this outfit? These creased to hell and back pants and checked shirt and tweed jacket and trilby? The shoes don't match, but then, well, they could be loafers, couldn't they? I want to look like a man even if that essential bit did go drifting away down the river/creek/running water/whatever it was in the Copse. Wish I could go do that again. Lie in the cool water, but it's cold today and the water will be cold today and I will realize sometimes it isn't worth a zombie actually feeling because it can be very difficult…

Ok, I will shut up.

Not much traffic.

Too early for it, I guess. I mean, who needs to drive through Arreton at stupid o'clock? Which it must be, the birds haven't cleared their throats yet and got singing. So why am I stomping along already?

Because sitting means thinking and remembering and I don't want to do that.

I can say that, but the picture of the basement, it was, wasn't it? intrudes and shows me what I left. Empty bed, empty bucket, table with no food, no doubt. If she was going to kill me, she wouldn't feed me.

Hey, Skullface, what was all that about the pet missing his master and the uneaten food and the empty flat and what else was it?

And I said the unwatched TV, didn't I? And I lied, didn't I?

It's what I wish I'd had.

Pets? They wouldn't allow them near me. Food? Rationed so I never put on an inch of flesh. Home? A basement prison and rings that tethered me so I couldn't attack them when they came in.

Oh I lived in dreams then and I live in dreams now. I also lie in them but do you blame me?

I wished for a remote or an OFF button for that effing TV, believe me I did.

Because, I couldn't change channels. I was stuck with what they decided I would watch. Some days, nothing but cooking, other days, quiz shows and endless chat, other days back to back Friends, at least they were funny, yet other days Discovery channel and I saw the world I would never see.

I lived vicariously and that is no way to live.

And I died and I never got to experience any of it. Now I am walking about in sunshine, cold sunshine but real honest to goodness sunshine and cool air and seeing green things for my very own self with my very own dead eyes which can still see. My flesh is dead and it feels. My heart is dead and it aches for the times I never had.

My body aches for the sex it never experienced. Ah, now we ask; what sex… and that is one topic we need to shelve for the time being. Maybe later we will explore that one a little further.

Perhaps.

I will ask one question, though, to keep the mind ticking as I trek up and up and up and will I ever reach the plateau, the top of this damned hill? The question is:

Do I have moobs or boobs?

Travelling Me

"Hey, Nevermore!"

Who the hell…

"It's me, Greyface!"

"Oh yes, I remember."

"Good! Want a lift? Where're you going?"

"Fishbourne."

"Oh, right. I'm heading for Yarmouth. I can drop you at the Racecourse roundabout if you like, if you can make your way from there."

"That would be good, thanks."

"You've not taken your makeup off yet, then."

"No, not yet. I didn't recognize you without yours."

"Ha ha! Congrats on winning, by the way."

"Thanks."

"Climb up, we'll get going."

Better than walking. That hill took a lot out of me. Ha! Listen to me, idiot that I am. I have nothing to give, especially now when the hunger is on me again, the craven crawling grasping clawing hunger. Greyface looks…

Stop it; he's doing you a favour, Skullface! And anyway, he's driving. That's considerably more than you're doing!

You're right again. Hell and damnation…

The sun's good, cool but good. This is a lovely Autumn; for me anyway. I missed Spring and Summer by being underground. Rotting. Wish I knew why it had taken so long to come back to 'life'. But on the other hand, whoops, that was a bad bit of road, the longer I'm out of the picture, the bigger the surprise when I knock on the door. And I'm going to have to knock on the door, she took my keys.

Among other things.

I'm getting some strange looks. Have I deteriorated that much? Hope not, Portsmouth awaits - and another feed. Oh God, the hunger!

Think of something else.

Like, do I have moobs or boobs? Am I male or female? Does anyone know? Bit of both doesn't quite cover it, not really. Everyone so far has called me Mr. and that will do for now. The jacket helps. So does the trilby. Whoever Mr. Pee-in-the-woods is; thank you, sir, for the clothes.

And the tickets for the convention. Sorry you missed out. It was good, apart from the music. I could have done without that. The rest was fun, including Glory Girl.

Here we go again, back to food. Sustenance, something that keeps me going. Like, it's a zombie's life essence. Sorry someone has to go die because of it but hell, I'm dead. Trade off. I'm dead but walking, you're just plain dead. Lucky you.

Back to the question. But then again, does it matter? What I am is dead. What I am is a zombie anomaly. What I am is effing tired of being dead and just want to sleep for eternity but there's something I have to do first. I don't think I can sleep for eternity until this task is done.

And then there's the Big Question, are the mediums right, do we not sleep but get a new different life and get to live on? Not sure I want that. Do we get to choose? What chance I can find a medium and ask them? Slim to nil, Skullface, slim to nil.

"Here you go, Nevermore! Fishbourne that way, Yarmouth this way. Been good knowing you."

"Thanks millions. Saved my feet no end."

"Easy as you go there, not like getting out of the cab, is it?"

"Thanks. Really."

"Good to do a fellow zombie a favour. Enjoy your life, mate!"

The pickup roared off left, I have to go right. I have to go right because food and time to hide from any police activity are high on the list of Must Do things.

I think.

Hold on. Hold on a moment or three, what's this? Flowers, someone died here? Hell, someone died here. And they, family, friends, remember who died here.

I didn't think it was possible to feel sick, but I do.

I had no flowers, no memorial, no friends coming with bunches of things, ok, so they rot and die, so they compost themselves and then they come with more, how much do I want to bet they didn't do that?

I feel sicker than ever.

And more determined to arrive on her doorstep.

Before then, FOOD!

Oh dear God do I ever need food… I'd even settle for roadkill but there isn't any.

Skullface, take a hold of yourself! Right now! You have to get to Fishbourne. It's a hellish long way from here.

No kidding.

So, how are you gonna get there?

Take a bus.

Do what?

Bus! You heard! You know, thing on wheels, two decks, seats, driver, people…

For sure you are insane.

No. I have money, look. £10 notes. Five of them. I can pay my fare.

And so you can. Well, there's a happening, you thinking instead of me. Congratulations, Skullface. You just woke up.

A bus should be along soon, I've just got to cross this flat out endlessly busy road. Somehow.

Like – now.

Made it.

Now to wait for the bus.

"Here, mate, you all right?"

"Yes."

"Want some help getting on board?"

"No thanks."

"Look, I ain't supposed to do this but –go sit down, all right? You look like you died and got up again. I can't take money off someone looking like that. Where d'you wanna go, anyway?"

"Fishbourne."

"Right."

Sometimes luck goes with me. The only person at the bus stop was me. And the half of my mind which argues with me. And the bus came in double quick time and now the driver doesn't want any money, more for me to use to get across the Solent quick and get me something to eat…

Stop thinking about food, Skullface!

Wish I could find some other clothes. These are pretty bad right now.

Think about it. Charity shops in Portsmouth? They'd let you buy something, change into it and take the old stuff for rags, wouldn't they?

I could look better than I do.

Ha! No contest there, Skullface! None whatsoever!

The question is: why does this feel familiar to me, the rocking of the bus, the sound of the engine, the feel of the seats, even the stares of the other passengers. I was not always dead so how come they stared back then –

Back when, Skullface?

Back when I was a kid. Back when I went on the bus to school and to the mall and to anywhere I wanted to go. Now I ask, why the effing hell didn't I get given a bike, like all the other kids? How come I had to stand like a stuffed muffin at the bus stop and wait for the blasted thing to come, hand over precious coins and climb aboard, enduring smiles and comments from the passengers, to go someplace.

Comments like: 'oh how cute' and 'fancy you going off on your own!' and once, from an older man, 'want to come and sit with me?'

No. I didn't. I sat near the driver that time for safety. He glanced at me, then in his mirror and nodded. He knew.

The question has to be, how did I know to stay away from predators like that? Instinct?

Whatever, I went with it and went on the buses and went places and explored all alone. No one ever played games with me, invited me to parties or tea or a trip somewhere. The others did.

The others. First time I've thought of them.

Wootton. There's a school down that road. Nice school, so they say. Mine wasn't.

The others didn't mind it as much I did.

The others.

I'm back there again.

Right, confront it.

Jasmine, Jay, Joanna. My sisters and brother.

Lay odds then that my name begins with a J as well. Families do things like that. Let's not go there; it might be something I don't want to dig up.

Ha!

Jasmine died.

No.

Not being truthful again, are you, Skullface? Come on. Get it right.

I killed her.

Stone dead.

With these hands. When they had all their fingers. Now they only have six and two thumbs. When did the other little one fall off?

Hey, bet it's in the back of Greyface's pickup! That'll give him a shock when he finds it…

Stop diverting, Skullface. You killed your sister. When?

What do you mean, when?

Before or after you were incarcerated in the basement?

Before. No. After.

You should know, you did it!

Yes, I should. After. Definitely after.

How do you know?

"Fishbourne next stop!"

Time to get up, to fight my way off the bus, to say thanks, to walk down that long, long road to the ferry.

"Thanks, Mister."

"Get on with you; go get yourself to A&E or something. You're very sick, Nipper, that you are."

"I will."

The bus leaves me standing. No one else got off. It stopped just for me. Now, could someone get the earth to stop turning just for me?

Slow walk, slow slow walk.

Don't want to think, though, these are dangerous waters.

More like quicksand, Skullface. Wondering if that wouldn't be the answer to all your problems.

No, not yet. When I climb the steps and ring the doorbell. Then I'll go find the quicksand, or the island equivalent. Might even go back to my grave in Firestone Copse, who knows?

The damn black shadow's back, Skullface.

So it is. My conscience. Won't let me be.

It's a long walk down this road.

Thoughts won't let me be.

I lied, again. No I didn't. It was definitely after She shut me in the basement. Jasmine coerced her way in 'to see my brother!' she told her. I heard her, wondered if she really meant me. I had been on my own for ages, no one talked to me; I was going mad.

She came in, all radiant and glittering with sunlight, sun I hadn't seen for weeks, months, forever. She seemed to bring the sun in with her. She danced in, light on her toes, then stopped dead and began to open her mouth to scream. What did she see in me is the question I have asked ever since. I know I look 'normal' so what is it she saw? The black shadow, a black entity, a devil peering over my shoulder? Something made her scream. I didn't want her screaming; it hurt my ears. I tried to stop her, shut her up, put my hand over her mouth, held her head, didn't realize I had covered her nose as well, didn't think I put that much pressure on, didn't know what to do when she slid to the floor, boneless, lifeless, breathless, dead.

These hands are big. Or they were; now they are diminished by the loss of a finger on each one. These hands can do damage still. I have to remember that. I have to be careful. Teeth only, to feed, to feed, to feed.

Thank God, it's the ferry port.

I can stop thinking.

For a while.

"One return as a foot passenger, please."

Strange looks, am I that bad, I wonder?

"Here." Muttering under the breath, price I couldn't quite catch. Thrust a £10 note at him, tick

tick click click spewing paper out of a machine, colour and black and white and it all comes down to one thing, I can get off the island for a while by simply holding a piece of paper. Bemusing. Never thought of it before. Remember the old jokes about needing a passport to visit the mainland? Now it's a bit of paper. Same thing, it just doesn't come in a cover, is all.

Nor do I; anymore. My cover is getting tattered and torn round the edges, like a worn out dust jacket.

Which reminds me. Soon as I get on that ferry I'm gonna go find out what size these clothes are. No point in going in a charity shop and looking for clothes if I don't know what I want. I look odd enough as it is.

And I want to take a look at my face.

You sure about that, Skullface?

Someone has to. It's for sure not your job to tell me if I look obscenely ill.

You're not ill, idiot, you're out and out dead.

And… Your thinking is?

You shouldn't be walking and talking and buying tickets and look, getting ready to get on the ferry and wondering why all the people who are also getting on the ferry are busy making a detour around you…

Their problem, not mine. I have a ticket, I have the ability to put one foot in front of the other, see me walk into the ferry and climb the stairs and all. What's their problem? See me walk, people? See my ticket, held out for all to see? Avoid me if you wish, let me get the hell over the water to Portsmouth!

Hovercraft would have been quicker.

Too far out of Portsmouth.

Catamaran? The bus would have taken you to the Esplanade.

Then I would have had to take the train to the pier head. Come on, give me a break!

And there is the big, big thing. The catamaran is no good to me. I want proper loos, with mirrors, sinks and cubicles. I want to check out my clothing size. Remember I said that? For sure I did.

You did. I'm just getting forgetful in my old age. How old am I now, two days?

How old are you really, Skullface?

Twenty nine.

You said that without thinking.

So it has to be right.

For sure it does.

Stop taking the piss.

Talking of piss, go sort yourself out.

Where are the loos… oh, that way. Oops, sorry, didn't mean to frighten the kid. Now, let me in there. Cubicle first. Right, pants, yes, checked and stored. Shirt, ok, collar size noted, shoes? OK, got that. Jacket? Yep. OK, I know what I'm looking for.

Now to go and look.

Fucking hell.

I look like I died and got up again, unquote.

Right, I want to try one thing before some idiot barges in here.

Smile.

Oh my God, my heart, my –

That's why Jasmine screamed. I think.

It's the smile.

It's –

Evil.

Did I sell myself somewhere down the line? Is that why I'm walking, talking, thinking, arguing and travelling? I'm dead, for God's sake! Dead, finished, not breathing, not living!

Gotta get out of here, fast. Oh my dear God, she screamed so hard, she was so terrified and I killed her...

"Excuse me, sir... are you all right? Can I get you anything, do you need help?"

"No, no, thank you. I'll just sit here. I'm – seeing a doctor when I get to Portsmouth."

"If I might say so, sir, that's very wise. Didn't you have anyone to travel with you today, to help you?"

"No, no family, you see."

"As long as you're sure you're all right..."

"Get the hell out of my face, sailor! I don't need this!"

Oh, that must have showed, he backed off pretty damn fast, Skullface!

Too right. Why can't people just leave me alone?

Well, the mirror told its own story, didn't it?

More than I wanted it to.

I'm being monitored. Oh, it's discreet but they're there, watching, waiting in case I keel over, or something. Ha! They're waiting for me to die! Oh what a joke...

I will fool them. I will sit here quietly until this floating coffin arrives at Portsmouth Harbour and docks and then I will go gently down the stairs, along the footway and into the town and there I will find someone and I will –

Feed.

And to hell with the world. I care not anymore. It has done me naught but ill my entire twenty nine years, ending however it ended by whoever ended it and that is the end of it.

Mainland Tales

Portsmouth. Hell on earth as it's always been. Too many fancy 'renovated' - for which read 'rebuilt' - boats, sorry, ships, too many fancy shops and a mall or three, expensive restaurants, if I can honour them with that title…

Oh come on, Skullface, you aren't buying anything in the fancy stores and as for the restaurants... your food comes on two legs and happens to be free. What more could you ask?

Clothes would be good. I'm getting strange looks.

Could that be because you're a strange looking zombie, I wonder…?

Nah. Why would anyone think me strange?

Look, a Cancer Research shop. They might have some clothes. Do I remember the sizes… yes I do. Here goes…

Getting those odd looks again but here, this shirt's a buy, thick and warm and bright colours. Is it… yes, my size. Good start. Pants, trousers, jeans, whatever, anything like that, I wonder?

Doing too much wondering, Skullface. Quit it. Concentrate. Get your goods and get gone out of here.

Jeans. Thick ones; look.

Ok, sweater? That one's a buy, too, deep burgundy, matching the veins on show in my rotting face… perhaps not. Beige or grey would be better. Here goes.

Shoes? Boots would be preferable, hey, I got lucky! Look at these! Like new and only £10.

Right, over to the cash desk. Oh my, I am getting strange looks.

"Thank you, sir. Are you all right?"

"Yes, thanks for asking. Been a bit off colour but getting better now." Or I will be, when I eat. It's been a while…

"Here's your change, thanks for shopping with us."

Underwritten by, get the hell out of our shop before you fall down dead – for the second time – and cause us all sorts of paperwork.

My plan was to change in the shop but it's clear I'm not welcome, so… looking for loos again… there we go.

Wish there was more room in this cubicle but still – oh this shirt feels good. Jeans, yes, holding all the bits in nicely. Nearly have a flat stomach with these. Good and tight. Sweater, yes, good choice, I'm telling myself. Jacket goes over it all and now it feels like it fits. Mr. 'piss-in-the-trees' was bigger than me.

Right, boots and here we go. Leave the old stuff here, someone else can get rid of it. I'm through worrying about litter.

Now for food.

Sometimes things fall into your hands, in a manner of speaking.

Look who's sitting on the bench, full of blood and life and energy, speaking to me as I walk past, admiring the shirt, no less.

"Hey, like the shirt!"

That was a come-on if ever I heard one.

"Straight out of the charity shop." Quick to answer, seeing all that lovely moving flesh before my eyes, tantalizing, stomach churning, drool inducing. Yeah, not nice but is meat nice, really? If you think about it?

"Good buy!" he said right back at me.

So I sat – carefully -and not once did he mention my face, my grey hands, the disgusting smell, nothing.

He was all Portsmouth; I was all island. He said he'd never been there. Told him he wasn't missing much. All lies but you have to keep the punters/walking food happy. Wondered what his game was until he began the 'I don't have any money to get a meal' tack. I went with it for a while, pretending I had some he could have – more lies- and then suggested we take a walk.

We walked as I wondered how desperate he was for money that he'd approach me, me who looks like something out of a cheap zombie film and smells like it too. I'd hate to think I was that desperate.

"I know somewhere we can go." Why didn't I ask why we were going there… didn't want to ask, went there, right round the back of a block of shops and outlets. What did he want, to mug me and steal my cash? Why else were we in such a secluded place? Right then every scrap of paranoia I had and

I have some, believe me! flared up and right there, in the sunshine, he lost all his worries about having no money to eat.

Took my jacket off as he watched, took my sweater off and then the shirt. Watched him stare open mouthed at the sagging rotting flesh. Watched him realize he had made the biggest mistake of his life.

The shock gave me an advantage; he didn't see I was so much of a danger, not straight off. Idiotic person. Idiotic homeless person, if he was what he said he was.

He fought back when I lunged for his throat, kneed me in the somewhat dilapidated groin area, thought he knocked something off, not that it matters any, not now, tried to scream but –

Thinking on this, thinking on this seriously, like I didn't think on the others –

Why not, Skullface?

Don't know. Don't ask.

Thinking how did I know that if I put my hand on his mouth and nose in just that way – he would stop struggling and then I could bite and the blood would fountain straight into my mouth and into my veins and into my non-beating heart and hardly a splash to be seen.

Then I hooked my fingers into the bite hole and – tore his face off.

This time I felt no remorse. He was a loser, big time. He had nothing in his pockets, so perhaps the money thing was right after all. Too late and anyway, I wasn't parting with any of mine. Hard earned, my money, I mean, who else would go to such lengths to win a best made up zombie competition? I crawled out of a grave, walked through Firestone Copse, got me to a zombie convention, was polite and nice to everyone I met… I only killed one person when I was there –

Conveniently forgetting the other two kills, I see, Skullface…

Shut up. I can do without reminders. They were necessity.

And Glory Girl was an impulse buy, like a bar of chocolate?

Like I said, shut up.

I've fed and I don't want to think about it. Or what I might be missing, thanks very much.

Got dressed quickly, turned him over so it looked like he was sleeping and worked out how to get back to where we were when we met up. Couple of wrong turns but there I was, almost back at the ferry port again.

My hard earned money's running away fast. Not much left of my £50 now. Enough to see me through perhaps a couple more bus journeys if I need to get on one and the driver isn't as nice as the one I had the other day. I don't need to pay to eat and what he gave me will last a good long time. He was full of the nutrients I needed. Says me.

I've said that before and still killed again sooner than I planned. Hmm, need to curb my appetite, methinks.

Sometimes you surprise me, Skullface. You actually make sense.

Shut up.

I've realised something: when I'm just fed, everything is exaggerated, the sunshine, the colours, the noise – I refuse to call it song – of the birds: can you call a crow or gull's cry a song? No way! All sounds are amplified. I feel good. I can take on the world.

And if he was truly homeless, that one who enticed me, then no one will miss him for a while and I can go back to the island knowing the trail has been diverted, when he is.

What a convoluted sentence that was! Try again, Skullface, you can do better than that! Overload of blood, you're drunk on it.

Right. If the 'meal' was truly homeless, he won't be found for a good while, which gives me a chance to get back to the island. Then, when he is found, the investigation will be diverted over here and give me a bigger break than I hoped for.

Check for blood, Skullface, before you hit the ferry again. They suspected something evil earlier…

I think I wiped clean. I can always say I'm wearing zombie makeup for a play or something.

Damn, why didn't you think of that earlier?

Such sarcasm…

Another damn. Missed a ferry. Now I have to wait.

Which means time to brood. I hate that.

On the other hand, Skullface, not that many people get a chance to relive their lives and sort it out in their heads. Take it and make it and go with it.

It's – not good.

Who's is? How many people passing you by now are not burdened with their own dark secrets? How many have their black shadows walking alongside them? Do you know? Of course not. Admitted, few will have your dark secrets or the denseness of the black shadow that haunts you but there you go, you're one of the lucky ones. You truly have something to think about and regret and take revenge on, or something.

Ok, so there's the gently rushing water, gently because it isn't pounding the pilings, rushing because it's on the move and the damn ferry is out there, sailing with clouds of smoke and lots of bow wave to the island, carrying people who have no idea what they'll find when they get there, anything could have happened whilst they were gone for sure and people who have no idea what they left behind on this side of the impossible stretch of water. It's a barrier, it's a defence; it's a pleasure. It's all things to all men.

Which I thought I was, for the longest time.

And the thing they left behind was me.

Zombie extraordinary. Zombie anomaly. Once a living being who didn't know whether he was male or female and who lost all track of time and who lived in a world dominated by a huge plasma flat screen TV he couldn't turn off.

So, when did this happen?

Nine years ago, give or take a month here and there.

Nine years of confinement. She put me there, she put me in the basement, she flaunted herself at me with the man with the flat stomach and abs standing at her side, grinning like something as demented as me. If I hadn't been chained at times, fettered at other times… I would have smashed his grinning face to flatness, that I would, as flat as the HD plasma flat screen on the hated wall of the hated basement. She took me by the arm, wrapped a chain around my neck before I knew what she was at, pulled it tight so I nearly choked, dragged me down the stairs to the basement I always feared as a child. Oh but it was not the same. No jumbles of rubbish to hide mice, rats or monsters, it was clean and bright, painted pure white with strip lighting behind cages so I could not get at it. There were bars at the window, set in concrete so I could not rip them out and cold cold floor with no carpet so I couldn't drag it up and use it in any way.

"Here you stay until I say otherwise!" The words were as icy as the floor was that day.

"Needs some heat down here, dearest," the man with the flat stomach said, with a leer in my direction. Sort of, 'look, I'm thinking about you, aren't I? That makes me the good guy around here, right?'

"Heat? Oh I suppose so. We'll get some piped in. Not having a heater in here, no way. Think what would happen with that!"

I knew then, in a blinding instant, that life as I knew it was over. Done. One act too many, one 'accident' too many, one step too far.

Twenty years of living the way I wanted to live, accountable to no one. Then, crash! Done. Ended. Gone. The ring I hated was used to secure me. The books I loved were taken away. I hated TV, she knew that, pap for the populace, I told her and she agreed. But there it was, already installed and working, showing me a world I would no longer be able to move about in. I knew that, without a word being spoken. No one prepares a basement/cell that thoroughly and then lets the prisoner/convict/internee walk free, do they? No, never. You know it, I know it. I knew it then and I felt what affection I once held drain out into that cold cold floor and never ever come back. Oh I loved her once, of course I did, that big big word, love. I knew it in all its forms.

It went.

It went completely, totally and absolutely in a nano-second.

In its place came implacable hatred. For her and for him. Who the effing hell did he think he was, being at her side? Offering advice instead of dragging her away so I could escape? Even though he suggested heat, that he had shown up that the bitch had overlooked the fact her prisoner needed to be warm, I hated him as much as I hated her.

"I curse you forever!" I told them both. I saw her scurry back a step or two; then she got her courage together and moved in again.

"You!" she scorned me with her eyes and her tone. "You know nothing! You think you're so bloody clever! Who has to clear up the mess you left behind, tell me that! Do you think I can stand you near me for a second after all that's gone down?"

"You talk like a cheap cop show," I taunted her. "You don't know anything, anything at all!"

“I know enough to make sure I don’t have the Old Bill on my doorstep!” A parting shot I couldn’t deny. She walked out and slammed the door shut behind her, a sound I was to hear a thousand times afterwards but never, never as horrifically *final* as that time. Later it became a part of the noise I lived with and never noticed. But then, then it was so terribly final I cried.

Sat on my hitherto unknown to me bed and cried and cried and cried until my eyes bulged and my head ached and my nose bled. And, unlike every other time in my life I had cried, no one came to hold me and offer tissues and comfort and reassurance.

There was none.

There is none now.

Only revenge.

And I will have it. One way or another. I will have it before I go back to the grave she put me in all those months ago.

Oh I know it was her, her and the leering fitness freak she had with her. I don’t need a medium to tell me that. I need a medium to tell me that the grave is not the end, like I don’t know that at this minute but I don’t know how I’m doing what I’m doing. How it’s happening, why it’s happening…

Unless the desire for revenge is so strong, always has been so strong, it’s overcome everything that should have happened. I should be rotting. I should be, if you believe the mediums, living free and healthy and happy on the other side of the veil.

And I’m not. And I’m scared senseless I won’t get there.

Skullface, I hate to interrupt the brooding and the walking in the past, but the ferry is docking and unless you want to sit here for another hour or so, I suggest you stagger to your feet and get on board.

Thank you. I was rather lost there.

Don't I know it…

Same ship, different crew. They're avoiding me. I have the plague; I have a bell around my neck, UNCLEAN! UNCLEAN! Everyone's avoiding me. Kids are running like hell to get away from the SCARY MAN! SCARY MAN!

No, physically I am no different from the zombie anomaly who walked onto this ship to cross over to Portsmouth, but the fact is, I've fed and I've gone back and those two things have brought out the very worst in me, admit it, go on, the thing that got me locked in the hellish basement for nine long endless eternal years.

It's a huge aura I seem to carry, shot through with flames and spikes of ice and glowing fire and hatred and – evil?

Why not, Skullface? We all know you worked for it and you got it.

I never thought of it like that.

This entire side of the ferry is deserted. It's a wonder the ship isn't tilting to starboard, so many on the other side, away from me. Ha! I should care. I want to be on my own, it's better that way. Better than –

A lot of things.

I am so tired of thinking.

I need to find somewhere to rest up tonight, recoup my limited strength and, if I must, continue this walk into my past, what I recall of it.

Right now, I just want to get back to the island where I belong. It feels wrong being off its soil, like I am attached to it in ways I never fully understood before or now.

Wish I'd taken the catamaran now and walk the pier if I had to. This is taking forever.

And forever gives me time to think and I don't want to think.

The damn shadow is back. Right there, look, behind the pillar, no, there, round the corner to the other side, no, right here in front of me, across the table. Get lost, shadow, get lost once and for all!

It's going nowhere.

Just like I am.

The sun on the sea hurts my eyes. I'd buy some shades… hell, why don't I go buy some shades?

Ha! God is with me, look at this! Shades left down the side of the seat. Oh my, just right for me, big wraparound shades, hiding the face a bit. I hope.

I remember my first pair. What was I, about seven or so? Found me some aviator type sunglasses, as we called them back then, not shades. They were way too big for me but oh I wore them, elastic hidden under my hair holding them on my head so I could get away with it. I felt so – adult, so superior, so streetwise and confident and assured. Wish that feeling had lasted into adulthood, I might not have gone seeking the black side to give me what I needed, to boost me, to make me feel less inadequate.

To find out who I really was.

Don't look at me like that, shadow, I know what I've done, where I've been, who I've damaged, better than you do. You stood by and watched; I did it.

Killed.

Time and again.

Started with small things, didn't it, like so many before me, what I could trap, what I could –

Eat.

I don't eat flesh just because I'm a zombie anomaly, shadow, do I? I eat flesh because I turned into a monster, didn't I?

A thought. I didn't turn into a monster, did I? I was always that way. From the start. You don't turn into a monster and want to eat flesh of any kind. You have to have been born that way, for sure. All those who think they're vampires or cannibals or whatever, are playing out a fantasy or a paranoia or are simply clean out of their heads. I was always that way.

I feel as if I should cry but I'm all out of moisture.

Isle of Wight, here we come, see Fishbourne glittering in the afternoon sun. Good job I have these shades. Good job we're nearly here, I need to recover from the memories I just dredged up from wherever.

Shadow, I keep saying God is with me but he's not, is he? It's the demons I summoned from hell who are walking with me right now, holding me up, see me walk to the stairs now the summons to disembark has gone out, see me go down the stairs carefully, shades are good but I don't always see the step too well…

Done.

We're back.

You and me and whatever is walking with me, shadow.

Now what, Skullface? What adventures do you want now?

No idea. Let's see what fate and fortune brings me.

They still avoid me, shades or no shades. I still have that invisible bell around my neck, still the plague carrier, the leper, the outcast. Should have got used to it by now but hell, it's only been two days. Wonder if I will get used to it?

No, it's something that goes back and back, Skullface, and you know it. When did you last speak to someone on a friendly one to one basis and they didn't look away or try and escape as fast as they could?

Ages.

About as long as it's taking to get this damn floating monstrosity docked at Fishbourne. The captain's acting like he never did it before. Come on, I want off, I want seclusion, I want –

Ok, here we go. At last!

Island Life

Back. I wonder if everyone feels like that when they've been off the island for no matter how short a time.

Good to just see the familiar houses again…

Come on, Skullface, how long's it been?

Years. Remember I went back in time – feel like I've been gone for that long.

"Hey, Mister!"

Is that me? Will I feel a fool if I turn round and it isn't for me?

Can but trust, I think he's calling me.

"You mean me?"

"Sure do. You're the guy with the zombie makeup, right?"

Ryde taxi. Ryde would be a good place to go. Wonder if-

"Well, actually it's real, but-"

"Ha ha! Good joke. I was at the zombie convention, saw you win the prize. Thought I recognised the jacket and the hair. The shades threw me for a bit but it's you all right. Get in."

No time to think, Ryde will be good, let me in – click and I'm in the car. Nice one, better than riding in the back of that pickup. Might not leave any bits of me here.

"I'm a big zombie fan, Living Dead and all that. My makeup's not as good as yours. Who taught you? Did you go to one of those theatrical makeup courses or something? Where can I take you, anyway? Ryde all right?"

Will he ever shut up and let me answer?

"Ryde's fine. I keep telling you, it's real, I'm a 100% returned-from-the-dead zombie."

"Yeah, right, good joke. Like it! I can tell everyone I had a real zombie in my cab. London cabbies like that kind of thing to tell their customers, the famous people they took from this place to that."

I could take off a finger and give it to him but we're doing 40 miles per hour down Quarr Hill at the moment and it wouldn't be sensible to have him go into a screaming hysterical fit, or maybe he wouldn't believe it, would think it's a trick I have to make it look authentic.

I won't bother. I need my fingers.

The smell ought to be enough.

Hey, there's a thought. How do I know I smell? Back in the grave I thought I did but since then…

"Good convention, wasn't it? What did you think of The Last Of The Living Dead? Island band, bloody good I thought, didn't you? The DJ was crap but then they all are, don't seem able to breed any good DJs here for some reason. What do you think? Do you listen to Isle of Wight Radio much? Or that other one, Jack FM or – no, no way would you listen to Solent Radio, would you? Too cool for that, I'd say. Right cool you are with them shades on and all. How did you get that colour tone for the blood coming out of your mouth?"

So I didn't get it all. I need a pocket mirror from somewhere.

"Well, you don't think…"

"It's not fresh, is it? It's dark, it has to be dark; I keep forgetting that. I go for the bright red of new blood and that's what spoils it. You got it just right, so you did. Did you get anything off any of the stalls? They're all mainland concessions and bloody expensive, too much for me. I mean, taxi-ing can earn you a decent wage but the overheads, the petrol, the insurance, the ongoing garage bills, all runs away with it. I get to eat but that's about it."

Eat you certainly do, my friend, considering you are crushed behind the wheel. You need a bigger car, a Picasso or something, where you can shove the seat back another six inches or so or you could go on the zombie diet and lose about 7-8 stone of your body weight. I have to say I could do with a bit more leg room, but then I'm having trouble with the legs lately, they want to cramp up. Could do with something to stop that but I don't think a doctor would be interested in giving me a prescription, more likely to send me off to the nearest teaching hospital for dissection.

Shut up, Skullface.

"Here you go, Cross Street all right? I'm gonna park up and get a bite from the Baguette Factory, not had much since lunch time and I'm driving for another couple of hours at least."

"How much…"

"Nothing, mate, nothing. Pleasure to help you out. I lost a fare doing that but hell, food called and as I said, right serious zombie fan, that I am. Shake on it. There, that's my fare paid. I met the star of the convention, what more could I ask?"

Had he not noticed my hand is lifeless, possibly clammy, ready to fall apart? Is he so star-struck? Hope so.

"Thank you, really, thank you. You've done me a huge favour."

More than you know.

"Good, pleased to hear it."

He's stomping toward the food outlet. I can't go in there, it'd kill me to see all that fresh crusty bread and not buy any to eat.

"Hey, they've gone and closed down!" So I won't have to go in there and die from seeing all the fresh crusty bread.

"I'll go over to that new place, that Frenchy thing, instead."

"Right!" He's pointing over the road, away from me. That's good. I'm trying to ignore him; food is his problem, not mine. I've fed. I have to re-orientate myself to Ryde, that's giving me a headache without his inability to buy a gut busting baguette.

And the place here, The Koffee Bar, looks cosy, looks welcoming; can't go in there either. I'd best not stand around; if he comes back he'll wonder why I've not walked off to wherever.

Now there's an oddity, he never asked if I wanted to go to Ryde for a specific reason, he never asked if he could take me to an address, he just scooped me up and dropped me here because his stomach called.

Good job mine isn't calling. He was very large and looked very tasty. But I already fed today. It's enough.

I've not been here for ages, on this street with its many shops.

Of course not, Skullface, at least six months…

No, long before that. Come on, not since long before I got locked up for crimes uncommitted and committed. Would that I had had been given the time to do all that I wanted to do before that happened! There would be a few less people walking around who shouldn't still be walking around.

Like?

Not getting into that. You know well who I mean.

OK, what's changed? Just realized a whole store has gone! Hayters, wasn't it? Gone, finished, demolished, like me. Unlike me, something new in its place. New shops. Not the same, not the same at all.

He's gone, Mr. Ryde Taxi Driver, over the road there.

Bookshop's gone, hey, what's this? Tattoo centre! Now, listen up, mind, I want one!

Don't be so bloody stupid, Skullface! What in the name of heaven do you think you're at? He can't tattoo you without finding out what you are!

OK. OK, I can dream, can't I? I'd like a barbed wire bangle, a Celtic swirl down my arm, a snake round my ankle and Zombie Anomaly on my forehead, although that would probably result in bits falling off. Perhaps just the blood trickling from my mouth, then, save me keep recreating the 'look' which zombie fans like. Or I could just keep right on eating.

Estate Agents. Oh, let me look, let me choose a home, the one I would have liked if I hadn't been kept locked up for so long.

HOW MUCH?

I've been away too long, it seems. Nothing's worth that kind of money; is it? Even if it is in some flashy area.

Forget it. I'll stick with my unmarked grave. Not everyone gets to live in Firestone Copse. Elite location, for sure.

If I could remember where it was.

My memory's shot, isn't it? Can't remember my name, can't remember where I lived; can't remember where I was buried… not much hope for me, is there? I'll have to turn myself in to a funeral director and ask them to arrange a suitable burial for me. And send the bill to her.

If I could remember her name and where she lives.

Meantime they could keep me in one of those chiller cabinets, couldn't they? You know, the cold rooms, the drawers you pull out and there's a body. They wouldn't have to waste a coffin on me.

She didn't.

Better than turning myself in to the police who really, seriously, would not know what to do with an unnamed dead person confessing to murders here and on the mainland.

Better stop standing in front of this window, the staff will get edgy and want me to move on. I obviously can't buy a house, flat, shed, garage or anything, looking the way I do. They'll know that for sure.

Oh look, a charity shop. I want a mirror, a little one for my pocket, so I can check for blood. Then I want tissues… one thing at a time. Cancer Research Shop; that'll do. They did me well on the other side of the water.

First, get across this road, busy busy, oh, thanks, nice of you to stop for me.

And again. Two pedestrian crossings and I'm right outside the shop. No, not exactly, this isn't fair. I'm right outside something called French Franks and people are eating and drinking and I can't and that isn't fair. That wasn't there when I was free and living; was it? Oh, that's where the taxi driver went. He said, 'that Frenchy thing.' There he is, with a bag of food, crusty bread, meat, everything I remember people eating at home. Back when. Not for me.

Going the wrong way for the Cancer Research shop, Skullface!

No, I want to go to this other charity shop, as I remember; it seems to have more bits and pieces in it. This one, Save The Children, look inside, see?

Good choice. Steady as you go, there's a slope.

Seen it. Yes, look, on the shelf here, little mirror, that will do fine.

"Are you all right, sir?"

Here we go again.

"Yes, I went to the zombie convention at Robin Hill, not got all the makeup off yet!"

"Oh right, yes, heard about that! Did you enjoy it?"

"Great fun. I won the 'Best Made Up Zombie' competition."

"You certainly look scary! Thank you. Do you want this in a bag?"

"No, my pocket will do. Thanks."

Good one, Skullface; nice thinking there.

That's what I thought. She's backing off, smelly me? Probably.

Now, tissues. Chemist? There used to be one down Union Street many years back, let's see… oh, pub, that was a store, I remember that. Clothes and material and stuff, called Fowlers, I think. Yes, see the sign? I was right. Not all the memory has gone. But it's a pub with the old shop name. Oh well, better than being forgotten, like so many are.

Like I will be. Probably am already.

These shops are new. Oh look, over there, the chemist. Just as I remembered it.

Some things don't change.

The staff has. Who's that elegant blonde busy with prescriptions… grab me some tissues, pay the other blonde, get the hell out of here. I'm not dressed for such a fine shop. Everyone's smart and groomed and looking at me. I must be the sickest person they've seen in a long time. The pharmacist has stopped pharmacing and is looking out at me, ready to ask -

Which way are you taking the word 'sick' here, Skullface?

Any way you like, it matters not at this late stage of my existence.

Out in the street again. Now what?

I need a rest. Back up past Save The Children, there's a churchyard next door, got benches as I remember. I can sit for a while. Then decide what I'm going to do next.

You decide? I think fate does the deciding for you, Skullface. That I do. You let fate carry you here, didn't you?

Yes, and I think there's a reason I'm here, too, I just don't know what it is yet.

A churchyard is surely the ideal place for a zombie to rest.

And this metal bench is ideal to rest on, it won't let me down. Wood, left outside for too long, lets you down. Like bodies, it deteriorates with age. Bodies especially deteriorate if left in a grave. Wood does the same when it's buried and left.

Stop thinking rot, Skullface.

I wasn't, I was thinking deterioration.

And what, might I ask, is rot?

I like my mirror. It's girlie, it has a flower on the back. I like girlie things, too long were they denied me. No one quite knew what to do with me, was I boy, was I girl, which one will we insist takes precedence. Let's not ask what he wants, whether he wants to be a she, let's go with it, let's pretend the additional bits are not there and register –

Hold on. Did anyone register me? I know you're supposed to, but… I wasn't born in hospital. The one who birthed me was unmarried, was scared, didn't go to any doctor or hospital or clinic, had no idea what was going on, only that she was growing and growing and finally the thing that was me emerged into the world. Part boy, part girl, wholly monster but they didn't know that 'til later.

I didn't know who my mother was. The person who raised me told me to call her Mother, so I did. Later, when I was in prison, she told me to call her Madam, so I did. How I got to be in her custody I don't know. No one told me. I was just – there. Somewhere to live, someone to tell me right from wrong – sometimes – someone to feed me the raw meat I needed. I heard tales of my birth from grandparents who were quick to condemn and slow to praise. I know no one quite knew what had hit them, how to deal with me, what to call me, what to do with me.

I went to school, yes, they enrolled me in a school, I had to learn, to possibly be useful at some time to the world, I guess.

But whether they enrolled me as a boy or a girl I can't remember. I just know they called me Jesse.

There.

I remembered.

Boy or girl, the name twists both ways.

I also know I referred to the others as my sisters and brother and they were, but really they were 'polite' sisters and brother. You know how you have to call people who are not related to you Auntie and Uncle for politeness' sake? So it was with these others. They were not related to me as full sisters and brother. They were –

I don't know. Don't ask. It's too much for the befuddled mind. The mysterious relationships that went on in that house were enough to befuddle anyone. Were all three of the others from one father? Now I doubt it. Then I accepted it.

The wonderful thing is; they accepted me, odd as I was; I was just Jesse, the boy/girl with more body parts than anyone should have.

"Too many drugs and pills while pregnant," Grandmother used to say when deep in drink and surveying me with eyes more bloodshot than white. The blue in the middle was faded to twilight most of the time. I didn't like listening to this, all I wanted was to hug and hold her, she was the softest nicest person in the place and it comforted me to have a hug. I didn't mind the smell of drink, the brandy, the whisky, the gin, the rum; whatever she could get her hands on. It mattered not to me.

It mattered when she died. Damn stupid thing she did too, fell down the stairs in a drink-fuddled state and broke her neck. Went down like a bag of laundry, Grampa said, tears leaking from his more-bloodshot-than-white eyes. She might have been a drunk but God, that man loved her! Loved her like no person has ever loved me, then or since.

You know why, Skullface; for sure you do.

Yes I do, but let's not go there just yet; I want to wander a bit in childhood first.

If it pleases you.

It doesn't but the roots are there.

Oh yes, the roots are there.

Not in the strangeness of me, for that was something everyone accepted. The physical me, that is.

The mental me was something apart, something no one knew of for a long time and did nothing about when they did.

I craved blood, simple as that.

It was just a craving for some time and then I tried to conquer it.

No. Lie. I craved blood but more than that, if I didn't get it, I went berserk. You know the proper meaning of the word berserk? I looked it up once.

Destructively or frenetically violent.

That was me. I would destroy everything in sight, no matter how valuable or precious or necessary to life it might be. Furniture, crockery, hangings, even doors and windows. I tried for walls too but they usually defeated me.

I had to have blood. The craving became a necessity, a life supporting necessity. When and how I turned into a monster I'll never know. Family might but family backed off and just humoured me.

I was fed raw meat, given black pudding, anything with blood in it. Fish wouldn't do, their blood was weak, unsustaining. I needed it thick, strong, raw and deep, deep red.

So family coped with me somehow. I had no school meals; that wouldn't have been possible. I skulked in the playground during lunch breaks, waiting for friends to come out so we could play. Teachers sent letters home about my not eating, letters which were ignored. No one could tell them the truth.

The fear was, if I didn't get my ration of blood each day I would bite someone and get it that way.

The ultimate fear was I would kill.

The ultimate act was – I did.

I can't stay on this bench all night; someone will see, someone will complain to – whoever; police, environmental clogs, social workers, you name it; they're out there, wanting to interfere with a zombie's life. I know it. I avoid them. If I can.

Where can I rest for the dark hours, then? Come on, brain, if you're not totally mush and you can't be, I still think, tell me where I can go to rest or what passes for zombie sleep around here.

Down on the Esplanade, maybe round the back of the water pumping station; maybe along the Esplanade itself, on the beach, behind the beach huts, come on, lots of places.

Just get yourself up on your feet and get walking. The boots are good, aren't they?

They are. Best buy of the lot, these were.

OK, let's move, Skullface!

Gets busy at night in Ryde. I remember someone telling me that a long, long time back. Before it all went lemon-pursed-mouth-acid-sharp wrong.

Look at them all, groups here, groups there, giggling girls, swaggering youth. You know nothing of true heartache, of loneliness, oh dear God the loneliness! Even now it cuts like a pathologist's scalpel clean through to the non-beating heart I still carry. I could tear it out but why mess up a perfectly good set of boobs?

What would they say if they did but know what walked among them...

They wouldn't believe it, would they? They who scream at horror movies would not believe real horror if it bit them. Lucky for them I am fed, or they would be bitten. For sure.

This will do, here, behind the huts along the Esplanade I'm sheltered from the night wind, I think, and there's reasonably thick grass. I also seem to be away from the maundering wandering aimless yoofs hanging around with little to nothing to do.

Did you mean maundering, Skullface?

No idea. It sounds good, though, so let's let it stand in these unwritten pages of my unwritten diary. Actually I'm pretty damn sure it's a word and the right one, too. When I next see a dictionary I'll check. That's if I can get into a bookshop or WH Smiffs or wherever to see one. If I live that long. Or the smell doesn't mean people stop me going in. Always a consideration, that one. Oh, and dropping bits of me. Which reminds me…

I've still got both goolies. How that happened I don't know. Gotta have tougher skin than I thought. There's me thinking I'm all feminine and soft and someone kicks rotting me there and nothing falls off.

Yet.

Anyway... here I am, comfortable on the grass, shielded from the wind, looking up at the stars – how long since I saw the stars like this? Like clear and bright and full of colours and what the hell are the constellations, never could remember them. It's just stars, a sky full of speckly shining things. Every now and then one goes nova and blows itself to bits. Like a lot of people do, only they tend to shoot a load of others first if they're mad. Or if they're a suicide bomber. I could do that, couldn't I? Blow myself up, shower the island with bits of me. Well, a small part of the island anyway. Would that be better than going back into the ground forever?

I remember – years ago, being terrified at the thought of forever. Of never ending, of infinity. The concept was beyond me, the thought of it was horrifying. Now I know it could be a blessing, sometimes.

Wish I could find a medium. Want to know so many things, so I do.

The church brought back a few memories I could have done without, like Sunday School, the dreary 'lessons', so-called, the emphasis on being 'saved', if anyone needed saving I did but no one would have understood that. I mean, what if I had held up my hand and said 'Miss, I need raw blood and meat every day to live, can I be saved?' Like hell I could do that. So I left the Lord Jesus to His preaching and teaching and went my own way, walking hand in hand with His counterpart, the Dark Angel himself, the one who was out to steal souls that Jesus missed along the way.

And if you don't believe in Heaven and Hell, then let me tell you what I went through as a kid, as an adult, as a zombie and see whether you think Hell exists, oh you who are not reading this unwritten diary of a zombie.

How It Began

My first kill was some Asian looking kid. Or Hispanic or something. Never did know for sure, the name meant nothing to me. All I know is, he had a dark skin, dark eyes and black hair and he seemed to like me a bit too much, sort of hero worship in a way and I hated that. Every time I turned myself around to do something, he was there, watching, sorrowful eyes, hesitant smile. He would have grown up to be a handsome, if not outstandingly good-looking man, but I put a stop to that in a single moment of anger and frustration.

I hadn't been fed that day. I went to school hungry and angry and ready to lash out at anyone and anything. Family was slow to recognize the need then, they soon learned.

There's this kid hanging around trying to attract my attention, offering me fruit, picking up my pen when I threw it, that kind of thing. It got too much. By lunch time I was in the middle of the gut crawling craven clawing hunger I hadn't got used to. I walked out of school and he followed. I didn't ask him to, he just did. Trotted along behind me like some well-trained puppy. He was shorter than me, had some growing to do to catch up.

I detoured through the park, he followed. I went behind some bushes, pretending to need a piss. He followed. I held him down, hands over his mouth and nose so he suffocated, tore his throat out and drank the blood, dragged him under the bushes and went home, after dunking my head in a stream to clear it of blood and quickly washed my shirt so it went pale pink and streaked and looked awful but better than being blood soaked. Scrubbed at my teeth and tried not to smile at anyone, even politely.

No one said a word but they knew I'd killed. I heard them discussing it. How they knew I don't know, perhaps because I wasn't berserking all over the place, if they'd realized it by then. They waited for the police; they never came. No one ever did pin that one on me.

I never forgot my first kill, the pure thrill, the pure ecstasy of drinking the fountain of blood as it came out, rather than dragging it from a piece of blooded meat. Meal times were never the same again.

Nor was I.

They treated me with cold respect after that, more like isolation in many ways, no more hugs, no more warmth; no more conversation. It was a complete turnaround. Suddenly the boy/girl/problem child became a serious problem person with needs they couldn't fulfill.

I wonder now if that was when the building of my prison began. They might have foreseen the need to shut me away. I can't remember the clearing out of the basement. It was chock-full of shit of all kinds, unwanted this, that and everything else. Maybe they discussed it then and began the sorting out of the unwanted after that. I never saw a mass clearing out.

In the future an unwanted person would end up in there.

My teen years were hell on earth. Rampaging hormones fought with blood lust needs. Drink, when I could get it, fuelled the anger that raged through me. I became more boy than girl; everything happened body wise, everything happened family-wise.

I had too much to drink one night, woke and found I had a steel ring round my balls. Welded tight. Too tight. "We'll do what we can to stop you procreating," they said. "We can't risk another monster like you out there in the world."

I was too ashamed of the ring to ever get into bed with anyone. They hadn't needed to make it quite that tight. The ring itself would have been enough but they didn't know that. Actually, I didn't know it either, at first. Then I got into a clinch with some busty thing at school who was after me for some unknown reason, realized things were being inhibited, looked on it as an insult to her and walked off. I think she was a after having a kid, she talked of kids like they were her aim in life, nothing else. She had me lined up for a future husband. She never spoke to me again. And I never tried again. I left them all alone. I didn't want any of that, thank you. Imagine having to tell someone I only ate raw meat and needed blood… so in some ways the ring was good, had its uses. Sometimes I even forgot it was there.

I think it was about then Mother said something about me wearing a hell of a lot of silver. I hadn't given that a thought, what the thing was made of.

Silver. A lot of it. That made it slightly better, if not a lot.

Staying away from anyone was a good idea, as it happened. I had a problem; I was as attracted to boys as I was to girls. The two sides of me were battling each other. Ha! The two sides of my mind are still battling each other, even though I'm good and dead.

Well, dead anyway. Not sure about the good bit. Can a zombie be good? And, I have to ask, am I a zombie? Really? I suppose in the strict sense of the word, yes, I am. I'm very dead, I lost a few bits, a toe is hanging off, my penis went floating; my pinky fingers have gone which is what you would expect to happen with a zombie who was walking about, bits fall off. But since I started feeding… it hasn't happened. I have all my toes still, the hanging off one is still hanging off, not gone, I don't recall losing any teeth and no more fingers have gone missing.

So I'm a zombie anomaly, more a zombie monster. Does that sound more like it? A monster who can kill and take the blood and think about it afterwards and have no remorse and where are you, black shadow, not that I could see you in this dark, dark, no-moon night.

I lost my conscience, though, killing never bothered me. Still doesn't. I try hard to summon up remorse and regrets and fail miserably. Sometimes I wonder if I am actually –

Ha! *Am?* Skullface, you're dead, in the name of all that's holy and sacred!

Yes, but I still think and walk and talk and feed, don't I? So that's a semblance of being alive, isn't it?

Ok, ok, what is it you wonder?

If I'm an Asperger's sufferer.

Well, if you are, tis a tad too late to find a shrink for you. I don't think you are. I think you're a monster, simple, sweet and concise as that. Something straight out of Grimm's fairy tales, just not as big and tall and not as empowered with otherworldly skills, like – well, like any of them. You'd make a good troll, though; hiding under a bridge, waiting for the clickety-clack of the hooves of the Billy Goats Gruff, or the high heeled footsteps of a dainty full-to-bursting-with-blood chick you could gorge on for several hours.

Not sure if that's a compliment or an insult. Whatever, I need to move on.

I decided to stop looking at anyone in 'that' way.

By that I mean, sexual, sensual or plain ordinary fancying people. Most women want you to look at them even if they aren't interested in you. It's an ego thing.

Damn sight easier to decide than to do. Big busted women walked around spilling out of low cut tops – how come when it's cold it's freezing everyone's tits off but theirs? They have their coats open and their tops too low and the goose-bumps are nearly as big as the massive tits swaying in front of them and what's worse, ask them and they'll say 'I hate my tits, I'd do anything to have them reduced' so put the bloody things away then. You don't hate them at all, or you'd not show them to the world all the time! And you complain we look at them and not at you. Wonder why?

And the ones with legs and the ones with chests and tight arses and the ones who scream 'sex' with every breath they take and every glance they give you and how the hell is someone tormented with hormonal changes supposed not to look, to be turned on, to want like it's life threatening to get them, to hold them, to try and do it with them…

Bitter? Me? Nah, course not. Much.

Are those maundering useless yoofs going home? Can't a zombie get some peace around here? Is the night so young still? Need a watch. Lost count of the chimes/dongs of the clock. No chance of finding a watch that works, it was fortuitous finding the shades on the ferry. A watch is something else.

I did my utmost to stop looking and after a while it got easier. After a while I saw it as so much flesh on the move and after a while more the hunger consumed me anyway, excuse the pun, and I saw it as meals on the move, not sex. In some ways that made it harder. Again, excuse the pun…

I gained a reputation as a loner. Little did they know it saved their useless ineffective unnecessary lives. I wonder if they would have been grateful for that had they known. Half of them were losers anyway; I knew that, destined for the dole queue and a lifetime on benefits. Bit like this lot hanging around here. They're looking for a quick fling and hope to get home intact, as in: no promises made, no ring attached to a finger together with a commitment for the future, home, brats and endless tiresome job until redundancy hits or even no job at all. The island was not exactly teeming with job opportunities then, probably the same now. Not having seen a County Press for 9+ years, I don't know.

I never had any of that because of the cock ring and the hunger. I knew I wouldn't control it. How could I, face to face with something living? I would have had to tear its throat out.

Would I have wanted the home, the brats, the wife, the job, the normality of it all?

Don't know. Never got the chance to even consider it as a possibility. It all ended before then. Long before then.

It grows late, for sure I heard midnight chimes and hey! the yoofs have at last gone. The night is left to the hunters, the squealing scuttling hurrying creatures who feed by dark light and those whose night vision lets them see the squealing scuttling hurrying creatures who are trying to feed and who scoop them up in teeth and talons and hurry them away to a secluded place, there to eat.

There's strong resemblance there to the way I have to live. I empathise with the night hunters. Go get.

Urban foxes; go seek the goodies thrown out by uncaring households.

Badgers; go see what you can find thrown out by uncaring households. You can fight the foxes for it.

Owls; there is food aplenty for you, take it before it reaches me.

Cats; catch the damn rats which are sniffing around my disintegrating legs.

I can't be asked to get up and move on. I like it here. It's comforting to sit and look at the stars, at lights blinking out in windows across the green and the road, in the Strand, somehow knowing people are heading for sleep leaves the night to me. The wind sighs its lack of energy at me and I respond with 'I know how you feel; it's been a long day.' And it has, for I have travelled many years this day and covered much ground. But there is a long way to go to bring Then to Now and reconcile myself to all that happened.

And still there are miles to go by bedtime and no candle to light the way.

Where did that come from? Is it 'how many miles to Babylon?' or 'Bethlehem' and 'can we get there by candlelight and back again?'

Heaven help us, why am I maundering those back roads?

A candle would be nice but the night wind would not approve and would puff out the small flame with one breath. So be it. We will remain in the dark.

Where you have been all your life, Skullface.

And I know it well.

I remember the time the first new man arrived in the house. Father had gone, left us, vanished into the darkness one night, leaving nothing behind but unpaid bills and worn out clothes. His good stuff went with him. So did a woman from our street. We didn't connect the two happenings at first; that came later.

I was surprised at the reaction, no one cried, no one complained, no one said a word. He was there, he was not there. Had I been so self-absorbed it had all gone over my head? Had the affection slowly dissipated and I never noticed it's going, being too aware there was none for me anyway?

And then this new guy arrived. Big, strong, nasty. Looked like an ex-boxer or brawler, street fighter, hard man. Who brought him into the house is anyone's guess. I had no conversation with anyone by then, just me in my little room and my sort of day job in a garage, learning to fix cars, wash windscreens, check oil and water. Apprenticeship, they called it. Slave labour I called it but still, it earned me a few pounds and I got to feel like a grown up person for a while. It was easy there to hide the cravings; near enough to home to go grab some blooded meat or cycle into town, slide into the butcher's and buy a steak to eat out the back before I started work again. No one knew. I was good with the pocket mirror then, checking for blood trails all the time. Wonder why it took me so long to realize I needed to do that now I'm dead and still eating? Not thinking, I guess.

This new guy refused to accept the way I was. He would cook the damn meat left for me and laugh when I stormed at him. He hit me once, sent me clear across the room and into the wall. Nearly did for the wall what I couldn't do when berserking. I remember Mother yelling at him that he didn't understand, I needed the blood and him yelling back that if he was going to live there then by God I had to eat what everyone else did, cooked food.

I went for him and got hit again. Then he threw me on the floor and stomped on my arm, breaking it in two places.

An uncle took me to A&E and got it set. I lost my job.

He got thrown out. Too late for me, the arm was never the same again.

I got a job in the supermarket, stacking shelves, then working the checkout but the arm ached something terrible handling all that stuff so I looked for something else. Persuaded the Job Seekers people to get me a placement on a computer course. Much easier on the damaged arm. I had a doctor's certificate by then, that the arm was pretty much useless.

Ha! Still is, isn't it?

And I avoided all emotional contact with females and males of any age as best I could.

And killed twice and no one knew.

One body was thrown into the sea, washed up months later with most of it missing, thanks to the fish, so they never saw the bite marks.

One body was left in Bouldner Copse or wood or whatever it's called and was never found, as far as I know.

I needed that thrill, that moment of fountaining blood, the freshness, the richness of it. Needed it more the older I got.

So we come to age 17, three kills behind me and a mountain of raw blooded meat consumed and goodness knows how many men who had come and gone out of the house by then. I cared for none of them and they ignored me.

At first.

Then I seemed to grow this aura, this madness; this flaming ice spiked thing which scared the living hell out of some of them.

And it is only now I realize, fully realize, they left because of me, not because of anything Mother did.

And it's only now I realize, fully realize, that Mother's hatred grew from a tiny acorn of dislike into full scale loathing because I was stopping her having a new partner. I was stopping her having any happiness in her life, such as it was.

The really terrible thing, only revealed to me now in a light bulb moment, was that she couldn't tell me to go.

Let me tell you by then the ring was tight, tight, tight on my balls. I hated it and resented it and wanted it off, so I could go make it with the chicks. All my intentions had gone, the hormones were roaring, the need all consuming. Night after night after night of sleepless tossing about, wanting relief, not getting relief, wanting to kill, not able to kill – because the people I wanted to kill were my family.

Grampa had long gone. Joined his wife in the earth. The other grandparents never came by once after Father walked out. No great loss, they didn't like me anyway. Mother was getting older by the week with the worry of it all and fighting the years to keep a man in her bed. It didn't work.

Jasmine was all tits and teeth and sexual allure and I wanted her and knew it would be the end of me if I did.

Joanna was all teeth and intellect and studying for some university or other and I let her be, could hardly bring myself to talk to her.

Jay was your typical builder's mate, big, dirty, fit for lumping bricks and cement and planks about and earning good money at it, too. He had some girl, Josie. Why the hell did she have a J name as well? She was a ditzy black haired thing, little to his big, smiley to his dour face, light to his plodding feet and he adored her.

Consequently, I hated her.

Didn't want her in the family.

Recipe for disaster, yes?

You'd be right if you said yes.

Are you following this sorry saga, this unwritten diary, this coming-to-terms-with-your-life, Skullface? Seems a bit erratic to me. I thought you only got to come to terms with your life when you walked through the pearly – or are they golden? gates and gave your name to St Peter as the newest arrival.

Or… you feel the heat and give your name to one of Lucifer's henchmen guarding the gates to hell, his task being to stop unwanted off course Christians from wandering in by mistake and contaminating the evil ones already there.

Shut up. Let me go on.

If you insist, Skullface, if you insist, but I have the strongest feeling you're making a mistake, that you won't like it when you get to the end.

My problem.

Back to where we were. Heaven and hell and all.

Guess where I was headed, but something stopped me, something held spirit and body together. Damn. I still need to find that medium and ask what in the name of God is going on here. Why can't I die? Why didn't I die, fully, properly, completely? Not even a ghost, or a spirit hanging around waiting to be recognized, I'm one being!

I don't much like it but there has to be a reason for it. Apart from taking out a few people along the way, that is and giving the police something to get their teeth into (excuse the pun.) And where was I during the six months I laid in my cosy warm earthen grave with the flesh slowly disintegrating and rotting and the bits inside deciding they no longer had anything to do and began to rot away, shrink down, become useless? Couldn't be an organ donor, could I? Who would want what I had inside me when all it had experienced was raw meat and blood? No one. Considering that some people take on the characteristics of whatever donor they had… hey, that would've been good, a whole new set of monsters walking about! Consider… eyes, liver, kidney; whatever else they could steal from me, all regenerating inside someone and turning them into monsters. Now that would set the medical profession in a tizz or two, would it not? They would no doubt blame it on the latest fancy-dancy drug they had invented and sold at great cost to the NHS.

No, I'm not allowed to procreate my kind. Which is just as well, all things being considered.

It's morning, time I moved on before someone sees me and thinks I'm loitering with intent. I am; I just don't want them to know it.

I need some money. What I have left from shopping and trips to the mainland and back may not be enough to get me over to the mainland again when I need to feed. I don't want to be stuck over there. My grave is here. I don't want to leave more bodies here. They're best left over there. Fate has been kind to me so far, I can only trust in Fate to be kind again and give me some cash. I have a feeling I'm going to need it.

On The Move

The dog walkers and horse riders are out, churning up the sea smoothed sand into lumps clumps and bumps. Not easy to walk on. They might be a tad more considerate, those with the looming animals with the teeth, mane and tail and which seem to be endowing their riders with a sense of superiority us mere mortals (am I?) could never attain. Not without a lot of money.

Money. I'm back to that again.

Do I steal it, demand it, beg for it; hope it falls into my hands? What?

What have you done so far, Skullface? Let Fate do it for you, right? So what's with the questioning? You don't need to buy breakfast. You do need to find somewhere to sit for a while. Let the world wake itself up and get going.

I could walk along the sand and see if any money has been dropped.

You could, so why aren't you?

All right, I will.

A penny. That won't get me far.

Where there's one, there'll be others. Go walk, lazy zombie.

For goodness' sake, treat the dead with respect, why don't you?

5p. Getting better.

Told you so…

I hate it when you're right all the time.

Hey look, a £1 coin! Now I'm £1.6p up on the fare to the mainland again.

At this rate you'll have to resort to begging, Skullface, or you'll starve.

No, can't do, don't want to draw attention to myself; I'll see what fortune brings me.

Fate.

No, fortune, that's what I'm after.

You're thinking someone's gonna…

Drop their wallet. Right. Ain't gonna happen, is it?

"Friend..."

"Me?"

"You. You look as if you are in need. Searching for coins on the beach is a display of desperation. Are you so in need?

"Yes."

"I have to say you look very ill, should you be outside?"

"I've no home, this is it; this is all I have."

"No more than our Lord Jesus had when He walked this earth."

How do they manage to say it with capital letters? And how come I get the religious one… hey, hold on, this could be fun.

"Fortunately for him, he had a few friends along to help out."

"Indeed He did." Looking at me with more critical attention than before. "Where are your friends?"

"I have none." Let's be honest, see what happens, shall we? "I endured being shut up in a room for nine years. Then I died."

“And came back to life?” Said with a disbelieving sneer, of course.

“Yes. I’m a true zombie.”

“You may be ill, friend, but dead you are not. No dead man walks and talks.”

“Jesus did.”

“He…”

“Spent three days in a stone tomb and then walked out, free as you like, visiting this one, that one and the others, appeared before crowds, gave them his blessing, before going up to Heaven.”

“That’s the bible story, yes, but…”

“You telling me that’s wrong? All these years of me believing it to be the truth?”

Skullface, you outright liar! You never so much as opened the bible you had!

No, but the Sunday School lessons have never left me. Shut up, this is fun. I love winding people up.

Could be that the winding up is what got you dead in the first place.

No, being shut up in that accursed basement got me dead. It was the winding up that got me in there.

Don’t think so. It was the killing that got you in there.

Whatever. Let me play, this is fun. The most fun I’ve had since I got out of the grave. No stone tomb for me, just a shallow trench in Firestone Copse. More than I offered that other poor guy, though, wasn’t it? The one I left in Bouldnor Copse or whatever all that time back.

He's staring at me like he's completely lost. Not used to someone arguing on my level and from my stance, ie: being dead.

"No, but…"

"You think the living dead are a figment of horror writers' imaginations, right?"

"Well, pretty much, but…"

"Look, friend, it's nice of you to want to talk to me, but you need to start from where I am, not from what you think you know. I'm dead. You're the only person I've said that to so far, well, said it in that way. I told them at the zombie convention I wasn't wearing makeup, that it was real and not a one of them believed me."

"It's pretty hard to believe."

"Sure, but we all have to believe someone sometime. How else would we know when to take an umbrella with us in case it rains?"

"Can you prove it? Prove to me you're dead?"

"Can you feel a pulse?"

"No…"

"Does that feel like living flesh?"

"No…"

"Right now one of my toes is hanging on by a thread. I could take it off and hand it to you but that's too gross for words, right?"

"Right…"

"Can you smell me?"

"Yes."

"Rank, isn't it?"

"Yes… but…"

"Now, let's talk Jesus and resurrection and what the hell you're doing standing here talking to me, OK?"

"Yes... I..."

"Jesus got up and an angel rolled away the stone and he walked out into the garden, right?"

"Right."

"That was a bit more positive. He was in the tomb for three days. I was underground for about six months, give or take a few days. I got out three days ago and have been wandering around the island since then. I need..."

Shut up, Skullface...

"...a bit of money to get me places, so I can try and find out what's going on, why I'm not properly dead, for a start."

"This is hard to believe."

"Even with all I've shown you?"

"Well, yes. You must admit it isn't every day a zombie walks up to you..."

"You walked up to me, friend, offering me the word of Christ."

"Yes, so I did. What can I do to help you?"

"I want to get in touch with a medium."

"Ah, oh, I mean..."

"Not something you want to get involved with, I take it?"

"Well, no... I mean, it isn't Christian. We're told not to speak with spirits."

"Really? What's Jesus, then? And the saints and Mary and what is, might I ask, the Holy Ghost?"

"For a zombie you're pretty damn sharp!"

“I have to be. I wouldn’t survive long if I wasn’t.”

“Why are you surviving?”

“Because I don’t think I can die properly until I come to terms with what happened to me and what happened to me is pretty bloody awful. It’s been worse than you can even begin to understand.”

“I think…” Extreme reluctance going on here, this is killing him. That’s just so funny. “…there’s some kind of clairvoyant thing going on tonight in Yelf’s Hotel. There’s a poster in the window. Take a look.”

“I will; thank you.”

“And take this, too.”

Notes in my hand. Different colours. Like he snatched them from his pocket without looking. Not going to argue. He means well.

“Sorry I worried you so much. And thank you for this; it’s a life saver, if I can say that.”

“You can. It’s all I can do for you, though, my friend. I pray you find the peace you seek. In Jesus’ name.”

Watch him walk away, puzzled, upset, unsure, but loving. God; he’s loving.

I’ve got £35 here.

Do you realize he’s an accessory to murder by doing that, Skullface?

Maybe, but he’s also accessory to giving this zombie anomaly a fresh feed, today or tomorrow. I’ll hold out as long as I can.

Skullface, I congratulate you, that was well done, even if it is still murder, whichever way you want to look at it.

Well, thank you for that. Now, let me go sit somewhere for a while. Tis a tad too early to go trailing into Ryde proper to look at the poster. I need a rest after that. Quite took it out of me, so it did.

This will do. Under these trees here, so I can watch the world walk by on their way to and from Appley Tower. I would like to go in the Tower itself but it's occupied right now.

OK, where were we before we got interrupted by morning, by evangelists and argument?

Ditzy Josie. Almost fits as a rhyme. She didn't fit anywhere. Not with Jay, not with the family, not in the world. Says me. Maybe she did, maybe I was wrong. I'll never know now. What I do know is, after a huge bust up with Jay one night, he was smoking 'stuff' and she hated it, she stormed out and I followed her. She got the bus, so did I. She sat at the back; I sat at the front so I got off before her and hurried round the corner out of her sight.

She got off and walked toward me, like it was planned. I had her round the throat and one hand over the mouth and nose and into the park before she could shout 'JAY, HELP!' Anyway, he couldn't, he was back home, stoned out of his not inconsiderable mind, full of useless junk as it was, and she had me to contend with, the me she had obviously blatantly and rudely ignored all the time they were going out. All of three weeks, if I remember aright.

It was the work of a moment to take her out; she was near gone by the time we got into the park.

I bit and ate and drank and all but shouted Hallelujah into the night sky but it took all the rest of the night to weigh her down with stones I took from here and there and then quietly and almost reverently roll her into the pond where she sank with no more than a bubble or two and a strange 'errrrrr' sound as the water rushed in. I had all night to do it; by then no one questioned where I went or what I did. I drank the blood as always and exulted in it and in ridding the family of someone they didn't really like. I knew, I overheard; I always got what I wanted in the way of information if it suited my plans. Jay shrugged off the loss, the fact she never came round again, the picture in the paper, the appeals for a missing girl, the whole bit. Acted as if he'd never known her – in every sense of the word. He went out the next night and came back with some other bit of a girl whose name I disremember but definitely didn't start with a J. Someone who didn't mind what he smoked. She ignored me too, but in a different way. Not rude, just – scared, come to think of it. She obviously saw more in me than the ditzy bitch ever did. She didn't last long, either, but it was relatively pleasant whilst she was around.

Josie never floated back up. No one's ever dragged the pond as far as I know, because no one suspected she – or anyone else –could be in there. They thought she'd met someone on the bus and that person abducted her. End of story.

It's easier to get away with murder than a lot of people realize, if you make sure you don't leave any trails. Killing as I do, there's loads of DNA but if you leave the body to rot in a deep dark wood or a shallow grave – which is what my family had in mind, obviously – or fall apart in a pond, lake or the Solent, it makes it much more difficult. Especially as I'm not on record anywhere, no DNA taken from me anywhere, any time. Oh, and be sure not to be noticed. I am normally Mr/Ms Average, ignored by all, so ordinary it isn't true. Only the flamboyant get noticed and I've never done that. Dressed outrageously for the sake of it. To me, putting a suit on is flamboyant and I don't do it unless I have to.

I didn't do it unless I had to, before you correct me, picky mind of mine!

This changed when I became a zombie but – the British tend to look the other way so many people only see me subliminally, 'oh my, odd person alert, look the other way!'

It was about this time I began to bleed.

I was treated as a male and acted and lived like one, so in all it took me three months to realize what was going on. I thought I was dying. I was too scared to tell anyone, so spent all that time in a state of abject terror. Then I overheard some girls talking about their periods and I sighed with such relief it almost killed me anyway. The other part of me was becoming normal. I was prepared for more and then it stopped and never came back. Quite why I had that sudden burst of 'female normality', albeit somewhat later than most, I've no idea. My body is different; it's a law unto itself. Then and now.

I don't question it anymore.

Time to start moving, slowly but surely, back into town. Done enough thinking for a while. I'm a way off being reconciled to anything, though, still got some distance to travel there before nightfall. What am I doing going back to silly nursery rhyme things again?

Losing it big time, Skullface.

For sure I am.

Hell, it's a long walk back to the town centre from here. Hadn't realized how far I drifted last night, looking for sanctuary for rest and thoughts. It's also got hellishly busy for a Thursday, never recalled it being this busy. Too many people staring and pointing and-

Pull the hat down a bit lower, Skullface, push the shades back up. That's better; you're almost a proper person now, albeit somewhat terminally ill. All you need is an IV stand trailing alongside you and a tube running into your arm.

I could stand that if it were pure blood being poured in, that would be good, wouldn't it? Save me all the trouble of making my way to Yarmouth to make sure I go someplace else for the next kill. It's Lymington's turn for the curse of the zombie. Or something.

Don't remember the taxis being here when I was alive and free to walk. Who moved them down here, I wonder, and why? Hey, there's my taxi driver!

"Hi, Nevermore!"

"Hey!"

"How you doing?"

"All right."

"You not got the makeup off yet, then?"

"Told you, it's real!"

"Sure, sure."

"Trouble is, it's gone into the skin and I can't get it off yet. Few more scrubs, I think."

"Yeah, it's rough stuff to shift, that greasepaint. You got rid of the blood trickle, though."

"That came off easy; it's the green-grey stuff that won't shift. It's getting me some funny looks around town."

"It would do!"

"Much business today?"

"Nah, everyone's walking everywhere 'cos of the sunshine. Likely to rain again soon, they said; then everyone'll be back in cars and on the buses. They're going out pretty much empty today."

"Well, best get moving. Time I sorted myself out. Good to see you. And thanks again for that lift, just what I needed."

"Any time! Good to see you again, Nevermore. Great name, that!"

He's telling the other drivers about it, a small moment of fame for him. He'll be retelling that story for some time to come, I think. Well, if it keeps him happy… saved me some slogging, and money. I'm not complaining.

Was Union Street always this steep? And busy? And crammed with shops that look as if they're prosperous but are they? Wonder how many changes there've been since I walked up here last? We're talking best part of ten years now. Over nine years in that accursed basement and at least six months in the ground. Don't recognize half these shops.

At last, Yelfs!

And yes, a clairvoyant evening tonight. 7.30 pm. £7 to get in. I'd best get a ticket…

Nice in here. Don't ever remember coming in when I was alive. Posh, isn't it?

"Can I help you, sir?"

"Do you have any tickets left for the clairvoyant evening?"

"There's two left, just the one for you?"

"Yes, thank you."

"The door will be closed at 7.30 precisely, so…"

"Don't worry, I'll be here."

"Excuse me asking, sir, but are you all right?"

"It's zombie makeup. I won the best made up zombie prize at the convention over at Robin Hill, having a job to scrub it off."

Big smile. Good job I thought of that. "I see! It's very realistic."

"Thanks! I worked at it for a long time."

"Nothing good ever came easy."

Never a truer word…

"Thank you. I'll be back later."

"The last evening went very well, I'm sure you'll enjoy it."

"Looking forward to it."

Lies, Skullface, you're pretty well terrified, aren't you?

Yes, but I have to do this.

I know. Go easy. You're radiating panic at the moment.

OK, best go sit for a while. How about the same churchyard I sat in yesterday? That'll do, won't it?

What, more thinking?

Listen, it's what I woke up to do. I can't rest – Ha! Until I sort this out in my head. The who, the what, the why. I might get a clue of what happened to me if I can think this through. Like I never did when in that accursed basement, because the accursed TV never let me rest for a minute. I know that was her idea, she knew I hated the bloody thing, the inane talk, the stupid patronizing adverts, the biased documentaries, the rawness of the nature programmes, the pathetic so-called 'celebrities' and as for the cooking programmes... let's not even go there. Let's talk to the viewing public as if they were a) rich and b) in school. The ingredients they used, disgraceful waste of food.

Like all this lot walking around, all this food on legs, look at it, masses of flesh wobbling and toggling and jiggling and all in front of my hungry eyes. It's gonna be tough holding out until tomorrow, but I can't kill again here, not yet anyway.

Question – do I smell a lot? I mean, I'm sure the remaining flesh covering my remaining bones is rotting but – is it? Not many people detour around me. Have I enriched it with the new diet of raw meat and fresh blood; halted the slow decomposition of my body? People are polite, they will ignore idiosyncrasies, outrageous dress, overdone piercing and tattoos but body odour they don't like and tend to move away, with that disdainful sniff only the British can do and I haven't seen anyone do that for a while.

So... it seems likely I can go to the meeting tonight, explain away the face with the makeup story and not worry about my flesh smelling of rot. That'll be good. I want to sit, I want to listen; I want to understand. I want to ask the question, if I get the chance, when can I die properly?

Hey, Skullface, I thought you were enjoying this adventure!

Well, I was but it's throwing up a lot of problems and if there's a chance, I'd just as soon lie down in a grave and stay there for eternity, provided I knew nothing about it. Otherwise it's gonna get the Universe's main prize for being the most boring occupation on this earth, or any other planet, come to that.

Oh look, no one's here. That's good.

So where was I?

Ditzy Josie and the new girl and the family and the rolling her into the pond and all.

OK. So there is me, late teens now, grown into all sorts, part man, part woman, part monster, I recognized that and accepted it and went with it.

No one else did. Family were on at me to go deliver myself to the medics and find out what I was. Refused, so I did, refused and told them to go **** themselves. They didn't like it, tough. I was there; I was one of them, wasn't I? This happened 'cos Jay caught sight of me in the shower. Shouldn't have been there, should he? My shower, my private time. He comes barging in, all bull headed, shouldered, chested and all and goes “oh my living Christ! What are you?”

And I said, “your brother.”

And he said, “no, part sister, part brother. What are you?”

I said; “what I am. You’ve not bothered about it before.”

He said, “not seen it before.”

I said, “lies, Jay! Damn boobs stuck out through teeshirts. I even bled a few times.””

You expect me to notice crap like that?” He stormed around the bathroom, smashed his fist on the cistern, cracked the bathroom cabinet mirror, God alone knows why. Shame? Embarrassment? Hatred? Disgust? His face gave nothing away, but his body language revealed outright savage rage.

I got scared. I turned off the water, snatched a towel, got myself out and wrapped it around me.

“Fuck off, Jay. My shower, my time.”

“I don’t share my home with any creature like you.” Then his face did change into the rage his thumping around revealed and the next thing I knew I was in the bath, blooded face; his fists hitting any part of me they could connect with.

The noise brought the rest of the family in, Mother screaming at him to stop, Jasmine tugging his arm, Joanna yelling in his ear. Somehow something connected and he stood back, panting and grinning so horribly it was like something out of a horror movie. I didn’t move; no breath, no will to get up. The towel was half round me, half off.

Jasmine stared and stared.

“You’re-”

"A monster," Jay finished. "That's why I was beating him up."

"Why?" She turned on him, which surprised me. "Why beat someone up 'cos they're different?"

"Why… 'cos, is all."

"Racist, are you, Jay?"

"Me? No. Everyone's got the right…"

"See?"

"Yeah."

He walked out of the bathroom, seemingly shamefaced and head hung down. I watched him go, knowing I could never trust him again, knowing I had to get a decent lock on the bathroom door, for the sake of all of us. He was too big, too aggressive, too – dangerous.

Joanna walked out too, but her face was expressionless. Jasmine got my arm over her shoulder and helped me up. "Hey, bro, is it OK for me to still call you my brother?"

"Course. Thank you. Thanks, Mum."

"Sorry we didn't realize what was going on a bit earlier, Jesse. It was sharp ears here who realized you were in trouble."

I got my toweling robe on, shivering a bit, trying to clean the blood off my face, trying not to think about the bits of me that hurt where his fists had connected, violently.

Mother left the bathroom, visibly upset. Jasmine got some cotton wool and scrubbed the blood off, so gently I hardly felt it.

"I've known you were different for a long time, Jess, just didn't realize how different."

"He called me a monster, Jas. I am. I eat raw meat and need blood."

"I know. You always have. You can't help it. It's the way you were made."

"It wasn't that, was it; that got Jay going?"

"No. He's racist, he won't admit it, not in front of us all, he daren't, but he is. I think it was the female/male bit that got him. Shocked me a bit, I have to say."

"Sorry."

"Don't be. Should have realized it a long time ago. All that hair; makes you look like a girl at times. Some of the guys at school used to ask if I had another sister instead of two brothers. I never thought it, just thought you were a bit more feminine in looks than the rest of them. I mean, compared with Jay, anyone's a bit more feminine, let's face it."

We laughed together, softly, not wanting Jay to think we were laughing at him – we were; we just didn't want him to know it.

From then on Jas and I were close and Jay and I were a million miles apart. He didn't speak unless he had to; he didn't walk by me unless he had no choice. I read hatred in his face and was careful when he was around. If he ever found out I'd killed his Josie… even though he didn't want her, not really, anyone he'd touched was his, highly possessive, that Jay. My life wouldn't've been worth living if he ever found out.

Not that it was much to go with anyway.

That was home. Hard work.

Daytime job was hard work too. Boring as hell, entering data all day every day, working with a bunch of people I didn't like. They were polite but distant and that should have suited me, but I wanted –

A friend.

I couldn't have one. Oh, I could have gone out for a drink now and then but beer was dangerous for me, loosened my tongue too much. I would give too much away. I had too many secrets. A teetotal friend is not always a good thing, people feel uncomfortable around someone who doesn't drink. I gathered this from the one teetotal person in the office, a woman of about 30 or so. No one quite knew what to do if we had an office celebration, what did they give her to drink? She usually settled for lemonade but that killed me, all that fizz. Tried it once or twice, useless. Threw it up immediately.

And of course I couldn't touch the eats. So I avoided parties, invitations to go out, pleaded studies – I had studies all right, how to kill and not be caught – couldn't tell them that, could I?

And staying out of trouble, so the police never ever got my DNA.

I learned to drive. That gave me freedom to get out of the county and kill elsewhere when the need was too much.

And that's about where I need to stop this night, if I'm to get to Yelfs in time for the meeting and not have the door slammed in my face.

Hell and damnation, Skullface, did you do some thinking tonight, or what?

What, mostly but yes, I did. And it gets better, doesn't it?

Well, clearer, not sure about better. Come, let's be moving, zombie anomaly. Time to meet your nemesis.

I'm cramped!

So? Get moving; time is a-wasting!

An Evening of Clairvoyance

"Good evening, everybody; thank you for coming. Nice to see every seat filled for our second evening of clairvoyance. I would like to introduce the two mediums we have for this demonstration, Mark Templeton and Jenny Campbell. Thanks for coming along tonight."

Chairperson, ordinary sort of guy, now why did I expect anything else? Mediums are not obvious, he says, looking at the other two. And why do I think the chairperson is a medium as well?

"Good to be here. Shall we open with a short prayer?"

Templeton, tall, rake thin, wearing clothes that fit like they were made for him and probably were. No one gets that quality off the peg. I'm jealous already. The shirt looks like the finest cotton going. Nice tailoring. Never had that quality clothing when I was alive and since then the quality has gone right down the drain. Not that the clothes I got in the charity shop were bad, it's the way I've treated them, sleeping rough and all.

Oh hell, missed the prayer. Never mind, I'm sure God won't hold that against me.

Anyway, he looks competent, assured; confident. That's good. The audience looks – mixed to say the least. Mostly middle aged and older, very few young ones here, maybe two-three, is all. It's a faith thing, isn't it, when you're young you know it all and you are never, ever going to die so what does it matter? No Christians here, unless they're Christian Spiritualists. Now how the hell do I know about them? Must have picked it up somewhere. There's a distinct air of anticipation, it's almost physical.

Jenny Campbell. Oh my, now there's someone to be wary of. Mass of hair, mass of body, if I can be that kind, years of experience etched in her face and the devilment of living life to the full in her eyes. She bothers me. She's got the way of checking you out that misses nothing, she's scoped out the room already, looking for – what? Her prospects? Who she has to go to? Not that I've been to one of these things before but someone at work talked about it. Said not everyone gets a message, never enough time but you get a good idea of what's going on in the spirit world by the messages the lucky ones get. She's looked at me several times now, wonder what she's thinking? Big flowing swishy clothes; bit more like what you would expect a medium to wear. Ha! The men couldn't wear clothes like that!

Skullface, you could, it would bring out the other side of you. Come to think on it… no, best not change gender right now.

Templeton's got the first link, rambling on about some old guy who used to drive a steam train… yes; the person's getting all emotional. Then comes the crunch, the sale of his house won't go through but not to worry, a better offer is coming and it will sell fast and go through with no problem.

Face goes from apprehensive to smiling in 0.3 seconds.

Stop it, Skullface. Let them get on with it.

Now it's her turn, precise, sharp, accurate messages, with humour, that's good, the whole place is laughing.

Then him again.

Then her. My, they're good.

My turn, isn't it?

No. No one gets a message as a matter of course. Come on, Skullface, you know that!

Yes but this is getting a tad boring.

For you, yes, for those getting the message, no.

The door's closed. Couldn't slide out if I wanted to.

Look, idiot face, did you or didn't you invest £7 of the hard earned arguing-with-the-evangelist-type-person this morning in buying a ticket for this evening?

Yes.

Then shut it and be patient.

She's pointing at me.

"I want to go to the gentleman at the back, the one with the strange makeup on. Yes, you, sir. Can I come to you?"

Me!

"You're wearing makeup, aren't you? It isn't your skin, is it?"

"I won the best made up zombie at the zombie convention at the weekend. Not got it off yet."

"Thought it was something like that. Sir, I have to say to you, there are voices calling out to you, some angry, some grateful. Would you understand that?"

"Yes, thank you."

Not sure, I will have to think on that when I get out of here.

Liar. You know well who she means. All the dead ones, dead at your hands.

"You have a burning question; I'll try and answer that later, when the demonstration's over. You will wait, won't you? I can talk to you afterwards?"

"I'll wait."

"Thank you. It's important, they tell me. Meantime I've been asked to say the life you're living at the moment won't last much longer."

"Good, thank you."

"You're not happy at the moment."

"No. That's right."

People are turning round. Do I sound that bad?

No, they're just nosy.

"There's much on your mind."

"Indeed there is."

"You're doing a lot of thinking."

"I am."

"They're saying this is good, you'll reach your conclusion."

"Thank you."

"I don't want to open this up any more in public, it's a bit personal. We can talk later."

"Thank you."

"God bless. Now, the lady with the blue coat, can I come to you, please?"

Left me shaking.

How the hell…

Skullface, you asked for a medium, fate gave you one, a good one. Now, what are you gonna do about it?

Talk to her, of course. I bet she knows more than she's letting on right now.

That's for sure.

The hunger is building. Tomorrow is a long way away.

Be quiet, be patient, she has things to say to you, Skullface. Be sure it will be something you will want to hear – I hope.

The room is remarkably silent for so many people – no creaking of chairs, no shuffling of feet, no blowing of noses, no rummaging in bags. I've not seen people this quiet in a long time.

And still the messages come, some long, some short, they're trying to reach everyone by the look of it. They're good, I have to say that. Not sure what I expected but it wasn't this precision. No one has hesitated in taking anything they're giving.

It's done. Let everyone go by me. A few are staring, but that's par for the course. I look strange, after all, and I'm the only person there wearing a hat.

I have to. Damn hair's falling out.

"When they've gone… we can get out of here." Jenny Campbell's standing by my side. "Do you have a name?"

"Nevermore."

"Good choice. Right, they've shifted their bodies; let's go through to the conservatory. I've said my goodbyes."

The words chilled me. I never got to say any goodbyes.

Perhaps you can, Skullface, when we knock on that door. When you remember where it is.

The hotel's busy but look, table for two in the conservatory, like it was booked for us.

"Here, you sit there, secure the table. I'll go get myself a coffee. If I'm right, you don't drink or eat anything normal, do you?"

"No, I don't."

"Thought not. Won't be long."

Houses opposite, wonder who lives there? So close to the hotel like this, surely there's noise? Perhaps they're cheap. Perhaps they're desperate. Perhaps I should shut up, this is diversionary thinking and that won't do. I need to be alert. Can I trust her?

Let's see how it goes.

"There, done, coffee will be here shortly. Right, let me look at you properly."

The eyes grow darker as she stares.

"You're not what you seem, are you? This might sound silly but I'll say it anyway. I think you're dead but walking about."

"You'd be right."

"Thought so. Never met a true zombie before. You look the part; you don't walk talk or act like one, though."

"You've got that from seeing the films. Not real people. I'm real people."

"I can see that."

"I asked the Universe to let me see a medium. I have this question."

“I knew there was one as soon as I clapped eyes on you tonight. Who did you ask?”

Coffee is served, brown/white sugar in a bowl. I am sore tempted but worried what it might do. She reached for and ate the biscuit.

“Some places offer chocolate instead of biscuits, much more sensible but this’ll do.”

The biscuit disappeared, washed down by coffee rich with cream. I feel a senseless surge of jealousy. She can’t eat raw meat and blood, why am I jealous of coffee, cream and biscuit?

Because they’re normal, Skullface, raw meat and blood aren’t. You’re not a vulture, hyena or jackal. Yet. Maybe the next life, eh? How much of a taste for blood have you acquired?

“I don’t know. The Universe, God, whoever. Spirit, perhaps. I just said, I need a medium to answer the question I have, please direct me to one. Or something like that. Then I was accosted this morning by some Christian who wanted to lecture me on Jesus and God and we ended up having a bit of religious argument. Then he said, ‘what do you want, friend?’ and I said, ‘a medium’ and very reluctantly he told me about this evening’s meeting. I bought myself a ticket with the money he gave me and here I am, with my question.”

“So, ask.” She’s smiling in such a knowing way, I feel as if my mind has been read before I even open my mouth. But I have to ask something else first.

“Do you want money for this?” I have one hand on the remaining money, ready to pull it out of my pocket if she says yes. I don’t mind paying.

"No. This is a gift for someone the likes of which I've never seen before. I'll be dining out on this story for ages, when I know you're back in the ground, where you should truly be, not before."

"OK. I want to know: Why am I not properly dead?"

"Do you want to be?"

"Not yet."

"There's your answer. Until you want to be properly dead, as you put it, you won't be. You're not human, you know. There's a big part of you that's not human and isn't going to lie down and play dead because the family wanted you to."

Ha! Family again! Hold on, I never mentioned them; she's reading this from spirit or from me.

"I feel like I've got to come to terms with them, what they did to me and all I did before I can be truly dead."

"And you're right. You only wanted confirmation. You got it. Good job you came tonight, Nevermore. Others might not've seen you for what you are and you'd have got yourself a load of gobbledegook. I'm not saying they're not good mediums, most of them are, but they haven't lived as much as I have. I've seen everything, on both sides of life. That's how I was able to recognize what you are."

"Am I a demon of some kind?"

"No. You could call yourself a monster, though, and not be far from the truth. You're part monster/part human. The human part is trying to reconcile the family's attitude to the monster part and you're trying to reconcile yourself to the monster part, too."

There's a sense of relief in hearing this. I'm not going completely mad: I am completely mad. That solves a lot of my worries.

"Am I obviously a zombie?"

"You look like one. You can go on getting away with the makeup story for a bit longer. How long do you want to stay alive?"

"Until I remember everything and go back and knock on the door and demand acceptance or something. Revenge, possibly."

"What's holding you back?"

"Still remembering everything, not remembering where we lived."

"Oh, right, small things, then. You'll remember. Believe. Spirit said so."

"Thank you so much."

"My pleasure. Like I said, I have a story to dine out on in a few months' time, when you're reinterred, whoever does it. Where were you buried?"

"Firestone Copse."

"Oh, not a proper grave, then."

"No. I'd as soon go back there if I can, it's a nice place."

"It is. Walkers and people and children passing you by, yes, I can see that. Good luck, Nevermore. Stay strong. It won't be for much longer."

She stood up and then looked at me with a strange piercing look.

"I'm finding it hard to believe we just had that conversation."

“Me too.”

“It isn’t easy for you, is it?”

“No. You got that right, for sure.”

“Well, time I went. Sometimes these evenings take it out of me but tonight was worth it, just to meet you.”

“Thanks again.”

She’s gone, a small proud talented lady with more insight than most people on this island. I wondered why she wasn’t afraid of me.

I feel better. Time I was gone too. I need another lodging place for the night.

Out the back door of the conservatory, avoiding looking at anyone, feeling the dagger eyes staring into my back, customers wondering who I am. I’m wondering how much they overheard. I mean, was that a surreal conversation or what? She totally accepted she was talking to a dead person.

Of course she was, Skullface; what else do mediums do?

No, you’re missing the point, I meant a walking talking living dead person, not a spirit dead person.

I did make the right choice, didn’t I? I know now what I am.

Monster/human.

The other question, which gender of human I am, didn’t get asked. I don’t think I want that answered anyway. I know if I was to go into a charity shop and buy a skirt and blouse and nice shoes with heels, put a necklace on and earrings, I could be a reasonable looking female. A zombie female, but it would work. It would change everything, though, and right now I don’t want that.

These jeans give me some protection from the weather, these boots are made for walking – there's a song in there somewhere, as I recall – the jacket's good and the hat covers up a lot. I guess I'll go on being a man for the time being. After all, I lived most of my life as a male. The female part was pretty well secondary all the time.

It would have been good to have indulged that side, though. Wish I had now.

So, tonight, where do I rest up and continue my ongoing deliberations? Sounds like a jury, doesn't it? The jury is out on whether I am entirely sane or entirely mad. Depends on whether you consider me entirely monster or entirely human.

On that point the jury is definitely out.

On the Streets Again

Well, sort of.

That wasn't easy. The yoofs are out in force tonight. I wanted somewhere quiet, not somewhere they would stumble over me and decided I was fair game. I don't think the flesh is up to that. Nor am I. I'm hungry but not hungry enough to take one of them out. That's Lymington's surprise tomorrow.

So I tried the Esplanade by the café and entrance to the pier, too busy. Tried the bowling alley, too busy. Tried the funfair, way too busy. So here I am, round the back of the boating lake, beneath the trees, dark and quiet and only the sound of the ducks and swans having a private hissing conversation to bother me. Oh, and the occasional car driving off but the yoofs, on the whole, haven't ventured this far tonight. I can retreat onto the golf course if I have to, but I might need that another night, depending on how long all this nonsense of remembering actually takes.

So I was at the point of Jay attacking me, as I recall. A few hours have passed since I thought about that and a lot has happened during that time, been rather busy, in fact. Learned a few things, accepted a few things, understand a little more than I did before Jenny Campbell talked with me. I feel a little more relaxed in the mind, but the body aches. I don't think all this sleeping – if I can call it that – on rough ground is doing me much good. But she said it won't last much longer. God forfend it doesn't.

Whoo, where did that medieval-type expression come from?

She talked to some people, so did Templeton, come to that, of people who walk with you from the other side. Wonder if I have someone looking after me? Certainly things keep falling into place, like the guy giving me the money this morning.

That feels like two days ago, so much has crammed into my mind since then.

OK, let's go back again, Skullface.

I wanted a friend.

I never did get one.

Ever.

I buried myself in music, blues and country and western, where the songs rip your heart out and you want to cry with the loneliness and heartbreak they sang about with such meaning. I did too, cry I mean, a lot and always, always alone.

Jas went on with her life, her sexy looks and her various men.

Jay left home to flat-share with some rather obnoxious yoofs. We weren't sorry to see him go.

Joanna carried on with her studies.

Mother/Madam kept bringing men home and losing them when they came up against the reality of me.

I carried on being me, needing blood and raw meat and avoiding everyone as best I could for fear of them finding out I was part female. At that time I thought it was something evil, best hidden from the world. Now here I am, wishing I had utilised it, flaunted it, accepted it, rejoiced in it and made the most of it. I could have had so much fun.

Well, that's one acceptance, Skullface. Now go for some more.

Shortly. Just had another thought.

How long have I been out of my grave? Not long. I think I'm gonna get home before the County Press comes out, good! Seeing it for real on the doorstep will be a bigger shock than seeing my ugly mug in the pages, won't it? Now that's worth hurrying up for, I think.

Actually, Skullface, you won't. It's Wednesday. The paper comes out on Friday and you've a way to go yet. So, she may well see it – then again she may not – before you arrive. You'll have the satisfaction of knowing, if she does see it, that you're out and anything could happen. Her nerves should be on edge by then. Says he with hope and what fingers are left firmly crossed.

Ok, more.

I got fired from my job. Someone said they didn't like the way I looked at people, as if I wanted to eat them. Ha! Like I'd eat any of those stringy half-baked bodies! But I've got to confess the hunger was there more times than not. That wasn't the reason they gave to get rid of me, though, that wouldn't have gone down well at an industrial tribunal, would it? They come up with a cost cutting exercise, shifted a few people, made it look like a regular downsize. Perhaps it was. They weren't doing that well, I knew that. I went with no regrets, I hated the place anyway. But it meant job hunting and that was difficult. I had this aura that put people off. I got turned down time and again for any job, shelf stacking, warehouse work, working on roads: you name it, I applied for it and didn't get it, where others did. I know that, I saw them doing the job.

Still I tried and still I got nowhere. The Job Centre people were indifferent, unsympathetic; downright hostile at times. They drew back, though, when they saw the 'me' underneath the subservient face I put on to go there. That 'me' rarely stayed hidden in the face of adversity.

Ha! I recall the visit to the dentist, oh my, he was scared senseless when he saw the teeth. "What kind of person are you?" he asked, whilst trying to discover the source of my perpetual ache. He finally found the rotted tooth but said all the others were shaped in a way he had never seen before. Like the teeth of a wild animal, sharp, fangs to tear and bite. "But of course," I said and he sort of laughed. Uncertain. He took the tooth out, I never went back. Never had to. Now I never will. One good thing, anyway.

So what happened in the last nine and a half years, then? Seems like some kind of plague has overtaken the human race. Like, everyone seems to be holding some device to their ear and talking loudly over the traffic and noise and if they're not doing that, they have wires coming from their ears and there's the sound of music as they pass me by. What I'm saying is, they're all locked in their own little world, whoever they're talking to, whatever they're listening to, takes them out of whatever they're doing at that moment and into another place, another time. Like they don't want to be connected to the here and now. Like they can't connect with people unless it's through a tiny handset. Like they don't want to connect with anyone. Like they need that distraction, that conversation, that song.

It wasn't as bad as that when I disappeared from society. I guess the signs were there, guess I should have seen it coming and perhaps if I'd lived a normal life out in the world, working, socializing, seeing people day to day, I would have noticed the creeping plague of electronic distancing.

TV showed me some of it, but TV tends to centre itself on different things, the sound bite; the 30 seconds of fame some people achieve or, if it's a programme about something in particular, the overall tendency of the human race to rush lemming-like into technology is not always apparent.

Come back into the real world, people! You have no idea what you're missing. I do, I've rediscovered it and am appreciating it even though I know it's only for the short time I'll be here. And I like it. Wish I'd been given more of a chance to appreciate it before now.

So, with no work I rather fell back into wandering the streets, terrorizing people without realising it, making a nuisance of myself at home, getting under people's feet and generally in the way. Joanna would snap at me to leave her alone, that she had studying to do. Jas would tolerate me but if she was getting ready for yet another date with yet another man, then she would push me out of the way.

‘Getting ready’ meant hours of preparation, clothes washed and ironed and I wondered why; they would be creased the moment she got in someone’s car. And the makeup would streak the first time she got into a pub or club that was over-heated – most of them were.

“It’s the first impression, Jesse,” she said once with infinite patience.

The problem for me was, the first impression was the true one and I terrified most people by simply being - me.

Not something I could do anything about. Jas told me, gently, that I had an air of menace that was almost physical; it scared off the toughest man.

Jay never visited, I can discount him.

Mother was in despair; would I never leave home and let her find someone else?

No. Not while I had no job and no woman/man to call my own. And who would want a half man/half woman anyway? Only someone with a kinky mind and they wouldn’t be after settling down in a little new build somewhere with a huge mortgage and a hundred bills to meet every month. Well, you know what I mean.

And the hunger grew.

I knew it, felt it, lived with it. It was harder to control by the day. I was hanging on by the skin of my not inconsiderable teeth to the fact that if I kept on killing, I would end up in prison and that would be the end of me, for sure.

I drove to far off counties, killed quietly and disposed of the bodies carefully, in the sea, down disused mineshafts, left on lonely moors for wild animals to dissect, in shallow graves in deep forests. No one asked where I'd been, no one checked the miles on my car. As long as I reported at the Job Centre regularly, no one cared. I faked the job applications, even going so far as to buy local papers in far off counties to show I'd been looking, taking the papers with me to the interviews. 'Look where I've been, job hunting, people, and still they won't take me.' It went down well.

Fools.

I covered up my activities as best I could for as long as I could. No one could have asked more of me. I was a walking blood sucking monster and only I realized it, until I found someone and ripped their face off or their throat out. Vampires, of course they exist, I am one. But I have no gift of immortality to pass on and not for me the gentle piercing with two fangs and leaving two neat holes. No, for me it is ravening hunger and a kill, swift, brutal and necessary.

Vampires don't exist really, do they? Not the way they're pictured in movies and books anyway. Zombies do; those of us get out of our graves and walk about.

Does that make me a mixture of both?

Always said you were a one-off, Skullface. Carry on, this is interesting.

Really? I thought it was pretty dull.

Well, let's consider this. I need blood; that makes me a vampire. I need flesh; that makes me a cannibal. I am dead and walk about, that makes me a zombie. A vamibalombie. Unheard of. Monster's a quicker name. More descriptive, too.

My next question, one I can't answer right now but perhaps when I arrive on the doorstep I'll get my answer is: who the hell fathered me that I came out like this?

And that, Skullface, is not for answering yet, as you said, but it's a good question. One you never thought to ask when you were here, did you?

No. I took Mother for granted, the father who walked out for granted, never occurred to me that I was so…

The hour grows late, or should that be early? I want to be on my way to Lymington this day, to make another kill, to satiate the need to eat before it drives me insane and I have to kill here, which is Not a Good Idea, is it?

No.

Tis early. The dawn is about to break. It's been a long night of thought and memories and a lot of it hurts. Wish it didn't, it would be easier if it didn't.

But there would be no merit in it without hurt, Skullface.

That is a cliché and a fact, for sure, but one I can live without, thanks very much.

You call this 'living', do you?

It is. I walk, I talk, I think. I tire, I would weep if I had enough moisture still to secrete from my over dry eyes and I certainly feel. That's why I'm complaining about memories, they're hurting. It ain't nice.

Nor are the memories, Skullface.

You certainly said a truth there, for sure.

Is it too early to go to Lymington?

Probably. Wait on a bit. Let the world wake up, well, this island's part of the world anyway.

Yarmouth.

Small as I remembered, quirky as I remembered, and as far from Ryde as I remembered.

That was not much fun, buses and people and traffic and stares, oh the stares, am I that peculiar looking or shouldn't I ask?

Every one who got on the bus stared at me. Those who got off seemed relieved to be leaving me there, in my window seat; watching the world go by. Newport. Need to go there, I think, next time I need a meal. Plenty of secret places to go and not be seen. If I wasn't so determined to get the hell off the island for this next one, I'd be there now, walking round the shops, eyeing up the meals on wheels/legs.

Too many memories on the ride over here too, Ningwood, there's a body there, can't remember the location. Buried, of course. Bouldner, well, I already talked about that one.

And now Yarmouth. No, not a place I would make a kill, I've too much affection for it without knowing why. Maybe it's because, like me, it's an anomaly. It's a funny historical place, has a castle of its own, narrow streets, lovely homes and yet is a busy working ferry port. The two don't really go together and yet they do.

"One return foot passenger ticket, please."

If they knew how hard this is for me, pretending to be a living person… but hey, I got lucky, casual glance, not a second look, one ticket, one lot of loose change and I'm free to wait for the great hulking thing to make its way across the often rather turbulent stretch of water. Today it's calm, the yachts are hardly moving in their berths. I'm grateful for that.

Look at all that money tied up there! Millions of pounds, I'm guessing. It was an expensive lifestyle when I was alive. And I've been out of circulation for a long time.

I don't count the time locked up as being alive. I wasn't free to walk about, go where I wanted, see what I wanted; be what I wanted.

Lies, Skullface, you were exactly what you wanted to be.

A monster. A killer. An aberration. An anomaly. Inhuman.

Hey, the black shadow's back! When did I lose it? Can't remember. But it's back, look, walking across…

To the ferry, where I ought to be.

Wake up, Skullface! You near enough missed this one. Thought you were hungry.

I am.

So let's go!

"Are you all right, sir?"

"Yes, not been well, getting there. Need to go to Lymington today."

"As long as you're sure…"

No, I'm not but let me get over there, please! You, in your smart uniform and strictured life can have not one tiny miniscule infinitesimal inclination of the ravening beast inside me clamouring for food.

I need to eat and soon. Otherwise I'll disintegrate without walking back into that hated house and confronting those hated people and demanding to know –

Some things I don't want to think about. Yet.

There's time.

That kid is eyeing me up. He'll turn away shortly – like that – bury his face in his mother's coat – like that – and he'll have bad dreams tonight of bogeymen coming to get him. He'll scream and she'll come running, comfort him, hold him, the way mine never ever did, no matter how bad my nightmares and night fears got.

Locked the damn door and left me to fight them out alone, yelling at me to 'shut the hell up in there, Jesse! Some of us have to sleep!'

No wonder I'm twisted and sick!

Blame the parents, Skullface, everyone does.

Well, back to that question, who fathered me? Some freaky weirdo? Who? If it was the man who abandoned us, who fathered him? What rogue genes were carried through to end up in me?

I get the feeling sometimes I'm a throwback to one of those freaks the carnies used to travel around with, exhibit them for a coin or two, let the people in to gawp at them and go home to be grateful for the healthy offspring they'd fathered/birthed. I'm not real, am I? Not by a thousand mile stretch am I real. If you set out to invent someone strange, unreal, inhuman and yet who looks human…

Frankenstein's monster didn't work because he was bits and pieces put together and brought to life. Scary story, yes, one of the good ones, ruined by

Hollywood's interpretation, most of which was farcical. Bolts in the head and all.

Now me… if someone wanted to make a film of me, they'd need someone average looking at first. I didn't make a habit of walking around drooling blood and only became vaguely monster-looking after I crawled out of my grave.

Inside, though, I am far worse a monster than any Dr Frankenstein could create. Heartless, consciousless, cold blooded killer. No, not cold, hot. The need for hot fountaining blood, not cold.

And here we are, stumbling off the ferry onto the mainland again. Well, I am anyway, stumbling, that is. Need to feed before I fall down.

And hell, got through some more thoughts; didn't I?

Gotta stop this travelling business, not good for me.

Last time. After this, killing on my own doorstep - in a manner of speaking.

Hello Lymington, what do you have for me…

It's shipified.

What? Skullface, you inventing a language again?

Pretty much. What else do you call a place which exists for boat owners?

Sensible?

Ok, try yachtified instead. Same thing. Boats and more boats. Look at them, clogging the skyline with their masts! Bit like Cowes but more so – nah, not really. About the same.

The streets are pretty, but – dare I say this, you could find places like this on the island. Maybe I'm biased, probably am, but there you go. I'm not here to write a travelogue on the place, I'm here to eat.

And I need to get out of town to do that. I recall country lanes, quiet places where someone might walk alone and meet up with a half-starved zombie.

All right, whole starved zombie.

So I'm leaving all the chandlery and the fancy shops selling fancy goods behind and trekking out of town. Anywhere away from the crowds, of which there are many and the looks, of which there are many. Naturally. I must be getting worse, but they'll have to put up with it until the day I walk to that front door and confront them all with my questions. Of which there are many.

Here we go. Peace. Nothing but birds, of which there are many.

Skullface, that is no longer funny. Quit it, would you?

OK. Need a rest.

If that's the level of the humour, you need more than a rest, for sure.

Stop bullying me. I told you before, have some respect for the dead.

This tree will do. Looks like it's supported many a weary person in the past. Even recently, judging by the fresh cigarette ends. Yuk. Filthy habit, so glad I never started that one. The ones I have are bad enough.

Listen up.

Going back to the beginning. Unmarried mother, don't know who, dumped with a family, don't know why or who or how or when, like: was I a babe in arms, was I newborn, was I walking.

Remembering, the woman I was told to call Mother. Suited me, she seemed sort of motherly, big busted, big hipped, lots to hug if I fell – which I did, often – lots to bang into in the small kitchen we had in that house. Not much room, I had to share with Jay and that probably started off the problems with him.

I knew from an early age there was something different about me, so I dressed when he wasn't in the room and undressed when he wasn't in the room and made damn sure I was covered up when in bed. He treated me like a brother, which suited me, as in he ignored me, fought with me, stole my possessions, such as they were, snatched my biscuits and cakes when he thought no one was looking and made my life hell. I thought all brothers were like that.

Jasmine and Joanna shared a small room. Not sure how they managed it but they did and, unlike Jay and me, never seemed to fight. If they did, we never knew of it. Mother had the bedroom at the front with the man she called Father, the one who walked out one day and never came back. I disremember his name, I disremember him, actually. Not an image remains of someone supposedly there to take care of me. It was because of that Jay could get away with bullying me nonstop. And did.

Not a fun place to grow up. Not a fun place to live when you are so different people are repelled by you. The men Mother brought home were repelled, big time. Often they took one look and said, 'that's one peculiar kid there, honey," and found an excuse to leave. The aura I mentioned before, the spiked one; must have showed from an early age.

The only friends I had at school were the troublemakers, the rebels, the class tormenters. I stayed friends with them to avoid being the butt of their torments. I had enough of that at home. The teachers turned away from the black eyes, the cut lips, the bruises down my arms, when they could have done something. I guess I was too peculiar for them to take an interest in. I noticed the ones they fussed over were the class sweethearts, the blondes with curls, the ones who excelled at lessons and sports. I didn't do either. And I didn't have blonde curls. I could have done, but Mother kept it cut short, in the ongoing pretence I was a boy.

She, Mother, was short tempered, quick in her movements, could throw a meal together in no time for all of us and make it taste good, or so everyone said. I would be there in the corner with my bowl and raw meat whilst they ate roasts and pies and sausages and pasta and pizza. I couldn't eat it. I tried, I puked. Sorry, basic truth there, not nice but a fact of life. My body couldn't take it. I wanted it but it didn't want it. As in, my mind wanted it because it all looked so good, but the body rejected it instantly. Jay soon learned to stop tormenting me physically by commenting on the quality and taste of the food instead. In the end Mother threatened to serve him with raw meat and blood so he quit it.

Crowded home, no love. No sense of belonging. I was just – there. Somewhere to live, a shelter, a place to lie down at night, somewhere to eat my food and rest my weary bones.

Love came from grandparents, which is how I knew the difference and grandparents upped and died on me but, unlike me, never came back to life.

Hey, how could they? Burned up, they were, in the crematorium, disappeared behind the curtain and into the flames. Sobbing relatives outside pausing to weep over the floral tributes and us kids in our best black. I hadn't realized how many relatives I had until they came to the funerals and I did wonder why I never saw them at any other time. When someone says 'I was his/her brother/sister/cousin' I got to wondering why I didn't know them, how come they all visited when I wasn't visiting and it put a nasty suspicion in my head, that my grandparents, although they loved me, kept me away from the rest of their family because they were ashamed of me.

My mourning, my grief was compounded by this thought. It tore me up for months.

Someone's coming! More than one, damn. Can't cope with two. Lies, I could, but how do I subdue two people at the same time?

Let them go. They'll never know how lucky they are.

Walkers. Proper walkers, with backpacks and sticks and maps and all. Just as well I let them go, they'd be missed. I want someone who won't instantly be missed, someone who is just out for a wander, that afternoon stroll in the Autumn air, preparing themselves for winter which, if I have anything to do with it, will come rather quicker than they anticipated.

The shadow hides beneath the adjoining tree, see it skulking there? Thinks I can't see it, foolish thing. I can. It's blacker than the shade it's in. Far blacker. Like my thoughts right now.

Hey, this is new, I can see ghost dogs. Spirit dogs. They're jumping and running and playing and fighting. No one's stopping them fighting, either. Oh, it didn't last long, they're back playing again. Never thought I would see spirit animals. Hope I don't see the mole; if I do, I'll have to ask for his forgiveness. I needed his blood but didn't need his skin after all. I was a bit scared back then, fired up with the need to get out of the grave but worried about what would happen when I did. Ask me now why I thought I needed the skin for a mask and I'll say I have absolutely no bloody idea.

The dogs have gone. Wish I knew what that was all about. A glimpse into the spirit world, where I ought to be, perhaps?

Should be, Skullface, not ought to be.

How much longer do I have to walk on this earth? How much longer before all the thoughts catch up with me, I accept what happened, I finally remember where Madam lives and can go confront her with my existence and then…

Then what?

Back to the grave? Can I rebury myself? Will I have to ask someone to do it for me? Will I be properly dead then?

Does anyone, anywhere, have the answers to these questions?

More important than that, even, will I get the answers to my questions?

That's in the hands of Fate.

As is the life of the next person who comes my way.

Whilst I wait, knowing full well someone will come along, I'm going back again.

We were all there together in the end of terrace three bed house with garage (for which read junk area – the car never saw the inside of the garage from one decade to the next) garden front and back and that most mysterious of places, a basement.

Few suburban houses have basements. I never did find out how this one got to have such a thing but it did and it was off limits to us kids. No matter who. Jay tried hard to get in there but got his ears boxed and his ass kicked for even trying it. I never did, I had enough to cope with – Jay was everlasting beating me up and Mother was everlasting ignoring what he was doing. I sometimes wondered if she had a scrap of feeling for me anywhere in her substantial body and had to decide in the end no, she hadn't. I knew she got paid for having me there, until I grew up. There was the motive, no love, not even affection, nothing. Money came first, especially after the man of the house walked out. I doubted that was anything to do with me. I wasn't displaying any of my latent abilities then; only the need for blood and raw meat and surely anyone could cope with that, couldn't they?

Probably not.

So, like I said, I never got my nerve together to try and get in the basement. It had a thick door with an even thicker lock on it, massive hinges fit for a church door; it was that heavy. No idea who did it, but I would say, if asked –

Ok, I'm asking, Skullface, who did it?

The people who had the house before us. We heard the stories from the neighbours and Grampa had a few thoughts on the subject. They were a strange couple, so the word went, both big hulking people, kept themselves to themselves, never spoke with neighbours, had everything delivered; hardly ever went out. A lorry came by now and then and took away a load of earth, another lorry came – and then one of those huge cement things where the barrel is rolling rolling rolling to stop the cement setting. It poured gallons of the stuff down into the hole the man made. People asked, got no answers, so they gossiped, what was going on there? Were they building a nuclear shelter of some kind?

"That's close enough," said one delivery man and that was all anyone got.

I wanted to know so bad it hurt but I was scared of being hurt any more so had to settle for not knowing. I knew I wasn't Mother's favourite person so asking, trying to wheedle information out of her, was a no-no. Jay couldn't find out so what chance did I have?

For the longest time I believed Jay was the only natural child Mother had, because he said so. He could have got away with more than he did, if she wasn't busy setting an example to the rest of us. Jas, Joanna and me, I was told, were fostered, in a manner of speaking. I doubt any social worker ever knew we existed; it was all done informally, people wanting to dump their unwanted kids knew where they could come. Or so I was told.

You think that doesn't go on?

Course it does. Everyone knows about kids being dumped on relatives, finding out their aunt is actually their mother, usually at a time when it's most damaging to their psyche. I knew I didn't belong there, that I was just a source of income. Jay was quick to tell me and then repeat it often, to make sure I got the message. Thanks, Jay, I got the message first time you beat it into me.

And so, we lived in a house with a basement.

Now you know about the basement. You'll know a hell of a lot more by the time we get through to the end of this sad scribbler's unwritten diary. I have to stop now. I hear someone coming.

Perfect.

Like I ordered it up, a takeaway for a zombie. No, a vamibalombie. Nah, too much of a mouthful and too long to write in the diary, too. But it has a certain ring to it, don't you think?

He's a scraggy teen, hoodie and all, slouching along like he has the cares of the world on his hanger-thin shoulders, from which a lousy tee shirt is suspended with all the grace of a jumble sale display. I can see the lower six inches or so of the tee shirt below the hoodie, which is grubby and as ill-favoured as its wearer. Trainers, of course, mandatory, that disgusting form of footwear. I am grateful Madam never put anything that dreadful on me, but then again, would she bury expensive or even cheap trainers when Jay might need them?

Jay first, foremost, up front always and ever.

I got brown slip ons. I always hated brown shoes. And she knew it.

Anyway, there's my meal on legs.

"Hey, Mister, you look rough."

"Thanks."

"You-"

He got too close. He got not another word out.

The hunger could not wait any longer. Behind the tree, blood stained clothing and drained body with lumps taken out of it discarded like the piece of rubbish it portrayed itself to be. No respect for clothes, for self, nothing.

I had a tiny pang of regret for his at least noticing I looked rough.

But Skullface, anyone dead looks rough. He was stating the ******* obvious!

Yes, but…

Give over, would you? Are you not fed? Are you not sustained for a period of at least 24 hours, enough to get you back to the island, to what you think of as civilization? And will that not stop you having to feed again for a goodly length of time?

Yes.

Then get the effing hell out of here, would you? Wish I knew why I had to remind you all the time to get away from the bodies when you've done with them!

Because it would be so, so nice to just sit here and digest my meal.

And insane.

Yes, I know, I know. OK, let me get up. Where's the mirror? Oh, here it is. Need some more tissues soon.

Get some before you get on the ferry. There's that shop you saw with everything imaginable in it and then some things you didn't imagine.

Ok, ok, ok, stop bullying. How many times…

I heard you the first time. Respect for the dead. You'll get no respect if residents find you here, blood dripping down your face, next to a chewed body.

Right, look, I'm up on feet and walking. Back to the town centre, back to the ferry, back to the island. One foot in front of the other, again and again and again… hell, this is boring.

Skullface, have you checked your clothes? Are you walking off with blood on the nice tweed jacket, by any chance?

Oh hell, yes.

Well, it's gonna rain, that's for sure. There's a Save the Children shop, you favoured that charity in Ryde. A raincoat might be good cover up. But if you can scrub some off…

Let's give it a try.

Nope. Best carry it, I think.

Inside out, Skullface, inside out!

How much money do I have left… enough to buy me a raincoat, I should think. I'll worry about bus fares when I get back to the island.

Hell, it's started raining. I look stupid carrying a coat when it's raining!

Ditch it. No good to you now.

I like it!

And?

I ruined it.

So you did.

No, damn it, I didn't ruin it! Hoodie ruined it! Fountaining his blood everywhere like that, faster than I could drink it!

Yes, that's right, blame everyone but yourself. Typical Skullface reaction.

Well, there we are, there's the shop. I'll just dump this…

There's a half decent raincoat, how much is it? Is that all? OK, that's for me, then.

Gives you a different look, Skullface. You've got your return ticket, yes? It isn't in the tweed?

No. Got it here with the money. It's safe.

Gotta say you look half smart in that. Almost normal. Almost living.

But not quite.

No, there's no way you'll ever look completely right. Sorry to say that.

Don't we always tell the truth to one another?

Sure, but sometimes we don't want to hear it.

"Are you all right, sir?"

"It's makeup, no problem. Thanks for asking."

"I was a bit concerned but yes, good zombie makeup, well done!"

"Thanks. I'll wear this now, if you can take the price tag off for me?"

"Of course. Weather changed suddenly, didn't it?"

Don't even think of smiling, Skullface, this is going too well. And don't, in the name of heaven, let her see you're two pinky fingers short of a full set. You really will freak her out!

"It did. I have to get back to the island."

"Oh, just over for the day, then."

Not a question, no need to answer.

"Thank you."

Coat feels good. Better than the tweed. Well, that was incidental rather than chosen.

Waiting on the ferry – again. Decided I am not doing this again. To hell with serial killer nonsense, the papers are bound to be full of it ere long; surprised they haven't started on it yet. They can't do anything to me that hasn't already been done, can they? Lock me up? I'll lose the will to live and they'll be left with a rotting body. Lucky them.

Lucky me. I will be glad when this is over. It isn't much fun.

I was about 18 when I realized the basement was being emptied and cleared. Like, seriously emptied and cleared. Jay was coming round way too much for my liking; Mother was paying him to do the work. Junk came out of there, was thrown in the skip she hired, along with half the neighbourhood rubbish, I saw the neighbours coming out with this and that and the other and throwing it in, taking advantage, but I suppose we all did that when a skip arrived.

I never realized how much junk we had in the basement, either. Not all ours, I was guessing, a good deal might have been left over from the strange couple before us. I saw clothes, rotted through and moth eaten, that would have covered people three times my size, so I knew they weren't ours. Even Mother wasn't that big.

Then paint arrived and other stuff and there was painting and hammering and drilling. It went on for ages, day after day. Jay would come up the stairs complaining about his back and his arms and his legs and the fact he had a headache from the paint fumes and on and on and on. Mother would tell him to shut the **** up and remember he was getting paid for it, this was not a favour.

So he shut up and got on with it. We didn't see him again for ages after the job was done, whatever he'd been asked to do.

You know how it is, you get used to something, never give it another thought. Like, nobody wants CCTV cameras everywhere, next thing they're so much a part of life you don't think about them. You go round getting photographed all over the place and don't worry about it.

That was the way it went with the basement. Whatever work was done was done, finished and the door was locked. I ignored it, it ignored me. Outside in the so-called garden I sometimes glanced at the barred window and thought, wonder why anyone would dig the ground away to make light in there, then thought, nothing to do with me, so what the hell… and it would go from my mind.

Stupid. Blind and stupid.

It had everything to do with me. I just didn't know it back then.

Island Life Part II

Here we are, back on the island. Maybe I can escape some of the strange looks. These shades are good but not big enough to hide three quarters of my face, just the top bit. So the rest of the zombie-look visage is on show. Kids are still running from me. Adults are wary of me. I really hope they put my photo in the County Press, people will then see what happened: I won first prize; I can't get the makeup off. That's my story anyway.

Ha! I was about to say was ever £50 won so easily. In some ways it was, in others, well, I had to come back from the dead to get it so really it wasn't, was it?

"Hey, Mister!"

Strange sense of déjà vu going on here.

"Mister! Over here!"

"Hello?"

"You the guy who won the zombie makeup prize, ain'tcha? You was on the Esplanade the other day talking with my mate Barry, weren'cha? Come on, I'm going back to Ryde; just got me a fare to bring someone out here and I didn't get a fare back. I was gonna go back on my ownsome when I saw you there."

"Fine, thank you, I'd appreciate it."

"No probs, we can do it, us taxi drivers like sommat different. Barry said you was one fine zombie. He's into all that stuff, I ain't but it don't stop me appreciatin' it, like, do it now? You done a fine job there… Mr?..."

"Just call me Nevermore."

"Odd name."

"The Poe poem about The Raven?"

"One of them horror things, ain't it? Don't know it meself but take your word for it. What's with the Nevermore bit anyway? Don't worry, don't really wanna know. That stuff scares me no end; that it does."

Do all taxi drivers talk like this, nonstop I mean? Saves me talking, which is no bad thing.

"Anywhere in Ryde in particular, Nev?"

I knew he'd do that, I just knew it!

"No, wherever. You taxi people congregate on the Esplanade, don't you?"

"That we do, big bunch of us, all good mates, never argue over a fare, well, not often anyway. You a Ryde man yourself?"

"Yes. Born here, lived here."

"Not an incomer like so many, that's good to know. Here, look at that idiot, how he's driving!"

And he's off. I can relax. The other guy did this, started on about standards of driving and I just let him talk.

This is good, more money saved. I can do with that.

I just realized I said 'lived' and he missed it. Ha!

One life story later we arrive in Ryde. My ears ache.

"Nice raincoat, by the way! Better than that old tweedy thing you had on the other day!"

“Thanks, and thanks for the ride. Better than the bus any day.”

“Sure is. Wish we could put a banner up like that, we’d get more rides. See you, Nev!”

“For sure. Thanks again.”

Full and satiated, not so weary in the body but oh the ears ache and the mind aches from all the trivia he threw at me, but here I am, back home again. The Royal Esplanade is as grand as it ever was, the tourists are as lemming-like as they ever were and I am as lost as I was before I went to Lymington.

Except I fed and got myself a raincoat. And it’s raining.

Is the rain bothering you, Skullface?

No.

Why mention it then?

Because… I’d like somewhere dry for tonight’s deliberations.

Town Hall?

What, round the side under the overhang? Could do.

Thinking more of the toilets. You could get in there and lock a cubicle door. Too obvious in the open, right opposite the Legion and all.

For sure. OK, let’s give that a try. Later. Before then, I need a bit of shelter. No need to get soaked for nothing.

Station. At the pier. That will do you. Look, just walk along here and there you are. Honestly, Skullface, how long have you lived in Ryde?

Listen, I never needed to find shelter before, right?

Yes, this will do.

How quickly people walk when it rains! Unlike the sunshine days, when they dawdle to feel the soft heat on their skin, even the harsh heat, we get so little of it really. Me, I've had no sun on me for nine years. I'm even appreciating the softness of the rain right now, although I really don't want to be here in soggy clothes. Not that I can catch anything, but the clothes are already fit for nothing and I don't want them to get worse.

If I had more money I'd go buy some fresh ones but time is short and I wonder if I should waste money that way. On the other hand, the charity shops could do with money, so…

I'll go check them out tomorrow. New jeans, shirt and sweater would be good, quilted anorak/zip up coat would be nice. The boots are OK, wonder if I can get some socks to hold the toes on?

I've a feeling the weather's changed for the worse. I've had my sunshine quota and very nice it was too, while it lasted.

My last two years of freedom were pleasant, while they lasted. Jasmine was dating some really nice guy who didn't seem to mind me too much. He didn't look away when I walked in; he didn't seem to flinch if I forgot and smiled at him. What he ever said about me behind my back is anyone's guess but that didn't worry me; I was well used to people talking about me behind my back, to my face, mostly acting as if I wasn't there. Well, perhaps I wasn't. Not in their eyes, anyway. Joanna was home/not home, depending on studies. Someone said she wanted to be a social worker. I didn't believe that for one minute. Solicitor or barrister more like, some profession she could use her skills to attack. She had the most cutting tongue I had ever heard and in my state of being, that is plenty, let me tell you. Social worker… biggest joke I heard in my life. She never spoke to me, so I didn't know what the truth was. I refused to ask, refused to show any interest. I could play the same game as her. She never bought anyone home, man or woman. Solitary person, like me.

I have just seen someone hurrying past with a dog on a lead.

We never had pets. Any of us. No rabbit, gerbil, hamster, goldfish or bird. No dog or cat. Here I confess that a dog or cat would have been short lived with me, as would the rabbit, gerbil or hamster. The goldfish would have been safe as would the sweet singing canary, had anyone wanted one. Maybe not a chirpy irritating budgie but they weren't worth bothering with; they'd be no more than a sweet in my mouth. Not that I ever ate a sweet. Not once. Never touched chocolate, drank wine, had coffee rich with cream, nothing. Ha! Back at the beginning of this adventure, which is how I see it – it's the only way I can see it – I said something silly about missing a fillet steak with big fat chips.

Lies. The truth is; I miss never being able to have such a meal.

No pet ever came to live at the house and, stupidly, I now regret and resent that. The unconditional love I see expressed by these animals has been denied me all my life. It still is. I will never see that, never know that. It matters not that logic tells me they would not have lived longer than half an hour if I'd one of my berserker rages on, but – I never got the chance to show I could care for an animal of any kind.

Add it to my list of grievances.

It gets longer by the hour.

Revenge is a dish best served cold, they say.

It doesn't come much colder than dead.

Dark comes early when it's raining, like it creeps out of the closet and makes its way across the sky to dampen our spirits as well as the buildings, greenery and earth – and all who get in its way. It seems to want to drive us indoors. I have no indoors to be driven into, rain, spare me a few moments to find a new shelter for the night, would you?

There are yoofs out there but not that many. I can cope with them, I think. Mostly they're securely fastened to a bar somewhere, guzzling beer and spirits. I could tell them about spirits but they'd think I'm as drunk as they're likely to be.

I could also tell them about being securely fastened but they wouldn't believe me. No one would.

I had a thought earlier. Those damn spirit dogs, they've bothered me since I saw them. I think they've made themselves known to me before, if I can phrase it like that.

Hell, Skullface, whose unwritten diary is this? You can phrase it any damn way you wish!

Of course I can.

Town Hall, as we talked about. Hey, the clock's stopped, when did that happen? Did I imagine the chimes across the rooftops and trees? Might have done. It was always there, now it's not. At least I'll get some peace during the night. Got me a lot of thinking to do.

The loos are cold. But then, so am I, being dead and all. What difference does it make? I can lock myself in here and try and get some privacy. Might be some coming and going but a wet night might send people home instead.

And so…

Two years left of freedom. Wish I'd known what was ahead, I'd have made more of them. We could all say that, if I'd known I'd have a heart attack I'd have – taken that cruise, seen that film, visited that beauty spot, gone on that holiday tour – whatever. But we don't and it isn't given to us to know.

Look at me, dead and don't know where or how I'm going to be reburied, even. You'd think I'd know a simple thing like that, wouldn't you?

Two years of going around the country, finding someone hapless and helpless and making them less hapless by helping them into the next life. Not that often, I had enough raw meat in between to keep me centred and at home. Petrol costs money and there's a danger in too many kills. I was well aware of that. Every so often someone would start a scare story of a wild animal, puma or something, roaming the countryside, killing hikers. I didn't mind that, it took the heat off a rogue serial killer. They were bound to be suspicious, though, when they/if they ran the details through their detection software to match it with similar 'crimes.' I didn't use a weapon and that would have thrown it a bit. I also tried to vary it a bit by not always tearing the throat out. Sounds ghoulish but I had my preservation to think of, did I not?

Two years of useless job hunting and of being stared at in pubs and clubs, so I stopped going. Twice I ventured out dressed as a woman, looked pretty good too. I know that, men tried to pick me up on each occasion. But I made the 'mistake' of smiling at them – deliberately – to put them off and it did.

Two years of hating that bloody cock ring which seemed to grow tighter by the week. Now I'm free of it, I'm not able to take advantage. How frustrating is that, in every sense of the word…

So somehow it all coming to a crashing end was almost a relief.

Is that someone coming in the loos? Yes. Silence, total silence from me. When they're gone, I can shift position; this loo seat is not particularly comfortable and is very cold.

Quick **** and they're gone.

Wish the clock was still working; I'd have some idea of the time. Could be anywhere from 8, when I got here, I think, to about 10, as the street noise seems to be quietening down. The rain's getting heavier by the sound of it. It's hammering on the car roofs. Or something is.

Madam had some new guy coming to the house, Greg or some such name. All big chest, flat stomach, bulging muscles and everything. Good-looking in a rugged sort of way. I could see why she liked him so much.

What I couldn't see was what he saw in her, middle-aged and more, big body, big ass, big mouth you could hear half down the street. Not what you'd call model material, nothing delightful to have on your arm. What was the attraction, I asked myself a hundred times… the equity in the house, the fact she was, to all intents and purposes, still married so he couldn't be entangled in an unwanted wedding, but then, would he?

Or am I doing the man a disservice, did he really like her for herself? Not unheard of but unusual. Or… and here we walk a darker path, did he have problems that were as difficult as mine and no woman could cope with them, until he met Madam, who had experience of a true freak?

I speak of him in the past tense for one reason only: I saw him once or twice during the early part of my nine year incarceration and then never again. I have no idea to this day if he stayed/left/died/ran away with Joanna or what. No one ever said and when they did come down into the basement it was for one of three reasons:

Clean the place up for me.

Feed me.

Beat me.

So, I never spoke to them. Not once.

Leaping ahead of myself, bad habit.

Madam/Mother had this new guy. I was spending more time than usual out of the house, to give them privacy and to avoid his searching looks. If he fancied me, as man or woman, I didn't want to know. Not any way shape or form.

So it was inevitable that in a town like Ryde, where three quarters of the pubs are in one small area, I'd run into Jay at some point and Jay would have a bunch of friends with him and they would all know about my part male/part female body and they would all be calling out crude things and generally being yoof-ish and unpleasant as only Jay's friends could be.

Which is exactly what happened that July. I was walking past the King Lud down on the Esplanade when this group spilled out onto the pavement - and saw me. Before I registered who they were, they had pounced, encircled me and were pushing, shoving, pointing, dragging at my clothes, saying the crudest of things.

Jay was on the edge of the circle, calling over their heads, "show 'em your tits, Jessica!"

He made two mistakes that day. I made the biggest mistake of my life, but neither of us could have known that. Jay's mistakes were:

Calling me by the name I hated above all other, one he used when bullying me and

Not realizing I hadn't had my full ration of blood and meat.

I flipped into full berserker mode – and lost it. I roared at the 'friends', smashed my way through the ring, caught hold of one of them as I went and sent him clean through the plate glass window of the pub. His scream energized me; I went for the second one and tore his throat out, wanting to drink the blood but aware that there wasn't time. The others scattered and ran.

"Jesse, for Christ's sake, what have you done!" Jay screamed at me, his face a mask of horror. He'd not seen me in such a state before. God knows what I looked like, must have had blood all over my face and clothes.

Realisation crashed in, the berserker me vanished, the shy scared boy came back. I turned and ran.

For a while I hid on the golf course, skulking behind bushes, trying to climb a tree to get out of everyone's sight. I finally found one and sat in the branches, numb. Totally numb. I knew I'd had blown it and that it was the end of everything. It was, but not in the way I thought. I had visions of police, barristers, trial; prison.

When I got weary and disillusioned with myself and the world, I climbed down and began to walk home. The King Lud would have had crime scene tape round it and forensic teams working on the person I to0k out. There were umpteen witnesses to the attack. Jay was probably at the police station giving some sort of statement. About a brother he hated. About a situation he deplored. About a situation he contrived to set in motion with his thoughtless bullying tactics. I bet he never told them that.

I crept in the door, wondering what reception I would get. Mother came from the lounge and looked at me, blood spattered and shattered.

"I knew it." She was so calm; so – prepared for this. "You flipped, Jesse, right?"

"Yes."

A chain came from nowhere, from her pocket, wherever. In a second it was around my neck so tight I could scarcely breathe. Then she dragged me toward the basement. I saw Greg following, grinning and flexing his muscles. If I could have got free, I would have smashed his face in. There was enough berserker left in me to want to do that, no, screaming out to do that.

I wondered where Jay was, even as she dragged me along the hall. Nowhere to be seen. He would have been there, delighting in whatever Mother had planned. Then I had a fleeting glimpse of a future that didn't contain Jay, as if he'd been wiped out.

She didn't know I'd feared the basement all my life, simply because I couldn't get into it and see what was in it. When you don't see something, your mind plays games, fills it with monsters and creeping things. I was terrified, the chain was choking me, I was going somewhere I feared and I had no idea what she had in mind. And still I clung to the hope that there was a way out of this ridiculous traumatic dangerous situation.

The reality was shocking.

The basement had been converted into a prison.

She pushed me down the stairs; literally, shoved me and I fell and then bounced once. Dazed, breathless, confused, I was an easy target for what happened next. She ripped my pants down, snapped the end of the chain onto my cock ring and put the other round the pipe which went from one end of the basement to the other. I screamed with pain at the additional pressure on my balls. The ring was so tight that even that clip hurt like hell. Then she backed away from me.

"Been waiting for you to flip, Jesse," she said with such presence I was almost in awe of her. "This has been prepared for you for a long time. Eventually a monster like you has to be confined. Now's the time. That chain's long enough for you to get to the bed, the bucket, the window and the food when I bring it. It isn't long enough for you to get to the door or reach anyone who comes in, unless they're plain stupid and walk toward you. For now the chain's padlocked. I'll get Greg or Jay to weld it shut in a day or so, you'll never get free of it. Here you stay until I say otherwise!" The words were as icy as the floor was that day.

"Needs some heat down here, dearest," Greg said, with a leer in my direction. He'd followed her down but was standing around, the 'spare prick at a wedding' syndrome. The leer was sort of, 'look, I'm thinking about you, aren't I? That makes me the good guy around here, right?'

"Heat? Oh, suppose so. Didn't think about that. We'll get some piped in. Not having a heater in here, no way. Think what'd happen if I left him with that!"

She looked at me. "This is your new life, Jesse, welcome to it. I knew it would happen; knew you'd never hold on to that monster inside you."

"It was Jay!" I shouted at her, ignoring Greg, he was nothing, just another man in her life; he'd go, like all the others. "Jay taunted me about my boobs in front of everyone!"

"That was enough to kill someone, Jesse? Jay's still at the police station, still talking about you, about the monster we had in the family. He knows what to say, that we didn't know about your murderous traits. Not to mention the blood and the meat. Not to mention the girl in you."

"I should have been fed today." Sulky now, trying to lay the blame elsewhere.

"I know." I didn't expect that. "I should have fed you and you're right, Jay shouldn't have taunted you. I told you to stay out of his way."

"I was coming home." Tears were flowing, a suspicion of my future life dangling before my mind, which was everywhere, absolutely everywhere, jumping from defiance to defeat and back again. "I was coming home and he came out of the King Lud with a bunch of low-lifes and started on me."

Mother sighed. "Like I said, I knew it would happen. I'm only surprised it took so long." She gestured to the basement. "This's been ready for you for two years. You held out longer than I thought."

"Did I - get home without being seen, do you think?"

She sighed again. "If you did, I'm stuck with you for a hellishly long time, Jesse. But if you weren't, your time in prison would be limited. What would you prefer?"

"I don't know."

Greg left, as if bored with the conversation. Good, it was nothing to do with him anyway.

"Well, until someone finds out you're here, this is your home. I got it ready for you, knowing you'd need it one day. All those hormones rampaging through a body that's simply not right, not any way you look at it; had to happen. You had to flip. I hope you like what I've done."

As if on cue the TV, which I hadn't noticed at first, flared into life. I stared at it in horror.

"I hate television!" I shouted at her.

She gave me the most evil smile I had ever seen in my life, worse by far than mine and that's saying something.

"I know."

I felt what affection I once held drain out into that cold cold floor and never ever come back. Oh I loved her once, of course I did, that big big word, love, I knew it in all its forms.

It went.

It went completely, totally and absolutely in a nano-second.

In its place came implacable hatred. For her and for Greg. If I said this before, forgive me, I can't read what I haven't written down. I recall something like that anyway and I definitely recall the next bit, because I relived it many times in the days and weeks and months and years I had left to me.

"I curse you forever!" I saw her scurry back a step or two; then she got her courage together and moved in again.

"You!" she scorned me with her eyes and her tone. "You know nothing! You think you're so bloody clever! Who has to clear up the mess you left behind, tell me that! Do you think I can stand you near me for a second after all that's gone down?"

"You talk like a cheap cop show! You don't know anything, anything at all!"

"I know enough to make sure I don't have the Old Bill on my doorstep!" A parting shot I couldn't deny. She walked up the steps and slammed the door shut behind her, a terribly final sound.

I sat on the edge of the thin mattress and looked at my new home. White walls, white ceiling, barred window, uncarpeted floor. Bucket in the corner. Bed bolted to the floor. It felt cold, it was cold. Greg was right, I needed heat.

The light blazed down from behind its wire cage, the TV blared it's nonsense, outside the darkness pressed down on the window I had seen from the garden and slowly but surely the full depths of her depravity and hatred dawned on me.

Crashed in, more like.

I was a non-person.

No one would know I was in the basement. Visitors would be steered away from the door and told it was full of junk, if they asked. People are usually too polite to ask. I would never be free again to travel, to kill, to feed as I wished. I would have to take what she gave me.

I would have few to no visitors. I would only have the TV. I could see no music in the basement, no stereo, no DVD player, no nothing but that awful nonsense I could hear and tried not to look at.

No books. No magazines. No newspapers.

No sunshine, no rain, no snow, no wind, no sharp frosty mornings and cool evening walks. No Easter. No Christmas.

The TV dominated the place. A huge plasma screen covered with something solid. I walked over and tapped it. Shatterproof, at a guess. She had no intention of letting me kill myself. Or anyone else, come to that. I walked to the length of the chain, dragging my pants back up as far as they would go; balls hurting where the damn clip was fastened. I could manage it if I left the zip down. It was not good. I needed all the clothing I could get to keep warm. And it was only July.

A basement is a cold place, it has to be. It's surrounded by damp earth and crushed by the house above it. It can't go anywhere. That reality didn't sink in immediately but it did later. Some nights I would lie awake hearing – or thinking I was hearing – the house creak and settle, scared witless and ****less that it would collapse and I would be crushed.

Then I'd think, OFFS, Jesse, does it matter? You've got eff all to live for! But somehow, no matter how hard it is, how dreary it is, what condition it is, the self wants to live. The self wants to believe that there's an end to it, that there's freedom at the end of the tunnel so long, so dark, so endless that it could model for eternity but surely even eternity must have an end. Nothing can be infinite.

But there were times when I believed it was.

Never so much as that first night when she slammed the door on the rest of my life.

There's light, Skullface, we've endured another night. Where are we in the great scheme of things?

I think it's Thursday. If it is, the County Press will be out tomorrow. I can't wait to see if I'm in it, to wonder whether she might see me. What fun! She used to buy the paper, probably still does. She was obsessed with the obituaries.

So, what plans?

Today we buy new clothes. I've just enough money if I'm careful and hold back a bit to go to Newport. I want to visit one last time. Don't even begin to ask me why I think time is getting short. It just is. I can't make it to Ventnor, Shanklin, Bembridge or any other place I once held dear. There's not enough time, not enough money and more than that, not enough spirit left holding this dead body together to let me do it.

Fair enough. One question before we depart this confining uncomfortable totally unbelievable shelter of a cubicle, what happened with Jay?

Oh yes, I said I had a vision of a life with him wiped out.

He immediately commandeered my car and wrote it –and himself – off in a major head on crash on the Calbourne Road three weeks after she put me in the basement.

I couldn't have been more relieved. Truthfully. I think I was the only one who lip-read him the one time he came down with her. I saw him say he would 'visit' me every week. I faced a lifetime of my bigger-than-me-bully of a brother beating me up every week and me, chained as I was, not able to do anything about it.

He didn't get to visit before he got wiped out. She saw to that. I heard them outside the door, heard the yelling and screaming, heard him demand the right to see me; heard her yelling he had no rights at all. She had the key and she wasn't giving it to him. I never did find out why she wouldn't let him, unless she was afraid of what he would do.

It could have happened; he could have got hold of the key. I was chained up in the basement shaking with terror at the thought of it. If he damaged me, I would die because she couldn't get a doctor in, or – perish the thought – paramedics. Not without a lot of problems for her and Greg. I bet that was behind her decision to keep him out.

Jay didn't let up, though. He would stand outside the door and yell insults and threats at me, keeping me in such a state that terror all but closed my throat for hours afterwards, scared senseless he would do something to get the key, that the door would open and he'd be there. Every time she came with food or to take the bucket away, I'd be shaking until I was sure she was alone.

She walked in one day, far later than usual. I think this was about five weeks after she imprisoned me. I'd noticed Jay hadn't been outside the door screaming his insults and threats but didn't ask where he was. I never did ask about anything. It was safer that way.

She came wearing head to foot black. I must have blinked in surprise or something, because she looked at me, smiled a bit sadly and said: "Sorry I'm late, been to your brother's funeral."

"Jay?" I felt my heart leap with relief and tried to smother it.

"Jay. Took your bloody car, didn't he? Wrote it off and got killed on the Calbourne Road." I saw tears gathering and I could almost, almost have hugged her in my relief but the hatred held me back. Please note; I wasn't empathizing with her loss.

She dumped my tray on the floor and walked out, looking as if she'd aged several years in a short time. Then I realized she'd been like that for some weeks, but I'd been too busy feeling sorry for myself to notice.

As the weeks went on, watching her change, diminish, lose weight and become grey and old with grief at losing her one true son, the only one she truly cared about, I felt the hatred deepen. She did this. She brought it on herself. If I'd been free, he'd never have taken the car, never tried racing a little car against a big one, which is what they said happened – Greg came to tell me all about it, she never did – and I and my car would still be alive.

I mourned the death of the car for months.

I also recall that was the last time I saw Greg.

So there I was, nearly twenty years old, with a birthday in the October which would see me turn twenty properly, heading toward leaving the teen years behind, with all that they held in the way of problems: needing the blood, needing the thrill of killing, needing the love and protection of a family. How odd, how strange in this modern world it was the first two which were easily obtained and the third an outright impossibility.

I suppose it's hard to love a monster but surely there must have been something likeable about me, no?

Skullface, you asking me?

No, you won't have the answers I need.

Good. 'Cos you're right, I don't.

Then I guess the answer is – no, there was nothing likeable about me.

So be it.

I get to live/be dead with that.

Skullface, stop with the semantics, let's go. 'Tis morning. There are things to do. Buy clothes. Sort yourself out. Get some more money from somewhere if you can. If time is running out, make the most of what's left.

I wish to hell you weren't right all the time.

Yet Another Endless Day

Too many of these, but still, it can't last much longer. Then there will be endless sleep and oh I crave that!

Where do we start with the clothes? What about British Heart Foundation? Just up the road here… open early? No, it's later than I thought.

OK, here we go; funny looks again. I know, wearing shades on a dark wet day, but hell, who cares?

These will do. Thick jeans. Thick shirt. No sweater, no coat? Can't win them all.

There's a couple more shops up the road. Age UK. Red Cross. RSPCA. Three shops, then. Don't like them too much but still…

It's a hell of a walk up this long, long slope. Getting all sorts of looks, guess I'm getting worse by the minute. Time's running out, I know that.

Skullface, have you taken any notice of the shop windows lately?

What?

Halloween. Look at that card shop, loaded with Halloween rubbish.

So?

You could –

I could, couldn't I?

You really are thinking what I'm thinking, aren't you?

For sure. Halloween. Sunday. I could go calling…

Yes, you could. What a surprise that'll be!

Right! Gonna do it!

Too many exclamation marks there for one unwritten diary, Skullface, but in the circumstances let it stand – just this once, mind. We do have standards to maintain, after all.

How come I missed the Halloween stuff?

Too busy being introverted and dreary and consumed with whatever you're consumed with at the moment; the need to eat, the need to re-live, the need to remember. But yes, yes and yes. This is perfect. What better time to come back to life than October and Halloween to cap it?

OK, Age UK shop. Not looking promising but – hey, good sweater here, thick and warm. Like it. No coat, though.

"Can you manage that, sir?"

One carrier bag? I should think so. But it's a polite way of asking if I'm all right, for a change.

"Yes, thanks."

"Thank you for shopping with us."

Out the door and up the road. Still need that coat. And socks. Won't get those in a charity shop. Toes are becoming a nuisance, rather loose these days and I need them to walk. Not for much longer, though, so I almost resent the money but there're two days to go and I need to be comfortable if I'm going places.

Red Cross, hey look! Just what I wanted. Hooded padded coat in my size. Cheap, too.

"That's been reduced, sir."

How come everyone says ‘sir’ to me? I doubt they do it to all the men who come in.

It’s that nasty aura of yours, Skullface, they’re terrified to do anything else but be oh so polite.

Well, that suits me if it keeps them from enquiring too much.

“A bargain. I just need it for a short time.”

“It’s a good quality coat, surprised no one’s wanted it.”

“Waiting for me.”

“Possibly.”

“Thank you.”

Right, loos, change clothes. No, look, let’s go in here first. Got to be some socks here. Yes!

Now I can go get changed. Get warmer. This is the first time since I came back to life I’ve felt cold. Sure indication of the deterioration, definitely going down fast. But there’s only the rest of today and tomorrow to get through, then I can plan my Sunday, my

Some days seem endless. Walking’s better with the new socks, nothing moving about. But killing time’s difficult when you can’t go sit over a coffee for hours, browse in stores for hours, go eat lunch and sit there for hours. I’m attracting too much attention. It’s raining and the raincoat can only absorb so much. The new coat is good and the hat’s in a pocket in case I need it. Using the hood helps disguise me a bit. Or so the ‘mirror’ shop windows tell me, those I can use to check my appearance.

If it would ease off a tad – oh, stupid, how come I forgot the second-hand book shop? I can browse there without attracting attention. I might even buy a paperback. I have enough left, I think. Let me check…

OK. All I have to do is walk up this endless hill…

Oh, what's this? Outdoor shop. Their socks might have been better, but no, look at the prices! Forget it. I only want them for two days. It'll all be over on Sunday, one way or another. Is it really this far out of town… I've passed it, for sure.

No, here it is.

Push the door, go in. The proprietor hardly looks up. I could be in full zombie attire and he wouldn't blink, I swear.

Yes you do, Skullface, but only to yourself. No matter what the provocation, you never swore at Madam, did you?

No. Not once. Perhaps I should have done.

No. You got your point across without that.

If I remember, the top floor is goodness knows how many flights of stairs up. It's the same guy running it. Fancy that! After all these years, he's still here. Nice to know some things are the same.

Wish I was.

Do you, Skullface? Do you really?

No, probably not. I need to be different. Can't live my life as a serial killer, can I?

Well, you could but it isn't recommended for an easy existence.

Need to buy a book.

Not sure if you've noticed, but this place is full of them.

Yes, I know. I want one I can read and not worry if I don't finish it before this ends.

I have one in mind, may/may not fit the bill. Jerome K. Jerome's Three Men In A Boat. You can laugh at the good bits and skip the boring bits – can't remember now if there are any – but most of all, it isn't a thriller or crime book you simply Have To Finish.

Tis the best thing you've said all day. Will go find a copy.

In about an hour's time, Skullface; kill some time while you can.

Books. Books. Books. Something I've not seen or handled for nine years plus some days. I've just realized how much I missed them. Oh my God, how I missed them! All these adventure stories, the thrillers, the crime tales, the historical sagas, the non-fiction to show me the world beyond the TV, the real world which comes alive when you 'see' the images in your mind's eye. The real world, not the one the film makers want you to accept.

God, I miss them! I want to scoop all these books up, surround myself with them, choose one at random and read and read until these dead eyes of mine fall from my useless dead skull.

Instead they're here, waiting for other hands, other eyes, other people to scoop them up, take them home and put them on shelves, there to be kept warm and safe and read and cared for.

If I had tears left, I would shed them. I want… I want these books!

Only one, Skullface, only one.

I know, I know!

What you want now is immaterial. You don't want a grave full of books to moulder with you. That would be unfair.

I know, I know!

We've been here long enough. Come, find a copy of Three Men In A Boat by the wonderfully named Jerome K. Jerome and let us be gone from here. I'm sure you can find a café and linger over a coffee without touching it. You can read some of your book even with your shades on, right?

Right.

Come, before the proprietor gets suspicious of us lingering here. You've looked at a lot of books. Now it's time to go.

I don't want to leave.

Leave what?

The books.

Oh. The books. But…

For sure I know I can't stay. For sure I know I have to leave these all here for others to find. For sure I know all these things, but walking away is so damned hard!

It never was going to be easy, Skullface, not for a moment was it going to be easy. Come, one floor down, we're sure to find a copy down there. Remember how the books are laid out? Nothing's changed in all the years the witch kept you locked away.

Yes.

I just added this to my list of grievances. Dear God; is it ever going to be a long list and dear God, are they ever going to pay!

Better. Much better. Now, let's get going!

Here, look, good copy for you, Skullface.

Right, thank you. Let's negotiate the stairs and out, shall we? Is it still raining?

No idea.

"Just this one?"

"Yes, thanks."

"Do you want a bag?"

"No, the pocket's big enough, thanks anyway."

"Here you go."

"Thank you."

Tugging the door, sticks just as it used to all those years back. Oh the memories!

It's stopped raining but everywhere's dripping. Good thought about the coffee, can't sit outside in this weather. My book would be ruined in no time.

You could try that Frenchy place.

I could.

I can't believe how good it feels just to have a book. Let's hurry.

No, don't let's hurry. Your toes aren't that good, Skullface… nor are your legs. Walk casual and slow, be sensible. You don't know how much longer your body will support you without food. You seem determined to go without 'til Sunday. Not sure you're gonna make it.

Nor am I.

You may have to feed tomorrow to see you through.

I hate it when you're right.

This French whatever-it-is place feels warm. Judging by people's open coats, it's warm. I can't feel enough to know for sure. It's not too full. If I sit in the window, I can watch the world go by.

And they can look at you.

Not with my hood and my shades.

Got the hat still?

For sure. Right here in the pocket of my new padded coat.

Leave off, Skullface!

No, it's fun. Do you realize... seriously... I haven't owned or worn a coat for nine years? Not till I garnered me a tweed jacket. It felt so good, so very very good, to be wearing something tailored. The raincoat feels good too. I'd forgotten how good it felt to be dressed.

And not have pants open at the front because of the accursed ring, too! I almost felt normal for a while. I even feel good having the raincoat folded over one arm like I'm the true man about town. Ready for anything.

"One espresso, please."

"That's all, sir?"

"Yes." And I won't drink that but you won't worry about that. Here I go, paying for something I won't drink. Stupid but it helps.

As I thought, no one's looking in at me. Got my book... got me a place out of the wet. It might not be raining but it's damp and horrid out there. My grave will be flooded now. She will have to find me a new one – if there's anything left of her to arrange such a thing. There might not be enough of her left to bury, come to think of it. Now that is a good thought.

Hey, this book is even funnier than I remembered.

Skullface, how can you wrap humour up in the same thought as leaving virtually nothing left of Mother to bury?

With the greatest of ease. She did me enough wrongs, didn't she?

And you did your fair share, as I recall.

We'll think on that later. Right now, let me have a read, OK?

Not sure what she thought when I left; I've not drunk any of her coffee, but the break was good for me, if nothing else. And that's what matters around here, not what people think. My time's running out, I want to please me during these last few days. The memories aren't pleasing, the days need to be. As best I can make them, anyway.

It's silly but I'm getting so much pleasure from simply holding this book.

And I have a theory why it's so pleasurable. I can, if I want, read this book from end to end without interruption.

I don't think I ever saw a TV programme or film all the way through. I doubt I ever did. She didn't set the thing to one channel and leave it there, she had it set, I'm sure she did, to change channels at random times. Not every half hour, or every hour, or every two hours. It was five minutes, or three quarters of an hour, totally random. I would be watching the news on the BBC and find it leap to some Western or something on Sky or back to Discovery and wild animals and then some soap or other. I couldn't keep track of storylines, follow news items or get involved in a film.

She was determined to drive me mad. No books, no music of my choosing, only what was on the music channels from time to time , no consistent TV to watch, no way to follow the soaps, not that I wanted to, but anything would have been better than nothing. It was designed to drive me insane. It nearly did.

Combine that with the desperate need to see anything but whitewashed walls, a barred window and a tiny bit of garden, the need to breathe fresh air, to talk to people, to walk further than nearly to the door and back, or the walls from side to side.

Imprisonment in every way you can think of.

At least in a 'real' prison I would have seen prisoners, guards, had exercise periods, have work to do to keep me occupied; have the prison library to utilize, studies, perhaps.

Instead I had nine years of intensive mind-numbing boredom.

I did exercises, my own devising, to try and stop the muscles atrophying, but even that seemed pointless sometimes.

Look, see the flowers in this shop here? I didn't see flowers, apart from on the TV screen which is not the same thing, that entire time.

Trees? Forget it. Those magnificent specimens that tower over us and contribute everything to our civilized world, I never saw them. I wanted to see them. I'm no tree hugger, never have been but I could have walked out of that prison and hugged the first tree I saw without feeling self-conscious or stupid. The need was there.

So much was taken from me. So very much. More than any state run prison could have taken from me. And finally, it took my life.

I think… really I do… that I'll take out whoever's in the house straight away; then start on Mother. One limb at a time. One organ at a time. I want her alive as long as possible. It won't compensate for all I went through during that time, but hell; I'll go to my new grave with a smile of contentment. For sure.

Skullface, watch the look. The evil's showing and you're attracting attention!

Ok, ok, sorry.

Fog coming in. The rain's stopped but the fog's coming in. Typical late Autumn evening. Cold, wet, foggy.

And there's the foghorn, mournful as ever, lonely as ever, as soul destroyingly sad as ever. A monotonous drone, rhythmic as a failing heartbeat. Warning ships off the rocks, warning us to stay indoors out of the cold damp air that makes us all feel lousy, chilled through and aching.

But I'm free. I'm outside in the fog, the damp and the darkness which is creeping in so fast I think someone dropped a blanket over Ryde. Thanks, I could do with one for tonight.

What, even with your new padded coat, Skullface?

Even with my new padded coat.

I'm free to breathe damp air, not reconditioned stuff, free to see the fog coming in, shrouding everything, softening everything, touching it with featherlight fingers and changing the outlines as if they are melting. The street lights are muted glows; I never realized they could be so attractive in fog. The people hurrying by are ignoring me, even if they're wondering why I am stood in front of a Halloween display with moisture all over my coat and yet I don't move. I can't tell them this is freedom, this is heaven. This is what I was deprived of for too many years. A man released from not prison but the grave has to take pleasure where he can.

Hey, I called myself a man. Perhaps the male part of me dominates after all. Even missing that essential bit hasn't changed the feeling. Well, would you think on that, it's taken my resurrection to tell me what I am. All those years I couldn't make up my mind one way or the other. I don't think Mother truly knew; she treated me like a boy but there were hints at times she thought of me as a girl. Especially when the boobs grew. Not big, but enough to be seen.

What do you think of the street decorations? Those 'ghosts with pumpkin' lights on the lamp posts? Pretty damn foolish if anyone was to ask me. What a waste of money.

Gotta say all this Halloween fun stuff is in turn freaking me out and inviting me in. I know now I can go out Sunday night and not be noticed, that's the biggest thing.

It's freaking me out because even though I know the end is near, it's nearer than I want it to be. Does that make sense?

Probably not but as no one will read this, it doesn't matter a jot, does it?

The Town Hall loos seem to be the only place I can get shelter overnight in Ryde. Everywhere else is tight shut or not suitable for all night and I want to do some more going back. Each step takes me closer to understanding what really went down there, each session of thinking releases memories I thought had gone forever. Really, when I came out of that grave I couldn't remember who I was or anything. All I need to do now is put it all together and the address will come to me. I know that. Before then I have treacherous pathways to walk – it will not be pleasant.

But then, none of this has been pleasant.

And I'm sure I'm gonna to have to feed tomorrow, the hunger's a rat gnawing at my guts and I'll never stand that until Sunday. There's also the small problem I could flip into berserker mode and that Would Not Do. It would end my chances of knocking on That Door and getting my revenge. After that, they can do what they like. I won't be here much longer, it doesn't matter a scrap. I just don't want to be denied that chance.

Let me see, tomorrow's Newport, my final visit to the county town, catch a glimpse of the County Press if I can, should be able to. They always used to put huge bundles of the thing in front of the counter in newsagents. I only want to read the headlines, see if there's a photo of the 'best made up zombie' on the front. If the picture's not on the front page then I might have to actually buy a copy. Got some dough now. That £5 note in the puddle helped out a lot. It dried all right inside my new padded coat.

That damned coat, Skullface!

Yes, all right, I'm pleased with it, OK? Even if I had a lot of life left I'd be pleased with it. The hood's making the world of difference in keeping me warm and helping me hide.

And that's the most important bit right now.

More Memories

More travels by the Memory Time Machine into the past.

I found a certain pleasure in the fact Jay wrote himself off in my car. It was as if I had a hand in it somehow, that I had taken out my arch-enemy myself. I hadn't; that was the only small cloud on the otherwise bright screen that said

JAY IS NO MORE!

I have to say the relief it brought with it was unbelievable. I doubt I would have lived for nine years if he had been there and 'visiting' me every week. I never knew such naked hatred in someone as he had for me.

Considering the terms of my imprisonment, maybe he would have done me a favour but the way of it would have been beyond acceptance.

The imprisonment, though, was unbearable. Mother forced me to sign the Power of Attorney she had drawn up. She boasted that she had cancelled my appointments with the Job Centre, told them I had run away after the murder. She said she told the police the same thing; that I was very likely somewhere on the Continent by now, having stowed away on a cargo ship or ferry. If they believed that, they'd believe anything but I wasn't there, nowhere to be found. If they searched the house for me, I never heard them and she never said. Someone who went as berserk as I did that night was obviously mentally unbalanced, perhaps they thought I'd fallen off the cliff or thrown myself off or something. Or I had actually run away, it does happen.

The car was written off; she reclaimed the tax and insurance, took the scrap value in my name, closed my bank account, took my savings, such as they were and sold off my possessions. All this she gleefully told me when my daily ration of raw meat and blood was delivered on a paper plate, along with a bottle of water. Nothing else. I had nothing else to drink or eat. I lived on that for nine years. At least when I was free I had the occasional beer, which I could tolerate for some reason. Provided it wasn't one of the dark beers, that is. The food remained the same.

Water gets boring after a while.

After she told me about Jay, after I watched her decline for a few weeks – don't ask me how long any of this was, I quickly lost track of the weeks, the days were there on screen but weeks, forget it – I decided to stop speaking to her. I was not going to give her the satisfaction of goading me into responding to her barbed comments. She was looking for confrontation; I refused to rise to the bait.

She hated it.

How easy it was to get my own back in tiny ways.

She had it all worked out well in advance. Every morning, a handful of wipes to clean myself up, toothbrush for a quick rinse, bottle of water to start the day. She took the bucket away while I cleaned up.

Every lunchtime, tray with dish or plate of raw meat and more water.

Every week, tin bath – believe it! – and lukewarm water. That's when she cleaned the basement. If I was safe in the bath, right alongside the pipe where I was chained, she couldn't be attacked.

The odd thing was, that was her paranoia. I wouldn't have attacked her for one reason: no one would have released me from the chain. No, I desired revenge from a standpoint of freedom.

That's probably why I got out of the grave, then, the desire for revenge when free of the accursed chain, the freedom to do what I really want to do, take her apart.

Before then, oh the fun I had and the information I gleaned…

When you refuse to speak to someone, they get irritated, they spout nonsense to try and provoke a response. If they don't get it, they try with something else.

It was this way I found out that Jay's funeral was only attended by a handful of his car mad friends. No family came. Her 'my Jay is so popular with everyone and so loved' fell on its little face in the mud and blood he spilled at the crash site.

But the real killer, for me, came some years into my incarceration. Forgive me for not wanting to go over this too much, but the dullness, the sheer agonizing monotony of 'living' in that confined space with nothing but interrupted TV programmes, day and night, cannot be described. I knew the reasoning, to show me the world she had taken me out of. I knew the glee she felt knowing I hated television and preferred the solitude of books.

The depths of her hatred could not be plumbed by someone like me. She needed help. I needed understanding.

She flipped one day when I refused to speak to her and began yelling she would get my real mother to come and talk to me, so I would act like a human being again. I just stared at her, waiting for her to tell me who my real mother was. I knew it was coming; it was like the approach of a storm, the air was thick with tension. She'd gone too far, she had no way of pulling back; she was committed.

"I'll get Joanna down here," she said finally.

My look must have said it all. She stared at the cold stone floor for a while; then looked back at me with savage hatred filling her eyes and distorting her features.

"Joanna came to me pregnant. Never ever told me who the father was, I didn't ask. I took the money for her board and lodging and waited for the kid to arrive. The intention was, get the adoption people round immediately and get you gone. But you grabbed the tit so hard you drew blood. You went on drawing blood, it wasn't a one off. The adoption people came, took details, took a look and walked away. They said no one would want you; there was 'something about you.' Well, we knew that. Joanna wanted nothing to do with you. Who could blame her? Fifteen, scared to death, got a baby that even without teeth bit and drew blood and screamed the place down if he didn't get it. No wonder she didn't want to know.

"I should have done away with you, cot death; no one would have been surprised. It would all have been over."

I went on staring, mouth open, shocked beyond reason at this revelation. Joanna, the cold hearted bitch who had ignored me my entire life, the person I had shared a table with, sat through endless evenings with, watched her studying wondering what she was going to be in life, called her my sister and wondered why she never spoke to me, was my real mother.

She had rejected me so totally I never had an instant when I would have thought that was the case.

Mother/Madam knew then she had finally reached me. Got to the core of me and hurt me for the first time. The incarceration hadn't appeared to hurt me; I made damned sure she didn't know how I felt. I wasn't going to give her that satisfaction.

"Surprised you at last, Jesse? Good. I thought you were turning into a blood pudding and just existing. Yes, she's your mother all right. I ought to know, I birthed you. I know what came out of her womb. You. Thing is, you looked normal or you'd have been a stillborn, no question of it. I've done it enough times for kids too young to be mothers. Got paid well for it, too. That back yard you look out on? God alone knows what's buried there, fetuses, stillborns, live ones that became stillborns. That's why it ain't a garden. No one's allowed to dig out there but me. I can just about recall where the last one was buried.

"You wondered why Joanna never looked at you, spoke to you, never been down here to visit you? Cos she hates and detests and loathes the very sight of you. You're a reminder of her foolishness, one drunken night, one unknown father. All she knew is he was called Tyrone and if you believe that, you'll believe anything. More a false made up name I never did hear in my life. One night stand, her first ever, she gets knocked up – with you.

"She's trying to make something of her life. You are NOT, I mean this, Jesse, going to interrupt that life. I love the kid like she was my own. Joanna's not her proper name, I gave her that name. I quite like you all having names starting with a J.

"One day I'll tell you about Jasmine, but right now you've got enough to chew on. Enough for a few weeks, I should think. I'll make you talk to me if it's the last thing you do!"

Slam. As it had slammed so many, many times before.

She left me alone.

With more ghosts and memories and thoughts than she realized.

And a bit more ammunition than she realized, too.

Because she lied. Oh, only in the last bit, all the rest was a shock to me. I admit it. A total shock. But she lied when she said, 'I love the kid like she was my own.'

She was her natural child, as was Joanna. I had all this bullshit about adopting/fostering and all and knew that's what it was. Bullshit. Not sure who was supposed to benefit from that deception, or why she'd insisted on maintaining it.

I'd gone burrowing in hidden places one day when they were all out somewhere and as usual Jesse was not included, as Jesse couldn't eat or drink anything on offer and if Jesse didn't get his blood and meat he'd tear the place apart and that would not go down well with whoever's home they were in. I'd gone burrowing and found an envelope full of birth certificates for Jay, Jasmine and Joanna.

All her natural kids.

By different fathers.

Another bus ride. At least it isn't raining, overcast and grey and gloomy but no rain. I'm almost tempted to hand the raincoat in at a charity shop, give something back. But not yet, I still like the feel of it, although a raincoat and a padded coat don't go together too well. Perhaps I will, before I leave Newport for the last time.

Damn it, I'm getting maudlin.

This time I paid my fare, got my hood up and my shades on and no one gave me a second look. Good, just the way I want it right now.

Newport. Bustling busy with over keen shoppers eyeing the Halloween displays in the shops. Come on, you don't want that stuff, do you? Come with me on Sunday night, I'll show you Halloween in all its gore and truth. A true walking dead doing a real killing. Maybe several, depending on who's there. Night of the Living Dead it ain't.

No, best not. You might get in the way.

I need a rest. Damn buses make me feel queasy.

Ok, this will do.

Skullface, do you really want to sit here?

What's wrong with the memorial cross?

Nothing, only you look like you're begging.

Hey, there's an idea! Where's the hat?

You're not… you are. Oh hell…

Look the part now?

Well, let's see if you get any takers or whether the police move you on. Begging's illegal.

I'm not. I'm sitting here quietly and if I care to toss my hat to the ground…

And sit peacefully for a while. Watch the girls go by. It's cold and Autumn-y and they're in skimpy tops and tight leggings or something and shorts so short they are hardly there and -

Thank you, sir, thank you.

OK, Skullface, I concede. This time you're right.

Oops, here comes one of the dog collar brigade.

"My friend, are you in need?"

"Not really, sir, I was sitting here for a rest…"

"Now I look at you, I have to say you have the appearance of a man who is…"

"Dying? Say it as it is, sir, yes I am. I came to Newport today for a final goodbye."

"I am so sorry."

"Don't be, I'm not. My time's almost done, it's the way I want it. I've had chances to say my goodbyes. This is one of the last. Tomorrow I'll say goodbye to Ryde."

"It seems so sad…"

"Give me your blessing, sir; that at least I can take with me."

"Of course."

Hypocrite, Skullface.

No, keeps the man happy, makes him think he's done something for this poor dying man.

Then he'll see the papers…

And know he blessed a zombie. So? Everyone has to do have one thing they're proud of. He can be proud of that.

Maybe.

"Thank you, sir."

"Here, let me add £1 to your small collection."

"Ha! That was unintentional. I put the hat down and someone threw a coin into it!"

"People are generous."

"Some."

"You're right. Well, I wish you peace, my friend; in Jesus' name I wish you peace."

"Thank you."

"Go with God."

He's going. OK, I got myself £1.50 I didn't have before, so let's go look at the County Press, shall we? Got some money now in case I need to buy one.

Now, where's WH Smith? Down the road here, where all the initials are, as I recall. HMV, BHS, WH Smith… what's this? HMV closing down? Hell, where are people going to get their music? Online, I suppose. I see enough 'online' references on the dreaded hated TV and she wouldn't let me near a computer. Of course. I might have told the world where I was and she'd be in trouble for harbouring a known murderer.

Hey, hold that thought. It's the first time I've thought of myself that way.

Does it hurt, Skullface?

No, it's liberating. I'm coming to terms with me. And there's one more to go before Halloween, too. Who will be the lucky one to end his life of trial and turmoil and worry? Don't they realize I'm doing them a favour?

And why did I think 'he'? I haven't fastened my dead eyes on anyone yet.

Here's Smiths. Pretty crowded, got to be careful, bits might get knocked off. That would never do, not yet. That can happen on Sunday, until then… I'm having enough trouble hiding the fact both hands have lost a finger and are about to lose another.

There's the County Press stack… Oh my God, there I am! Front page, full colour, a ghastly looking creature. Am I really like that?

Of course, Skullface, of course.

No wonder I won first prize! And look at the headlines, 'Serial Killer Loose On The South Coast' - right next to my photo.

And no one will realize for the longest time what that juxtaposition is all about.

That I like. That I like a lot.

Well, that has pleased me. She'll see it for sure.

Whether she recognizes you as Jesse is anyone's guess, Skullface. I mean, you look pretty horrific. Come to think of it, you still do, hood, shades and all.

She should recognize the person she had locked up for nine years!

Yes. She should but if she doesn't, it'll be even more of a shock when you arrive, won't it?

Should I buy a copy?

Any reason why not? Your money was added to this very day by well-wishers, all two of them.

Might have got more if I'd stayed there.

And got yourself moved on by the police? Skullface, we are so close to the end, don't blow it now.

Damn it, again you're right. I hate that.

The hunger is intense, like really intense, like I can't describe how it's tearing me apart. Got to feed, but where and who?

Where; that stretch of river before you hit the town proper; that would be good. I could walk along there, sit for a while; think about things; see who walks into my web.

If they don't make it soon, I'm likely to jump someone right here in the street and take them out.

And lose the chance of revenge?

I know, I know… but it's – torture is what it is. Pure bloody torture.

Listen, if you can't stand it, how are you gonna get through tomorrow without killing and then all of Sunday?

I'll make it, because it's thisclose to The Time. Like; thisclose.

Go buy your paper so we can get going.

For sure.

Are these assistants programmed to ignore eccentrics? Not so much as a flicker at the sight of my hands, minus their little fingers and another half hanging off. Oh, put the rotting thing in my pocket, why don't I… That's better. I'll knock it off otherwise. Clean off.

And scare the living **** out of someone if it happens.

Look at me, a proper islander again. Here I am, clutching my County Press, waiting for a chance to say somewhen or even better, anywhen. Haven't said those words in years. I want to feel normal again, even if it's only for a day or two. Is that too much to ask?

Probably.

In which case, I'll take what there is and make the most of it.

Here we are, greenery, lots of fallen leaves; lots of solitude. No one around, just as I thought. I can bury someone under fallen leaves; they'll stay hidden for a few days, with luck. Long enough for me to get my revenge and then who the hell cares after that? Like I said before, what can they do to me?

Nothing.

I'm gonna change my nice new padded coat for the raincoat. Then if the blood goes everywhere – it tends to do that – I'll have a clean coat to go back with.

Now let's read about me.

Hmm, the convention a great success, x hundred people there, brilliant bands – I'd take issue with that if I had an address to write from – and a wonderful winner of the Best Made Up Zombie competition, Mr. Nevermore. The organisers said 'it was the best makeup they had ever seen.'

Ha! They'll never see the like of that again, will they?

Your moment of glory, Skullface.

That it was. All the rest is unsung, isn't it?

And has to stay that way.

Halloween can't come soon enough.

What can come soon enough is the right meal on legs for this vamibalombie. Time someone wandered along here…

Yes! Another yoof, female this time, for a change, sweeter blood, I hope. On her own.

Whoops; almost fell. "Can I help you?" She's all solicitous and helpful and -

Oh yes, little one, you can.

And that sets me up until Sunday. That's a promise.

Cover her with the raincoat and leaves.

Where's my mirror? Here. Not too bad, let me get at the water for a moment, there, that's better. Clean and fresh as before. I feel a thousand times better. Throw a few more leaves on her… and I'm out of here.

Goodbye, Newport. You're as bustling busy as I remembered and as unattractive as I remembered. No great loss to me.

Back to the bus station; get the next bus to Ryde.

Before anyone connects me with the body that will be discovered ere long.

Return Home

A walk along the Esplanade seems like a good idea after the hustle and bustle of Newport, of too many shops gone and others taken their place and probably they've had a change of ownership too. The place feels transient, very few fixtures. I think that's why I went to the memorial cross, it felt permanent in the midst of change.

The Esplanade here in Ryde, on the other hand, always seems permanent. The hotel, the pub, the cottages along the road, Ryde Castle, which looks like it's been damaged, was that a fire, I wonder? Lots of work going on anyway, scaffolding and all. Oh, the Chinese restaurant roof's changed from a thatch to a slate one and looks different. It is different. New name. Wonder what happened there? Another fire? Nothing else would surely have meant changing such a lovely old building. Still a Chinese restaurant, though. It's that sense of permanence which imbues Ryde with its atmosphere. The boating lake looks no different, nor does the odd old Appley Tower. I like it here, I'm comfortable here. I'm right pleased I made it to Newport one last time but equally right pleased to be back.

I really don't want to go back to those loos tonight; I think I'll lose myself – excuse the pun - on the golf course somewhere, climb a tree; crawl under a bush, whatever. It's not raining, I can cope.

It's not that good an evening that people are out and about still. I can see the Esplanade clearing from here, my seat by the Tower. They're hurrying home to a warm house, good food and comfort. I'll overlook the fact they'll all be slumped in front of a television before you can look round but still… their choice. I still have my book and that's good enough for me. I keep touching it to remind myself I own a book, the first in nine years and six months, at a guess. That's a long time to go without a book when you love them. I still envy the Rydeites their warm house, good food and comfort. I wish so much I had been normal, could have eaten the burgers and beef, the ice cream and chocolate, the multitude of vegetables and fruit I saw in greengrocers' windows and longed to try. Apples, gold and red, bananas, rich yellow, grapes, red and green… I could go on. It'll depress me if I do, so I won't.

Instead I want to watch this miracle, the sun going down painting the sky more shades than can be mixed on an artist's palette, for sure.

Now we come to something, a big confession/admission for this unwritten diary. I would have loved to have been able to paint. I would love to have sat before an easel in the countryside and painted the skies. I love skies, clouds, sunrises, sunsets, would love love love to have been able to do that.

I never could. I tried, oh how I tried! Whole pads of artists' paper used up, whole sets of paints, all different kinds of brushes and hours of time all that came out was a splodge of colour that in no way resembled what I'd envisaged. My hands wouldn't do what my brain directed them to do. Hands? I tried both. I thought it might work if I used the left hand, activated the right hand side of the brain, see? I tried everything. I had to admit I was talentless. Never could do it. School never got me to paint anything half reasonable. The best they could say was 'Jesse tried.'

Now here's a huge thought to conjure with this late Autumn evening.

Is reincarnation for real? If so, perhaps I can choose to become a painter next time I return to this side of life, if I haven't blotted my celestial spiritual copybook by my many murders and my revenge and my hatred and my desire to wipe out an entire family, one by one. Small things that just might get in the way of my coming back to do what I want. Might mean some time in the spiritual equivalent of therapy, methinks.

Or will they understand I came here in a strange half/half body which could only exist on blood and raw meat, with a mind which flipped into savage berserker mode so fast even I was shocked by the change - and I was the one doing it. A monster in human form. They would know, wouldn't they, that there's no such thing as a vamibalombie - but I am one. A unique creation caused by mutated genes and probably drugs of some kind. I'm a monstrosity, a freak, a complete aberration of nature. Something the doctors and scientists would love to have to prod, push, preserve and work on. Hard luck. I intend to ensure no one does, once I've done what I came to do. No one pulls Jesse to bits to find out how he/she ticked. I'm going to destroy me just enough that no one will want to do that, says he hopefully, but leave enough to bury. I do want a proper grave.

I don't think it overly matters, Skullface.

It does to me.

But you'll be in pieces and…

And what? The pieces can be gathered up, put in a carton and buried, right?

And you are going to write this in your will?

No, it's right here in this unwritten diary. That's legal and binding on the world. As far as I'm concerned.

You, Skullface, are off your head.

You, mind, are out of order. Shut it.

I will.

Good.

Someone, an outsider, came to visit me one year.

Mother took a huge risk in doing that. I found out later it was a doctor who'd been struck off. Figures, no proper working licensed doctor would've come to see me and not gone away and reported it to every authority there was to report to. Not even a retired one.

I can't recall properly what was wrong with me. It had to be serious or she wouldn't have gone to all that trouble. You don't find debarred doctors in the local surgery, do you? Must have taken her some time to find him.

What mattered to me was, someone strange had come down into the basement carrying a bag of bits and pieces, looking at me with intense curiosity.

I returned the look. I hadn't seen anyone in years and years and years. All right, maybe four is all it was but it felt like eternity.

"This is Dr. Green, Jesse. In case you're wondering, he's retired from practice." Oh so polite and nice, nicer than she had been for – well, four years. Oh, retired, has he? He's way too young to be retired. That's when I knew for sure he'd been debarred for something or other. She admitted it later, said she didn't want to say it in front of him. That I can believe, it would have been embarrassing – for him. I didn't care one way or the other. I just was pleased to see another face and speak with another human being.

"Hello, Doctor."

"Hello, Jesse. Your mother tells me you're not as well as you could be."

"Need some fresh air and sunshine," I said, tempting fate and Mother's anger. She only smiled.

"He gets exercise, Doctor, and fresh air. I just can't let him outside. He's too strong to hold back when he wants to kill."

"Not 'wants', Mother. Needs."

"Shut up, Jesse. That's just semantics. The doctor needs to examine you. You've not been right lately and I got a bit worried."

So he got busy with stethoscope, blood pressure monitor, spatulas and all and checked me out.

"Bad chest infection going on here," he told Mother. "Here." He handed her a packet, I guessed it was antibiotics or something. He couldn't write a prescription, could he?

"Thank you."

"Take the pills, Jesse, you'll be fine in a few days."

"Thank you, doctor."

I wanted to say, but I don't feel ill but perhaps I did. The strange wheezy sound coming from my lungs had bothered me but I put it down to years of breathing stale recycled air. I had also ignored the hacking cough, same reason. But I admit now the blood streaks had bothered me. I don't mind other people's blood; I hate losing my own.

I did hate losing my own.

He looked round the basement, nodded at the TV and smiled."Something to watch, at least." Well, not exactly but I wasn't going to say that. He looked at the bucket, the bed, the bars and then the chain.

"Is that necessary?"

"Yes. He's quiet now, Doctor, but believe me, he can flip in a moment and destroy everything in sight. Like I told you, he can only digest raw meat and blood. If he doesn't get that, he goes berserk. In every sense of the word. We have to make sure he doesn't attack one of us."

"True aberration, then."

"Yes."

"Scientists would love to take a look at him." They were moving toward the steps. I heard the doctor say, "he looks so normal, doesn't he?" just as they reached the basement door.

I didn't hear Mother's reply, the door slammed as it had done a thousand times already. I didn't even care what she had to say. It was enough for me to have something else to think about.

At that moment the TV switched to some hospital drama. Serendipity or what?

How did she find him? How do you go about getting in touch with a struck off doctor? What did she tell him? ‘My son’s imprisoned in a basement, all mod cons you understand but he has to be chained up or he’d kill everyone. What did she say?

“Attacks one of us.” There’s only one person who came down there, day after day after day. If there were more, it would be better for me but she has no intention of that happening.

I waited on the pill. He’d drawn attention to my illness, which I’d been busy ignoring. Now I wanted to get better. When the chance came to get out, I would.

Fool that I was; I really believed I’d leave that basement as a living being.

I had very few visitors to break the tedium. Very occasionally Mother would bring a stranger, usually a male, down to the basement. Then I knew it was a serious relationship – for a while – as the transient ones didn’t know I was there. Those who were going to stay around for a bit needed to know why there was raw meat in the fridge, meat that disappeared on a daily basis. I didn’t speak to them. Hardly any of them spoke to me. They were not part of my life in any way; I couldn’t have cared less about Mother’s sex life. It was not something I needed to concern myself with, was it?

Not until one came down alone one day and started beating me about the head with the broom handle she used to shove the tray nearer to me each day. I was screaming blue murder when Mother came charging in and snatched it from him.

"What do you think you're doing?!" It was an outright bellow, the loudest I had ever heard from her. She swung the broom handle round and clouted him on the head, nearly knocking him out. He got up and ran for the stairs but she bashed his knee and he went down like a skittle. By this time I was getting myself together, going to the farthest wall of the basement out of the way of both of them. I hurt everywhere on my head and shoulders.

"What the fuck you think you're doing?" he yelled back, clutching his knee. "You said you hated him!"

"So that gives you the right to come down here and beat him up, does it? Get the fuck out of my house!"

He finally scrambled to his feet and got up the few stairs. "I'll report this!" he said as he opened the door.

Mother went after him. "If you do, I'll have things to say about you beating up a helpless male tethered in my basement, Don! And what you get up to with my daughter!"

He went red and I knew then that he hadn't known she knew. Fool. Mother knew everything that went on under her roof.

"You can't admit to having someone chained up!"

"Wanna bet? I can say we play sex games; that he gets turned on by it. It's a game, right?"

I saw his face fall. She had him then, fair and square.

She looked round at me. "You all right, Jesse?"

"Hurts."

"Sure it does. Let me get rid of this opportunist lowlife and I'll bring you some painkillers."

"Stupid bitch!" The man slammed out of the basement, it's the only word to describe it, and I was left with a mother who had admitted to a stranger that she hated me and yet had flown to my defence and attacked my intruder without a second thought.

I wondered then, as I do now, did she really hate me that much –as much as I hate her?

If she didn't, then why imprison me?

If she did, then why defend me?

Questions that have no answers this cold October night.

Maybe I would ask before I took her apart.

Maybe I wouldn't. Maybe I don't really want to know. Either way it wouldn't be pretty, would it?

And so the confinement continued for some years, dreary, crushing, endless, demoralizing years, a whole thesaurus of words thrown into a whitewashed cold soulless basement and the demoralized crushed vamibalombie which lived there. Only I wasn't a zombie then, so I was a vamibal. No, not even that, just a vampire. I didn't get human flesh then. I doubt Mother could have conjured that for me.

That doesn't sound half as interesting.

I only found out about being a cannibal when I got out of the grave. So first I was a zombie, then a cannibal and then a vampire, or was it the other way round and-

Skullface, will you shut the fuck up?

I think, oh mind, that at this point of my 'existence', I am entitled to total insanity, extremely stupid and outrageous and ridiculous thoughts. I doubt any other person in this town of how many people? 30,000? are anywhere near my level of 'existence' and therefore entitled to my level of insanity this night.

I repeat, Skullface, shut the fuck up! This is getting you nowhere but entangled in such a mess of stupidity you won't see clarity come the morning. And right now, clarity is what you need to avoid drawing attention to yourself. Remember, your photo and the 'serial killer' headline was juxtaposed in a way that could bring attention you don't really want. Time is getting short and you need to be aware that it could all go wrong so very very easily. If you aren't careful.

And that kind of twisted diabolically insane thinking will ensure you are not careful.

And I repeat; I hate it when you're right.

I also think you're overly fond of the word juxtaposition. Ok, it's a flash word for a late October evening but still… let's not show off in this unwritten diary, yes? No?

If you can't show off in your own unwritten diary, Skullface, when can you show off?

One of the things I missed so much, apart from books, during that long time was the ability to write. Words, letters, memos, cards, anything. That sounds foolish, I'm not a writer, never could have been, no way of putting words down that mean anything in an order that would interest a reader, let alone asking them to pay for it, but writing. The physical act of writing. The pen in the hand, the flowing ink, the transcribing of thoughts, the wrapping up of a letter and tucking it in an envelope and sending it off, the finding of words to put in a card and writing them, signing it

JESSE

with a sweeping curlicue to finish it off.

Almost forgotten how to write, how to hold a pen properly without cramping the fingers – now that would be interesting, the fact the fingers are coming off, one at a time – how to space a letter on the paper, yes, paper, I was and am old-fashioned enough to want to send letters, not emails. So the next best thing is this unwritten diary, which will never see the daylight – or would that be better expressed as never see the light of day – in an effort to keep the brain cells from degenerating so much I can't function another day. I have to get through the 30th and then… Halloween will arrive - and so will I.

The question on everyone's lips is… what time should I arrive, what time would be best for the dreaded knock on the door, the best time for the raven to sit and watch and utter 'Nevermore' as I finally, finally, take my revenge. If I could find and train a pet raven in that time. Or even one that didn't need training. Don't all ravens say 'nevermore' when you ask them the time of day or how they are?

Hey look, never seen that before!

A cruise ship going out, on its way to far off places, loaded with lights – how many decks is that? Like a tower block on the waves! Wow, that's something – wonderful to see this dark night.

And I just realized how many lights there are down the pier, too, a whole row of them, beacons in the darkness as well. And there goes a train, rattling its way to the pierhead, flashing lights into the dark. It's a miracle the dark persists with all this light being thrown into it and at it, but that's the nature of dark, it smothers, it crushes, it dims and it destroys all that is light.

I've missed a lot in my life. Missed seeing cruise ships, not realizing how good the pier looks, forgotten how long it's been since I went on a train and now there's no reason to do it. Not been in the right place at the right time to see these things and not being anywhere for the past nine years and some months.

Missed out on the steam trains too. Fool that I am.

I want to see a bit more before it's all over. Just a little bit more. If we take any of these memories into the afterlife with us, then I want them to be good ones.

Playing Tourist

What happened? It's dawn, look, the pink of the night is now the pink of the morning but subtly different. Where did I go all night?

Stiff now, damp from the dew of the early morning, can't remember half of what I was thinking or dreaming or drifting or whatever I was doing. The night hours have gone. Vanished, like my life. Like the nine months I was resting underground, waiting for this time.

My time.

Today is going to be difficult. My last day before D-Day, Death Day; that is.

What shall I do with it? Today, I mean. I know what I'm doing on Death Day, for sure.

Suggestion, Skullface; no more than a suggestion. Feel free to dismiss out of hand, if you have any fingers left to dismiss anything with.

Go ahead, might as well hear it as not.

Have you any money left?

Some.

How about you make your final trip round the island, get on one of those open topped buses and go for a ride round the entire island, say goodbye to it all as you go? You were bewailing, as I recall, the fact you couldn't get to Shanklin, Bembridge and so on, right?

Right.

That would do the job, wouldn't it?

It would indeed. Sometimes you are so exceptionally smart and intelligent I stand back in sheer astonishment at your cleverness.

Sarcasm, they say, is the lowest form of wit.

And the highest form of intelligence.

The fact you are arguing with yourself, Skullface, tends to confound that particular argument.

Ok, let's quit that and think about that bus ride. Sounds like a good idea to me. There's a couple of things I'd like to do before tomorrow, they would fit in with the bus ride very well.

And they are?

Walk along the front at Cowes, see the yachts and money, come across on the floating bridge to East Cowes, maybe get as far as Osborne House and take a look…

How come I never did any of this when I was young and free?

Because when you're young and free you never think it's gonna end.

Right. And I hope that all this distraction will distract my stomach from realizing it's empty. I have to be good and hungry for Halloween. No matter what.

It has occurred to me, Skullface, you could eat and not spoil your appetite for Halloween, by buying some raw meat in a butcher's. It might make the difference between a studied satisfying revenge and a berserker flip-over revenge, which will not satisfy you.

That's the best thought you've had in days. I'll do that.

It's early yet, I'll wait for the buses to be warmed up and the day to be aired.

Hey, know what's been missing from life lately?

That black shadow. And guess what's just come back into my life?

That black shadow.

And now I know for sure what it is.

Death. True proper everlasting sleep death. Or, sleep long enough to get taken into the spirit world, anyway. Death as in the body not getting out of the grave again, not needing money and food and air and comfort and stuff.

Does that sound like heaven or what?

Money's getting tight. Too tight for my liking. Wish I could go knock on the door now and ask for some money from whoever answers, but it won't work like that. If I knock, that's it, end of story. Halloween has to be the end of story.

Skullface, every time you've needed money, something's happened to give you some. Stop worrying.

How much is the fare on the bus… £10. OK, I can do that. It's the best idea ever, apart from the raw meat, that is, my chance to properly say goodbye. Never thought I could do that.

"Hey Nipper, you sure you're well enough to go on this trip? You look dreadful, if you don't mind me saying that."

"I'm – dying right now. This is a 'goodbye to the island' journey for me."

"Is it? Looks like it, I have to say. OK, forget the fare, then. I'll put it in for you. Least I can do. Go sit down before you fall down."

"Thank you so much."

"Not often someone's as ill as you gets on this bus, Nipper. Believe me, I've not seen anyone that sick in my life. Like I said, go sit down."

See, Skullface? Sometimes everything goes right. Now, small suggestion, get off at Ventnor, small place, should have a butcher's shop, you don't want to walk miles to find one.

You're right – again.

I feel so utterly sad. The island didn't mean quite this much to me when I was alive, took it for granted 'til she shut me away. Then I missed it with a hollow gut wrenching missing but – the question is, did I miss the island or the freedom to go see it when I wanted? When I had the chance, I took the ferry, one or the other, to the mainland, didn't I?

Because you needed to kill, Skullface. How many did you take out in the end?

Don't know. Twenty? Thirty? More? Don't know. Never thought to keep a running list. Never thought it would end. Stupid, wasn't it, to think like that?

The black shadow has nothing to say. See, he sits on the opposite seat and says nothing and, even worse, no one has noticed him. They double back and look at me, acting as if I don't notice; no one looks at him/it. He's watching me the whole time. I know it's Death, but he'll have to wait on a bit. Tomorrow night, friend, it will all be over.

It feels like a lifetime away.

We're moving.

Travelling fast over roads I walked to find somewhere for the night. I saw little of it, being too pre-occupied with finding a sleeping/thinking place.

You also see things differently from the road, Skullface, you walked the pathways.

So I did.

Still am, only I'm walking the pathways of my memory now.

I swear the shadow's smiling even though I can't see a face.

Bembridge. House boats, always wanted to be on one. Quietness, if I can use that word. So different from Ryde.

No, I'm not turning this unwritten diary into a travelogue. No way. No need. I know where I am and what I'm looking at and that's all that matters.

But it hurts more than I thought it would.

I'm adding that to my list of grievances; that I lost so much time of seeing and being on my island.

Right now it is 'my' island. Mine in its entirety. Every down, every town, every byway and highway. I need to make up for nine years imprisonment and six months' death. I know I'll rest easy when it's over. This is how to say goodbye to life.

In style.

On a bus touring the prettiest coastline ever.

Right, Ventnor, here I come.

"You sure you're all right, Nipper?"

"Yes, thanks. I need to get something, is all."

"Don't lose your ticket. You'll need it to get back on the bus."

"I won't."

Zip up pocket inside my new padded coat will take care of the ticket. Now to take care of the hunger which is rolling and biting and clawing and I would definitely not have lasted until tomorrow night without flipping into berserker mode and ruining everything.

Like the ending of this unwritten diary. It would have been chopped off in its prime.

Shadow, get the hell out of here. This is my journey, not yours.

Right, here's the butcher's. Drooling, I am, over a window full of raw blood filled meat. What can I afford?

Empty shop.

Good.

"What can I get you, sir?"

"I'm looking for something to eat right now."

"It all needs cooking first.

"No, it doesn't. I eat my meat bloody and raw."

"If you will forgive the comment, sir, you look very ill. Are you sure you need raw meat?"

"It's all I've eaten all my life. That piece there, that beef, it looks good."

"If you can prove to me you eat meat raw, sir, I'll give it to you. Well, half of it."

"Half will be enough. Are you sure?"

"Of course I am. You're something – out of the ordinary, I have to say."

Clunk with a huge knife and the beef is in two parts. I can't contain myself much longer. Hand it over, in the name of God, hand it over!

"Here you go."

"Thanks."

The first bite is always the best. The richness of the blood, the fibrous meat ground down in my teeth, then the second and the third.

His eyes have got so big I wonder his head can contain them. I know my colour's changing, improving as I eat this perfectly gorgeous piece of beef. Good job there's no customers, they'd be shocked senseless and run screaming from the place, that they would, for sure.

"Now I believe you."

"I knew you would."

"What are you?"

"Truthfully? A monster, a freak. I've lived on raw meat all my life. But that life's running out fast. I'm doing the Island Breezer tour to say goodbye. It'll all be over soon."

"You look a little better now but not much."

"No, it's all gonna end very soon. I'm more grateful than I can tell you. Thank you."

"Worth it to see you eat it like that, never thought anyone would, or could." He held out a bloodied hand to shake. "You feel like death already got you."

I can see the dark shadow haunting me, despite my telling it to get gone.

"He has."

"God go with you, Nipper."

"Bless you and thanks again."

Now to wait for the bus. I feel satiated, nearly as good as after a kill. And look, it didn't cost me anything.

I really want to go to Cowes today. I really want to walk on the floating bridge. I really want…

To stop hurting. It's all hurting, all the memories, the time I missed, everything.

I remember the one time Joanna ventured into the basement. She'd never set foot in the place; shook me up quite a bit, that did.

Especially when she did nothing but hiss venom at me. How much she hated me, how I'd blighted her life, not being a bonny baby she could flash at the world, not get admiring compliments and baby gifts. She wanted a showpiece baby, she got a freak.

She overlooked the fact she'd had a fling and ended up pregnant with the freak, me, and vowing never to see whoever fathered me ever again, good job. He wouldn't have wanted to know and that would've been worse.

She told me all this, standing on the top step, way out of my reach and anything I might have to attack her with. I didn't have anything. Not a single weapon. If I had, I would've ended my enforced captivity long before. Mother/Madam knew it and made sure there was nothing I could use, ever. She wanted me to suffer.

Joanna stood there and threw hate at me. Everything she had bottled up for all those years spilled out, pouring acid into my heart and mind, creating a soothing balm for her. If it did that, I didn't mind. I knew it was; I could see the way her face changed, the way her eyes changed as she ranted.

I almost blew it, almost called her Mother; instead I opted to say nothing. I could see some of me in her, the blonde hair, the dark blue eyes, the shape of her face, such as I remembered from my 'mirror-abled' days. I could not see in her the ravening need to kill; she was softer than me, normal. I almost cried.

Then she walked out and left me feeling even more bereft and alone than I had in all the long, long, empty time I had been confined. And lonely. Intensely overwhelmingly lonely.

The TV flipped into a music channel. I hated them usually, hated the raucous music I didn't understand but this… this was different. This was someone saying he wanted to know what love is.

Then I did cry.

Back in Yarmouth and thinking, how come I'd ignored this little place for so many years? Went through it to get on a ferry and back out again, never gave it proper consideration. Or any consideration, come to that. Now I like it, now it's too late to think about having a home here.

Now I need to think of other things: how the hell do I get to Cowes from here?

Got that silly song in my head, the one from Peter, Paul and Mary, 'planes and boats and trains'. No trains here, no planes either but there are boats, loads of them.

I wonder if…

There would be a chance of a lift, if anyone's going to Cowes…

How the hell do I find out?

Let fate do it again for me? It's worked out pretty well so far –

So let's wander a bit down on the marina and see what happens.

Money, Skullface, just look at the money and how much do you have left in your pocket?

Can't think that way. I had no job for years before I was locked up and then locked up I got no money for years. And no one paid me for my time in the grave, did they?

Equally, no one asked me for taxes or rent for the plot of land I was occupying, did they?

"You're the zombie, aren't you? The one on the County Press?" He looks like a sailing type, got the right gear on, anyway.

"That's right."

"Congratulations on winning first prize. Pretty realistic, I have to say."

"Thanks. I like the look so much I'm wearing it a bit longer."

"Don't blame you. I'm a fan of zombie stories myself, as it happens. You doing anything particular in Yarmouth? I mean, if you're not busy, can I buy you a drink?"

"No thanks, not right now, not feeling particularly good in the stomach."

Understatement of the year, Skullface…

"What I'm looking for is a fishing boat or something heading to Cowes so I can have a lift. Getting the bus from here means changing in Newport and I don't feel up to that."

"You don't look that brilliant under the makeup, I have to say. Let's see… I know most of the owners around here."

"I'd appreciate it and perhaps I could come back another time and have a drink with you."

"Fair dos. I'll give you my mobile number before you go."

"That would be good."

"Look, see that one down there, the *Daisy Lee?* He'll take you to Cowes."

"I'm short-"

"He's due to sail there anyway any time soon. Hold on there; let me go talk to him."

"Appreciate it."

So far so good, Skullface… I'd suggest some finger crossing but you might lose a few more.

"Right, all fixed up. He's a mate, he likes zombies too, he saw your photo in the old County Press and all; he's well pleased to be doing you a favour."

"Thanks…"

""Nigel. Here's my card, got my mobile number on it. Call me when you're back in Yarmouth, yes?"

"I will. Thanks again, Nigel."

"No problem. Good to have met you, Nevermore!"

Put it safe in the pocket of the padded jacket. That will give them – whoever finds it or me – something to think about after tomorrow.

"Nevermore, isn't it? Bill Duffield, glad to have met you."

"Thanks."

"Incredible makeup. Must have took some time."

"It did! But it was worth it."

"Right, sit yourself down there out of the way, let me cast off and we'll be in Cowes in no time."

"Is that right, Nigel said you were going there anyway, you're not going out of your way for me, are you?"

"Nah. Have to go there somewhen; this is as good a time as any. Here we go."

Rushing about, untying this, coiling that, stowing – is that the right word? - things here there and everywhere and I feel like the useless lump I am, busy trying to hide my deformed – as in fingers missing – hands. I want to hold on to the 'I'm wearing my prize winning makeup' mask for a bit longer.

Until tomorrow. Halloween, anyone can be out and about and who will give me a second look?

We're moving, what did he do to make us move? Wish I had learned about sailing. Too late now.

Too late for so many things.

Add it to my list.

Which is growing longer by the day.

Not many days left, Skullface.

Just as well. No one's gonna live long enough to satisfy my desire for revenge for all the things on that list.

"You all right there, Nevermore?"

"I am, Bill, enjoying this."

"Done any sailing?"

"No, funny you should ask, I was just thinking I ought to have done some of this earlier in my life." If I hadn't been chained to a bloody pipe by a ring so tight I wonder how she got it off me without slicing my balls off. She didn't. I still have them. Just.

"Water gets a bit choppy just out here; hold on if you think you'll lose your balance. Would hate to see that makeup washed off!"

"Me too."

He wasn't joking. We went from bathwater to jacuzzi. Hell!

"Won't last long, Nev, no problem!"

Why do they do that? I suppose if I'd let on my name's Jesse I'd get called Jess.

"I'm all right!"

I am too, this is fun. If you can call being tossed around on a wild sea fun. But then Bill would no doubt say this isn't a wild sea, but a bit of turbulence, or some such. A real wild sea is when the lifeboats go out, isn't it?

Only if some idiot gets into trouble, Skullface.

I'm an idiot but this is fun and I think Bill knows what he's at.

At least, I hope so. I want to knock on that door tomorrow, not end up in a watery grave, thanks very much.

Oh, that's better.

"You'd make a good sailor, Nev."

"Thanks!"

"Any time you want to have a bit of a go at sailing, come on over to Yarmouth and I'll take you out."

"Appreciate it, very much. Thanks."

"Nige give you his card?"

"Yes."

"Good. You can call him and he'll let me know you're coming. Good guy, that Nige, good friend."

"He was good to me and he'd never met me before."

"That's the kind of guy he is. Good old Nige."

No one's ever gonna say good old Jess, are they?

They could say it, but they wouldn't mean it, Skullface. If you want, I'll say it for them.

Not the same thing at all.

I just realized something. I've not had a sense of smell, not properly, since I got out of that grave. I should be smelling sea and I'm not.

What do you want, Skullface? All your faculties? Come on, you're dead!

Yes, yes, but I'm missing out. Here I am on the *Daisy Lee,* having a great time and part of it's missing.

Part of you's missing. Does that mean you're not enjoying things?

Well…

See?

OK, point taken.

"You know what, Nev, if I didn't know different; I'd say you were a true zombie."

Whoops.

"What makes you say that, Bill?"

"Well, no one can really get that depth of realistic makeup, says me."

"You'd be right, too."

"Really?"

He's lit up like a Pompey firework display.

"Really. I got out of the grave seven days ago. This's my eighth day of 'life'."

"Really?"

"Yes. Look." My hands look odd without their pinky fingers. "They fell off."

"So you are! Oh my God, I'll be able to tell everyone about this!"

"Go ahead, it's the least I can do to say thanks for this ride."

"No wonder you didn't want to go on the bus!"

"Oh, been on the bus, here, there and everywhere. I just did the coast route on the Island Breezer."

"But you didn't want to do it anymore."

"Well, Yarmouth to Newport to Cowes… bit of a drag, that."

"Sure is. I am so made up you wouldn't believe! Wait till I tell Nige!"

"Tell him thanks and I'll try and give him a call for that drink, but I can't promise anything, I really don't know how long I can stay alive."

Lies, Skullface.

I know.

"You're not like a zombie."

"I know, I don't drool blood and walk around looking for brains to eat."

"That you don't."

"I'm a zombie anomaly, so I am."

"I like that!" He's laughing so hard I'm scared he'll fall overboard. I can't sail this thing by myself.

“Right, here we are. Let’s see if we can get you to the steps, so you don’t have far to walk. That OK with you, Nev?”

“Sure thing. Bill, I appreciate this more than I can tell you.”

“You gave me something worthwhile, I met a real zombie. Never thought I would.”

“Well…”

“Here we go. Steady as you get out there. All right? There you go. Bye, Nev, best of luck!”

“Thanks, Bill!”

He turns that thing like it was a saloon car and he’s parking it neatly somewhere. Oh, I’m feeling such a sense of loss I won’t get to do that.”

Skullface, you were on about reincarnation one time as I recall, right? If it’s there, if you get to come back, choose to be a sailor – as well as a painter. See, I remembered!

Yes, I could, couldn’t I? OK, that makes me feel better.

Right, here we go.

Cowes, here I am.

No travelogue, Skullface, you promised.

I did and I meant it. This is Cowes: water, yachts, yachty places and people. Money and class. I’m not lingering long here, just wanted to see it again, that ‘one last time’ syndrome. The butcher’s gift has kept me going but it won’t for much longer. Gonna need some rest.

And the final memory to reconcile myself to/with. If I can pluck up sufficient courage to go there.

Skullface, with what you've been through already, surely this one last step won't – excuse the pun – kill you?

It might. On the other – depleted – hand, it may give me the incentive I need to knock on that door. So afraid I will chicken out at the last minute and go to my new grave unfulfilled.

No way. You're gonna make it, big time, Skullface! The County Press headlines will be sensational, mass murder and the remains of someone dead these past six months to confound and confuse the forensic mob! Fabulous, who could ask for more? The dailies will jump on it as well… not exactly the sort of publicity the island needs but hell, any publicity's better than none. Right?

Right.

Shops, restaurants, bars, offices, nothing much changes here. A timeless place. Yachts and yachty people. As always. Makes me feel there is a permanence to life after all.

And down the road to the floating bridge/chain ferry. Which name does the world prefer? On the sign, chain ferry. In local parlance, floating bridge. Lot of us foot passengers waiting for it, quite a line of cars, too. No one seems impatient. I noticed that years back, nine years, to be precise. When you use the floating bridge, you learn patience. First, it's never on the side you are. Second, everyone surges off and on at the same time so you have to wait for the foot people to clear the deck so you can drive on, carefully, over the lump of iron which is all that's between you and the water. You take note of the man standing there, waving you down the middle, or each side. Nonchalant as always, as immovable as always. These guys have been working the bridge for years. They look like it, too, weather beaten, easy going, no rushing, time to talk to everyone.

Like Cowes, there's a timelessness about this facility, too. A bridge pulled by chains.

Huge chains. There's usually a heap of new ones by the side of the shelter, as I recall.

My chain was small, very very small in comparison, but it did its job, keeping me away from Life. These chains take you from one side of the river to the other, clanking and rattling and sounding as if any minute the bridge will stop in the middle and cause havoc to the shipping. And it always gets there. Every time.

Here I am, waiting. And it's on the other side. Of course. Always is. Sod's law, that is. Like I said, it's part of the bridge's charm, it is always on the other side. You wait patiently with the cyclists, buggy pushers, shoppers, late night revelers, depending on the time of day.

Getting some strange looks. The hood and the shades aren't doing it, are they? I've gone too far for that. Hard luck, people, I want to be in East Cowes for a while, want to look at Osborne House and all. My last visit ever. Be nice to me.

I didn't say a word out loud but they've looked away.

I wonder if they've seen the black shadow that's walking with me.

Here it comes, the chains clanking and banging as always. Used to amaze me back when, still does.

Something this old, this cumbersome, crossing the river a hundred times a day. And still doing it, too.

Foot passengers pile on, cars pile off. Same ritual as always. Nothing changed here. Wonderful feeling. Hm, nice car that one just driving on, convertible, good for an Autumn day like today. The sun's out…

Got his radio on. Or CD. Or something.

Got that damn Foreigner song on. You know, 'I Want To Know What Love Is' and I can't escape. Too late to get off and anyway, I want to go to East Cowes and to hell with the music. I don't have to listen, do I?

But I remember the last time I heard it. When my mother came into the basement. It hurt then.

God, it hurts now.

Hold on, Skullface, we can get off now, get away from it.

Too late. It's in my head.

Come on!

The bridge makes contact, lowers the iron plate, we all surge forward en masse, mind, you might knock bits of me off, you people! For once no one's trying to avoid me, all too keen to get off this heap of rusting metal and into the town. There are as many waiting to make the crossing back.

Wonder why? What's so important – oh. Look. Brand new sparkling bright Waitrose. Oh. Now I see. All those people coming across to shop there. Looks nice, wish I had time…

No. Lie. Doing it again, lying to myself.

Wish I had the energy and more than that, the ability to go in there, buy something – other than raw meat –

Stupid. I can do that. It might help me through tomorrow. I only had that bit of beef, didn't I?

How much money have I got?

Few pound coins.

OK. I will go visit and see what I can buy.

This is –nice. This is clean and fresh and loaded with food I can't eat. But there is food I can eat. Look, chiller cabinets, that's what they're called, isn't it? full of packs of meat. And look here, a counter full of cuts of meat and someone waiting to serve. Now, what should I do…

Buy a pre-pack, Skullface, it would be rather embarrassing to get the guy to cut you some meat and you can't afford it when he tells you the price.

Right.

This will do; this pack. It's not a lot but I don't need a lot.

Tomorrow I eat. If I feel the need. Might just let go. Probably will just let go. No eating. Put up with the pain, the clawing hunger.

Tomorrow doesn't matter too much. It'll all be done by nightfall.

I like that word. Nightfall. Rather fits with nevermore, doesn't it?

Hurry, before someone else asks if you're all right…

Yes, yes, look at me hurrying.

You call that hurrying, Skullface?

Best I can do.

Oh well…

"Thank you, sir. Do you want a bag?"

"Yes, please."

"£3.72, thank you."

Small coins in the change. I don't need them but what the hell…

"Here's your charity token, sir, drop it in one of the boxes by the door."

"Oh, right. Thank you."

"Take care, sir, and – go easy."

He's clocked the sick look so politely it's not true. Now, what's this charity thing? Oh, that one will do. It matters not to me, but it might to them.

Think I'll eat this meat now, rather than carry it. Might energise me, might not, I have to try. I have to get through to tomorrow. It's a mantra, isn't it, but I guess I need it.

If only to try and get that damn blasted song out of my head.

It isn't working.

The meat's good, better than the butcher gave me earlier. It was all right, but not as succulent as this.

Listen to me discussing meat like a true gourmet. Well, I am, I've lived on it all my life. This is good.

Whoops, upset that elderly lady, looked at me with utter disgust. Sorry, Madam, I have to eat.

Madam. Will she be there tomorrow?

Shadow, FFS, get out of my face!

I'm done eating. The mirror says I'm clean of blood. This bag might be useful, roll it up and stuff it in the pocket of my new padded coat.

Will you give over, Skullface, with the padded coat business!

Why? I'm still proud of it.

Come on, get going. It'll be dark before you know it.

York Avenue's as steep and as long as I remember. Not sure if I'm gonna make it, but I think there's a bench or something further along… gotta keep going, gotta keep going…

Why can't I get going? I've had food.

It's that damn blasted song. It's hurting so much, it's dragged up so many thoughts; it's made me so bloody sad it's not true.

I want to know what love is…

Tears.

Thought I couldn't cry anymore.

More tears.

Can't see where I'm walking.

Shut up, Skullface, FFS! Cry if you must, but shut up talking!

I want you to show me…

No. No. No.

Can't do it. Can't walk hurting like this… go away, song, let me be!

"Hey, Nipper, you all right? Can you get up?"

"Think so."

Vicar? Samaritan? What is he? Can I trust him? He's young enough to help, old enough to know better.

"Hold on to me. Where you heading?"

"I…"

"Sorry?"

“I was going to Osborne House but don’t think I can make it. I really need to get home to Ryde.”

“Give Osborne House a miss. I’m going to Ryde, come on, I’ll take you.”

“Th… thanks. You sure?”

“Can’t leave you on the pavement like that. What’s your name?”

“Nev…”

“Nev. Ok, Nev, I’m Paul. Let’s get you in my car. Whereabouts in Ryde d’you wanna go?”

“Oh, Lind Street will be fine.”

“All right, Lind Street it is, then. My God, you look ill! You sure you don’t want to go to St Mary’s instead?”

“Hospital can’t do much for me. Sorry, I got overcome then, couldn’t go on.”

“It’s all right, good job I came along. You don’t have to explain. I’m going to Bembridge, no problem to drop you off on the way. ”

“Th… thanks so much.”

“Don’t talk. Rest. You look as if you’re on your last legs. Promise me you’ll get some help.”

“I will.”

Damn song won’t leave me. It hurts. It hurts ‘cos it’s all I wanted and I never had, not once, not really, apart from Grandmother. I wanted a mother’s love; it got thrown back in my face. I wanted a lover’s love, never got the chance. Who would love a monster like me?

No one.

You know what, Skullface; you’ve got the luck of the devil. For sure you have. There you were, down on the grass verge, crying your eyes out –

you'd be in trouble tomorrow without them, that's a fact, when this guy comes along and stops, where thousands wouldn't.

Means God's on my side, doesn't it?

Him or Lucifer, one or the other.

Right now I don't care which one it is, as long as someone is. I need a helping hand. Or two. Mine are pretty useless right now.

"Here we are, Nev. You dozed a bit on the journey, you don't look quite so ill now."

"Thanks so much. Can't believe how kind you've been, Paul, I really appreciate it."

"I try and do one good deed a day, if I can. That was today's, I'm free to run riot now if I want."

"Don't think you're the type, but have fun trying! Thanks again."

"See you around, Nev!"

He's gone. I'm in Lind Street. He was right, I did doze off a bit, can't remember the journey. Smooth driver, didn't talk nonstop like the taxi drivers, either, I did get lucky.

Damn, lost my shades!

All that crying stuff, Skullface, never did anyone any good.

Need to go sit for a while.

Here, my favourite churchyard seat.

What in the name of Heaven did that damn song do to me?

The Penultimate Night

One of the problems of being on a holiday island is that there are holidaymakers. Now that's so bloody obvious I wonder why I said it, but it needs to be said.

The holidaymakers come with kids. Little ones, toddlers, bigger ones, all looking for something to do. Close-to-being-teens, wanting something different, interesting, outside the noise that's being pumped into their ears nonstop or the damn mobile phones glued to their hands.

The problem is: they have holidays.

There are two problems, actually. They have holidays. They have families.

I had neither.

The constant reminder of holidaymakers was a curse to me throughout my growing up. And afterwards, too. There were the people walking along with their kids – I could never have a relationship, let alone a kid of my own to hoist on my shoulder, lift up to see the beach and the sea rolling in, to walk along the sand and look for seaweed or something interesting to give them. Couldn't buy them an ice cream and fight off the starving (ha!) seagulls that would try and snatch it from their hands. See the men look into the eyes of the women with them, their wives; the person they loved. I never had that.

They spoke with accents that told me they came from other parts of the United Kingdom, places I saw only briefly when going specifically to kill, buy a local paper and hurry back before anyone noted the car and me in the area of a murder.

For the longest time I never thought of it as murder. To me it was survival. But in truth it was murder, wasn't it?

I'm a serial killer.

I admit it.

I hate it but it's a fact.

I couldn't go to those upcountry places for holidays; there was never enough money for that. I wanted/longed to go abroad, to see Spain and France and Germany and Italy for starters. So close, so far away for someone with no money and the inability to travel, for how would I eat when away? You can't go distributing Spanish, French, German or Italian corpses all over the place, although it would be easier to get away, for sure. The problem would be chatting up the person or finding the right place to hide and wait for a victim in a strange land. I got away with it here, I had a pretty good idea of the layout of most towns, scrap yards, dumps, back alleys, they were easy to find. Abroad was banned to me, by my nature, my needs. The Consulates would not appreciate dealing with someone who went berserk because he didn't get raw meat and blood, would they?

So much has been denied me in this life. Travel, relationships, children, pets, love.

Back to that damn song again. It broke me up the first time I heard it on the music channel and then to have it again on the floating bridge, well, that really was too much. Knowing what I'm going to do tomorrow made it worse. The people who should have given me love didn't and they're the ones I'll take out on the most hallowed night of the year, for us monsters anyway.

There's 'Halloween' people walking about, there's jack o' lanterns on walls and on windowsills. Are they making tonight, this Halloween Eve, into the 'real' night, because it happens to be Saturday? If they are, that's good for me; I'm camouflaged by their fancy dress. At least, I hope it's fancy dress and there's only one true zombie out this night. The world couldn't stand two of us, that's for sure.

If the kids are out tonight collecting their candy, that's fine and I could use them as cover to do My Terrible Deed, but I have to do it properly. I have to make sure it's the right night to send them all direct to the hell they kept me in for so long. And that won't work on any other night.

I've done my deal with the Reaper. He and I have been talking these past few minutes, bit like the way this diary's been written, mind to mind. He's not my conscience but I knew that anyway. He's the Reaper, he's Death. He's the final countdown. He's the supervisor of graves, the conveyor of souls to wherever.

You want to know something, oh reader of this unwritten diary?

There's no Heaven and no Hell.

Heresy! I know it's true. What happens is, we go where we are directed, into the white tunnel of light to the ones waiting for us and a chance to review our life and all we have done/not done, or taken into the greyness, the darkness, the nasty cells that await those who are truly evil, dictators, mass murderers, conscious-less people. You needn't ask where I'm bound. The Reaper and I aren't saying. I'm looking for the in-between state until I come to terms with what I was/am.

What I will tell you is he's gonna give them a terrible shock before letting them go on into the white light. A shock they will take with them. That satisfies me.

The other reason for not doing the Terrible Deed tonight is I've got one last thing to come to terms with. It's been there all through and I've backed off from it time and again. Now I have to confront it, live through it, accept it happened and be ready to make my peace with the Reaper later. Like 24 hours from now.

He doesn't know yet but I'm planning on going to church tomorrow morning.

But that's tomorrow. The true Halloween. Made for people like me. Well, there is only one of me, but you know well what I mean, you reader of my unwritten diary.

Wish I knew what this was all about. I mean, why I think of it as an unwritten diary. Reminiscing is enough, surely. Thinking logically about my life and how I got into the situation I did, ending up in an unmarked grave at 29.

And yet, thinking of it as if I'm writing a diary has helped, I've worked out a lot of other things as well as my past, haven't I?

More than you realize, Skullface, more than you realize. Now, you planning on staying here until they lock the gates?

No. Best move on.

Let's wander, down to the Esplanade again. Must be my favourite place, keep going back there, don't I?

Oh, oh, beggar alert.

"S'cuse me, mate, got any coppers to spare?"

That's rich, asking me!

"Do I look like I've got any money, friend?"

I have, I don't want to give it to him. I've got to put something in the collection tomorrow.

He takes a good look and backs away. "No, sorry, you've prolly got a bigger need than me. No offence, mate."

"None taken."

"Here, do you want any money?" He's thrusting coins at me. That's a surprise and for a moment I'm tempted. But no. Really, he looks like an alkie and he needs it more than I do. I just don't want to contribute to his booze.

Let's see what happens when I tell the truth.

"Friend, this is my last night on earth. Tomorrow I will die, along with those who got me into this state. Don't worry about it, keep the money you have, you'll need it where I won't. But thanks for the thought."

"You having a laugh?" Belligerent now, I can do without that. He needs to be careful, I only had two bits of raw meat today…

Flip the hood back, Skullface, show him the zombie reality.

OK, I will.

"Oh. You're one sick man, aren'tcha? Sorry, mate, real sorry. You look like you're dying right now."

"That's what I said. You just took a look at a real zombie, friend; one whose life ends tomorrow. I've been walking dead now for eight days and getting mighty sick of it too. I'll be right glad when tomorrow gets here and my revenge is complete. Then I can die properly."

"You're freaking me out, mate, gotta go!"

And he does, fast too.

Wonder if he'll tell anyone?

Really, Skullface? He's gonna admit he spoke with a walking dead man? Methinks not. Anyway, who's he gonna tell?

You're probably right, as always.

And I hate it when you're right, you know that.

From Day One, Skullface, from Day One.

Not too cold tonight, I can sit here for a while. This is a good place, sheltered, I can watch the buses coming and going.

And the taxis.

And see if my friend is among them tonight.

Busy, lots of people passing by.

Sit here till the sun's gone, then you need somewhere safe to rest. But yes, this will do for now.

You realize the King Lud'll be tipping out later; I want to be gone when that happens. Too many bad memories.

Or good ones?

Or good ones, yes. I did actually enjoy that moment of pure mayhem. The way that guy went through the window, like something from a film, it was. And the way the others scattered when I took the other one's throat out! If I hadn't been gut scared of the police I would've enjoyed that even more. Showed me what I could really do when I went berserk - and Jay too. Never did know what he thought of that evening, what he had to say at the police station, what the police thought when they went looking for his brother Jesse who vanished from the face of the earth.

All the time he was under the face of the earth.

Never thought of it like that before.

You wouldn't, Skullface, you were too busy being under the face of the earth. And a bad time it was, too.

For sure.

The worst ever. I thought being unemployed and hanging around feeling useless was bad, being locked up was the ultimate in disaster scenarios for me. I needed freedom, needed to kill; needed to drink fresh blood now and then. Being shut away… felt worse than prison. Like I said before, if I'd been in prison I'd've had people to talk to.

Oh yes, the list is long and revenge will be fulfilling, no doubt of it.

Hey, Skullface, you missed a chance to say 'for sure' there.

So I did. For sure.

All right now?

For sure.

OFFS!

It grows darker by the second. The street lights are haloed; must be misty tonight. No foghorn yet, good. I can live without that mournful sound, thanks very much. It resonates too deeply with me. How many nights have I laid awake listening to the endless 'stay off the rocks! Stay off the rocks!' call adding its music to the rattle of the train as it crashed its way into St Johns Road station, there to sit humming its dynamos or whatever while they change driver and guard and chat about the journey, all five stations of it… do they still have dinosaurs painted on them? I haven't seen the trains since I got out, not been in the right place at the right time. Even sitting here is the wrong place for that, damn things rattle along the tracks right behind me.

Does it matter?

No. Memory is all that matters. I know what they look like, old London Underground trains still running after all these years. More than you can say about me.

If we're talking sounds… night sounds especially, so much more vivid and clear than daytime, it's the foghorns at times, the trains and the music of the wind through the trees, the sirens as yet another problem erupts somewhere involving police, ambulance and firefighters, together with the honking of car horns, scream of engines as someone tries a superfast exit for whatever reason…

Sounds. So many of them.

I lived with my ears filling in the void for nine years, not my eyes. Nothing to see in white walls and a TV screen. Nothing to look at but a bit of muddy weed infested garden. So I listened to the sounds of the world I couldn't reach, adding in barking dogs, yowling cats and endless repetitive birdsong. It was all something to listen to. During the day the seagulls add their cacophony to the mix. Arrogant opportunist creatures. I envy them their freedom. Have done for nine years.

I worked at separating the sounds, identifying each one. Anything but listen to the damn blasted hated TV. She had it pitched just so that I couldn't ignore it, ever. I won in that I hardly looked at it, but was forced to listen to it. I hate television more now than I did before she shut me up in that basement. It's pap, mindless pap, brainwashing pap. I know, I suffered it 24/7 all that time.

Ok, let's move on before the mob gets the wind under its collective tail and looks for problems. I'm way too fragile to stand up to them now. Not even sure if the Skullface Evil Look will terrify them, not sure how terrifying it is any more. I want to work on that, need to terrify them when I get there.

You can look in the morning, Skullface; you'll see b-all in your mirror in this light.

I agree. Now, let me get the hell out of here and go somewhere for the night. I quite like the idea of going back to the Tower and the quiet I found there. Good enough for my last night, I think.

Tonight the Esplanade feels as if it's added miles to itself. It's a trudge, I'm getting tired; obviously, I don't think I had this much of a job to walk here last time. I must reach the canoe lake eventually; it hasn't moved itself since the last time I came here.

No, there're the swans, pale blobs in the darkness, fluffing feathers and muttering through their beaks at one another. And the fake swans, the ones you paddle yourself, clustered against the island in the middle.

But then, it's all winding down now, so it's academic whether I'm more tired than before.

For sure.

You had to do it, didn't you, Skullface?

But of course.

One problem – or is it a blessing? - with the dark full down now, I can't see that accursed shadow. But I know it's here and it isn't a shadow any more, it's real, it's the Reaper himself. He knows my time's getting short; he's after me because I escaped his realm, his domain, his kingdom. Ha! I did, didn't I? Got me out of his clutches and back into this world to get my revenge. He didn't count on that.

How come I thought he was my conscience back then, when this adventure began? How come I didn't recognize him for what he was/is?

Because you didn't want to, Skullface. You made your mind up on the spur of the moment, when you needed to throw your conscience away and go on killing. Not that you could help it, you've been a killer most of your life. Dead and alive.

And your point is?

No point. You chose to throw your conscience away, not realizing that the shadow wasn't your conscience. It made no difference; you still threw your conscience away. But I ask you this, Skullface, did you ever have one in the first place?

That's a question I can't answer.

OK, this will do, under this tree, dark enough no one can see me. I can see the mainland, Pompey all lit up. What's that tall thing with the red lights on it, I wonder? Don't remember seeing that when I walked the Esplanade back when. How come I missed seeing it last time I sat here? Not looking, probably.

Guess some new building went up whilst I was shut away. No newspapers to tell me about it. No newspapers to tell me anything, only half heard news items and they didn't mention a new tower, not that I recall.

I missed out on so much, didn't I?

Changes in Ryde, changes on the island, not being able to vote in elections, not knowing accurately what was going on in the world and, after a few years, not caring, either. Life reduced itself to the white walls, the ever blaring television and the daily visits for food and bucket removal.

And there is the root of one of the problems I had during that time. The torture, which wasn't always physical.

Like: a request for a new roll of toilet paper was not always met. She would claim she had none to spare. So I sometimes messed my pants and she would beat me with the broom handle for the 'crime'. My clothes were never ironed, not that I was going anywhere but it was part of the ongoing suppression, in a way, washed but not ironed clothes thrown at me. Left me feeling scruffy all the time. Razors were not changed very often; I'd cut myself with blunt blades and end up with sores and scars. You can't see them now, the death/life has erased most of them in its greyness but I knew they're there. Haircuts were a one man job, I would hack at my long hair with scissors she gave me whilst she watched, then took them back by lifting them out of my hand with a hook she put on the end of the broom handle. That thing was her tool, her weapon, her way of keeping me away from her and anyone who happened to come with her. Not that it happened more than say once every three or four years and then usually because I had a problem, like the time the doctor came. I cut my nails with clippers she allowed me for a few minutes, no more than that.

I never, in all those nine years, had physical contact with anyone until Jasmine –

Not yet. Not ready to go there yet. No way.

You have to, Skullface, it's the last obstacle.

I know, I know, but I am not, repeat not, going there yet. There's time.

Not a lot. It's the 30th.

Like I don't know that.

You sometimes need reminding.

When I want a social secretary, I'll ask for one.

Not a social secretary, just a reminder that time is truly running out and you are backing off from The Big One and that Will Not Do.

I wish to hell you were wrong occasionally. Perhaps once before I go back to the grave?

Nope.

Bunch of yoofs down there. Hope they don't see me.

It's dark enough here.

Shouting, yelling, drinking. "It's midnight, Mike, we'd best get home!"

Ok, so it's midnight. Good job he told me, the Town Hall clock's been silent all this time and I had no idea.

So, it's officially and finally Halloween.

That means…

The Final Countdown

This is my last night/day.

Thank God!

Not that it's been all bad, saying goodbye to the island was good. Some of it has been very good. Some of it has surprised me; the kindness of strangers, the gifts I've been given, the money in my pocket. Even the unwilling contribution of the coat, hat and zombie convention tickets were a gift in their own way. I'm right sorry the guy didn't get to see the groups – or perhaps he's lucky he didn't get to hear the groups – or the zombies and Goths everywhere, but I did and it funded my 'trips' to the mainland, not a bad thing. I couldn't have conned my way onto the ferry, could I? Wightlink wouldn't have stood for that.

Come to think of it, nor would the hovercraft, the catamaran or any Red Funnel ferry, either.

So thank you, Mister, and the sudden need that drove you into the trees that day, your loss, my gain. Big time.

There is not long to go. Not long to summon up the memories, deal with them, accept them, move on to – what? The Reaper isn't saying.

Hey, you, don't you have any other people popping off tonight? No heart attacks, no asthma attacks the sufferer doesn't get through; no falls downstairs or head on crashes, like stupid Jay did? No old people breathing their last and glad of it?

Or are you not THE Reaper, but one of his minions, delegated to watch over this vamibalombie for the rest of his unnatural life?

Or not quite a minion, someone a little higher than that. Someone more a superintendent of some kind, because I'm not your average human-about-to-reach-the-end-of-their-misbegotten-life; am I?

Whatever; let me be for a while, OK? One last biggie to get through, memory-wise and then one last biggie act to get through and then I'm all yours.

Forever, if that's what it's all about.

In my nine years of incarceration, I had only four visitors:

Madam, daily.

Doctor, once.

Joanna, once.

Jasmine, once. The shame was; it was her last time on earth.

I heard her outside, yelling 'I want to see my brother!' I had been locked away for all of nine years by then. I had no idea what she looked like, why she suddenly wanted to see me, nothing. I had wondered about her but kept to my non-speaking and never asked and Madam never said. I didn't know if she still lived at home or had gone off with some jerk who wouldn't treat her right or some really nice guy who would.

All I knew was, the love I had for her was a perpetual ache that never varied. To hear her voice outside sent my heart thumping madly, wildly, longing for her to come in, knowing it would make the ache worse if she did.

She came in, all radiant and glittering with sunlight, sun I hadn't seen for weeks, months, forever. She seemed to bring the sun in with her. She danced in, light on her toes, then stopped dead and began to open her mouth to scream.

No. Lies. That's what I said last time and it wasn't entirely true. She danced in, yes, and I realized two things as she did that.

One: she was carrying a baby.

Two; there were a whole load of spirit dogs between her and me, as if they were guarding me, or were they guarding her? I'll never know. They were the same dogs I saw in Lymington, I recognized them, a white and tan terrier, a lumping great black Labrador, a beige-looking poodle and a Border Collie.

She came across the basement floor toward me, coming as close as the doctor did, too close, too tempting, too much for me to resist. I knew it then, I know it now.

It was an accident waiting to happen - and it did.

"Jess… this is my baby…" she held the child out…

"Get the hell away from him!" Madam screeched so loud I wanted to cover my ears. But it was too late for that, too late for anything, I hadn't fed that day and there was a succulent meal right there, being offered to me. I snatched the baby… tore its heart out with one bite and threw it to one side. She began screaming demonically and I panicked, it hurt my ears, I couldn't stand it, she had to stop. I put my hand over her mouth, held her head, didn't realize I'd covered her nose as well, didn't think I'd put that much pressure on, didn't know what to do when she slid to the floor, boneless, lifeless, breathless, dead.

All the while Madam was screaming the ceiling down. When, when Jasmine hit the floor, there was a long silent moment when none of us moved. Jasmine couldn't, the baby couldn't, I was in shock, realising what I'd done and Madam was – terrified. The only word I can use to describe the look on her face.

Then she went as berserk as I did when denied meat. She snatched up the broomstick and beat me over the head so hard I blacked out.

When I came to I was alone, of course, what else would I be? Physically alone, anyway. The spirit dogs were sitting by my side, as if on guard, two on one side; two on the other. I never did know where they came from or why they chose me. I didn't recognize any of them but – got to say this – they were all dogs I would've chosen if I'd been able to have a pet.

In a frighteningly lucid moment I knew why I'd done it. Nothing to do with not eating. Madam blamed it on that later, blamed herself for the tragedy, should never have let her down into the basement without warning her to keep at chain's length from me, should have made sure I'd been fed, yada yada yada. I said nothing.

The truth is – Jasmine had a baby. Therefore, Jasmine had been to bed with some yoof. Whether he was with her or not didn't matter, she had done it; she had experienced sex with a male.

It should have been me.

All my grown up knowledgeable life I knew I wanted her, no one else, just Jas, the sparkling teeth and perky tits and cute ass Jas. The one ever pushing by me in the kitchen, brushing those tits against me, butting me with the ass – excuse the pun – you know what I mean. Whiffs of her perfume hitting me as I passed her by, having her hang over my shoulder to point something out in the paper or to find out what book I was reading. Jas, acting like she wanted to make out with me. And never did. And then I got locked away and she never could.

Jas had sex with someone else.

I saw the child as living proof she had sex with someone else and I lost it.

I didn't mean to kill her but she could never have sex with anyone else again. If I couldn't, no one could.

She did scream, I remember that, whether it was the look I flashed her as the realization hit me or the black shadow I will never know. That was in the instant before I snatched the living proof of her infidelity to me and killed it.

And filled my mouth with rich fresh blood like I had never had before.

Madam didn't feed me that day. Whether she got someone to help her get Jas' body out of the basement I will never know. Blacked out, gone, lost best part of 24 hours, I believe. The same programme was on when I came to, one that seemed to roll around at much the same time each day if no one had switched channels and by then they were getting very lax at doing that.

I had double vision, blinding headache, taste of stale blood in my mouth and stains everywhere - I had lost control of everything. The smell was atrocious.

So was the noise from outside my window. I crawled over there to see Madam, with set white face, digging a hole, a big one, not far from the house. She said she knew where the corpses were; I guess she had to move nearer the house for something as big as a grave for an adult.

The pain in my heart was worse than the pain in my head or the ache of the two loose teeth I soon discovered I had.

The ache in my stomach soon overcame even the pain in my heart. It was hours since I'd been fed and I needed blood, fast. Lots of it. I could feel the anger flaring and consuming me. She knew it; she looked at the window two-three times and carried right on digging. No need to give me the finger, she did that by looking and then carrying right on with the digging. She could've taken time out to feed me. It didn't need cooking, after all.

I saw the bodies being dragged across the grass, dropped in, a flower thrown in afterwards, then the earth being packed down. I saw the grass placed carefully on top. I saw how Madam distributed the displaced earth around the garden. I saw how she continued to look at my window and then carry on.

She finally came down into the basement, without my usual tray. She looked utterly calm, cold, no, more than cold, icy. I felt a chill from just looking at her but I didn't truly anticipate the next thing she said/happened.

"Been thinking, Jesse," she said, standing well back from me, one hand resting lightly on the broom handle. "Been thinking all the time I buried that poor kid and the poor baby. A boy, in case you were wondering. She called him Jay after her other brother. The one who cared."

I wasn't wondering, but I might have guessed if I'd thought about it. And Jay never cared, I did, too much as it happens.

"Been thinking this has gone on long enough. I'm through with it all. Fed up with the meat and the blood, fed up with worrying about you down here getting ill and having the doctor back again. I had to do some real fast talking last time. Don't like it, don't need it and, more than anything, Jesse, don't need you. So this is it. Your turn. I've no more room in the garden, you'll have to be buried somewhere else. I've got someone to help me, no problem there."

I went to speak but it was too late. Way way way too late.

She lashed out with the broom handle which had a new hook on the end, a large brass one with a filed down point.

I just about remember the pain as it ripped my throat open.

So there you are; reader of this unwritten diary of a zombie, that's how I got to be buried in an unmarked grave and how she got away with it. How do I know she did? No idea, but I believe it. No, stupid, if she hadn't, I'd've been dug up, dissected, reburied somewhere decent, or cremated or whatever. The fact I was still in Firestone Copse said she got away with it.

She would've continued to get away with it – assuming no one ever found out what she'd done - if my burning desire for revenge for that great list of – what? offences against me? What are they? had not driven me out of my grave.

Whatever you want to call them, they're my reason for being here now, quietly rotting away. I know the blood isn't working any more, I know the body is disintegrating; I know I could begin to smell any time soon, if I'm not already doing it. Part of the problem is wearing the same clothes all the time. No wonder the beggar stopped me!

I've drifted through my final night 'alive'. Drifted on a pain of intense deep sorrow that I lost Jasmine to another and then to my own violent insane jealousy. Drifted on a pain of regret that a child never got to live, part of her that would have gone on to create more parts of her in the future. A moment of utter madness destroyed two lives - and then mine.

Not that mine was worth living, I have to say. It was no great loss to me. It's just that I would have wished a better grave, a more respectful one, with a marker and all. But I realize how stupid that is, how could she have got a death certificate for me? What would the pathologist have made of this mixed up body of mine? And how would she have explained my throat being ripped out?

And the biggest question of all is, how come I hadn't noticed that wound all the time I've been 'alive'?

Because she sewed it up, Skullface. Small neat stitches with flesh coloured thread. That's why. And, if you think about it, it's a perfect addition to your zombie makeup story, isn't it?

No one's commented on that.

No one's commented on individual aspects of your so-called makeup, either. They say how good the overall look is, right? So the stitched up throat is just part of that. If they even noticed, that is.

Probably didn't. People aren't that observant, are they? And I've been wearing thick check shirts buttoned up to the neck. OK, I can go with that.

But I can't go with what I did. Unforgiveable. Shadow/Reaper, are you listening? Of all the lives I've taken, they are the ones I regret. Jasmine's was not for food or my ongoing existence, even, just my berserker mode trying to shut her up because the screaming hurt my ears. The baby was a mistake. A big big mistake. One I can never make up for, in this life, anyway. What you do with me when I finally relinquish this lousy rotting body is up to you. I just need some way of making recompense to her spirit if I can find it, whatever side of life it's on right now.

And at long last comes the morning, comes the dawn, comes the pink I like so much, so delicate, so impossible to capture in paint.

It's the last one I'll see. Thank you, God, it's beautiful.

And doesn't last long enough.

See that huge container ship slip sliding its way into Southampton? Wonder what's on board? Chinese goods aimed for our stores, silks and spices from India, clothes from Cambodia? At least one item I bought in the charity shop was made in Cambodia. Would you believe such a thing? We can't make clothes here in the UK anymore.

Stop preaching, Skullface, it doesn't become you.

Too late to preach, anyway, I'm doomed as at now. I just don't know what the Reaper has in mind for me. He isn't saying a word, damn his black soul.

I'm not going anywhere yet this last Sunday morning. I will let the town wake itself up, stretch its communal bones, drink its communal coffee and tea, fry up some bacon, eggs and sausages and then roll out into the streets and head for church.

And I will be there, right alongside – no, right at the back of them. I've never heard Sung Eucharist, it will be something to take with me into my new grave, if I get one, or into the fires of the crematorium, if that's what they decide to do with the wreck that is me.

I won't care one way or the other. My spirit will at last be truly free, with a stack of memories it didn't have before, images it didn't have before, freedom it didn't have before.

One of the first things I'm gonna do is come back to Jenny Campbell and say thanks for the help. She was amazing. If I can, of course.

Hey, the shadow's actually nodding! Thank you!

Watch it, Skullface, he might be leading you astray.

Probably is, can't trust a shadow, can you? Can't trust the Reaper, he's a slinky snidey person in his black and –

Wonder if he has a skull for a face, like everyone draws him?

Do you?

No movement of the head this time. I'm left unsatisfied on that question.

And about ten million others, too.

Ryde streets are aired and fresh, people are moving about, dog walkers have appeared and crazy dogs are racing everywhere, busy ignoring their owners' shrill calls to come back to them. Nothing changes where that's concerned.

And I need to start moving; everything is taking that much longer now. I need to be at All Saints by 10, so I can slide in when everyone is in place. Damn it to hell, I wish I had my shades! The hood will have to do for now.

Skullface, take a quick peek in your mirror.

Why? Oh yes, I said I wanted to see if I was terrifying.

Hell. I am. Well, they'll just have to cope, won't they?

Here we go. Oh, I'm walking like an old, old man. No walking aid either, not much good to me at this late stage of life. If I can call it that.

Come on, Jesse, get yourself motivated. It's nearly done.

It's Halloween. Come on, all you dark ones, come give me a helping hand here. I'm virtually one of you, aren't I? I mean, how much more do you want? Part zombie, part vampire, part cannibal, the only thing missing there is ghost. I don't believe in ghosts anyway, so that would be a tad difficult, to put it mildly.

Skullface, are you concentrating? Only this is not the smoothest of pavements and if you tumble, some people are going to be left with unwanted souvenirs of trying to pick you up.

Sure, sure, let me walk, OK? Walk carefully, then, as you insist.

At last. The church looms over the town like some old man, like me, in fact, windows like eyes staring out and watching our every move.

It's cool in here. Cool and dark. And only half full. I can sit here; no one will take any notice of me. Got me a book already. Hey, my second book to hold! I loved Three Men In A Boat, it thrilled me to own it and look at it and read bits from it. I might try and finish it today.

Oh, we've started.

Oh, we've done.

And in between, Skullface, you were on the verge of making a giant fool of yourself with tears again. What is it with you lately? Falling apart? Sorry, no pun intended.

It was – deeply moving. The singing, the prayers, the talk, the singing, the prayers, the taking of the bread and wine and I wished I could have, it might have settled me.

No, nothing can or will settle you until Madam and everyone are in as many pieces as you are, emotionally and physically. Now, you've gained another experience, let's get the hell out of here and go sit – favourite churchyard? And wait out the day, shall we?

And be still. Moving about generates hunger and that means problems. You're terrifying enough without the hunger look to go with it.

I won't eat again. I have no need to eat tonight, just to kill.

I hated to give the book back.

You're getting possessive about possessions, Skullface. Not good for a zombie with no grave to call his own.

I'm grateful for the possessions I have, this book, this padded coat…

OFFS, Skullface!

…the part of me that continues to argue, no matter what and this comfortable bench – well, sort of – where I can sit in the Autumn sunshine. If there are better times to come alive, I would like to know what they are. Golden leaves, brown leaves, golden flowers, winding down time, so right for someone to wind down their strange existence and bring it to an end before winter sweeps in with coldness, frost, snow and ice. I will be long gone.

And I wish to hell that song would get itself out of my head! All they can show me is why they hated me so much. Nothing else.

But then, I ask nothing else.

And I will ask only for a moment to speak before I take them out.

Once and for all.

Golden times. Golden days. Golden leaves and flowers.

Golden memories.

The bus ride, the nights on the Esplanade, the cruise ship in all its golden glory sailing away; sailing away to golden places.

And although I hate to admit it, a golden oldie in this song plaguing me. It says so much in what could be trite lyrics, yet they somehow go deeper than their obvious ploy, 'write a song to grab the heartstrings and go to the top of the charts.' If it was only that, it wouldn't be so well remembered now. And it is; I know it is. It's there. I don't need anyone to tell me about it.

So, question: did I become psychic during my temporary death? I seem to know things, not much but enough to say I am different even now from when I was here before. Or did the enforced custody bring out aspects of me I never knew I had? Or is this just one giant joke being played by the Reaper to drive me mad before I go wherever I'm going this one last time? See him there, on the other bench, watching every move I make and saying nothing, doing nothing, not a gesture, not a movement of the head, nothing.

Shadow reaper, speak with me just this once! Have I changed by being in the grave for so long?

Oh oh oh, the smallest inclination of the head! Wow, I got me an answer!

Another question, dare I ask another question, I wonder…

Does Madam know I am out?

Another small inclination of the head.

Now that is so so so so good. I now know she will be looking for me, scared of me, probably told whoever's in the house 'don't open the door, no matter what!' but that won't make a scrap of difference. If they don't open the door, I'll slip into berserker mode and smash it in. What the hell, I know the video ends with the singer embracing the girl he obviously loves. No one is going to end my time with someone embracing me because they obviously love me. They will be running scared out of my reach but they will also know, will they not, that when Jesse flips, Jesse cannot be stopped. By anyone.

Look, even Death couldn't stop me!

Gonna move. Gonna go sit in that new town square thing outside the supermarket, it wasn't there when I last walked the streets. That takes me a tiny bit nearer Well Street. When the ghouls come out to trick or treat, I'll move. Before then, hey, I have a book to finish.

And put back in my pocket. I intend to confound everyone when they find what's left of me. They'll say, 'does this mean anything?' They'll bag it up and put it in evidence when it means absolutely nothing. Just that it seemed like a good idea at the time.

Wonder if I should call the police when I've done redecorating the place with the latest shade, freshly spilled blood, or let someone stumble over the crime scene…

Depends on how soon the Reaper takes you, Skullface. Don't make plans he might disrupt. He's a law unto himself.

For sure.

I like to speculate, gives me something to do with the bit of mind I have left.

Fast being consumed – Ha! by my need for food. Excuse the pun. That was accidental. I'm suffering the ravening clawing need again. I don't want to eat. I want to finish with this travesty of a life and be gone. If I eat, I re-energise myself and have to start over again. No way. I'm done. Finished. Terminal. Gone.

Back to the book.

Wish I could have gone there, walked the Thames where they sailed, seen all they saw, but this is good, this is vivid, this is –

Taking my mind off what I will do in a few hours' time. The climax of nine days of walking talking thinking and suffering regrets, torment and agonies of jealousy, lust, loneliness and every other adverse negative emotion there is. And then some.

Come close, Reaper. We're nearly there. I will need you at the last. Come be with me, sit with me, warm my freezing flesh, my frozen heart. Let that damn song reach me and fill me with the longing I need to carry me through this final act.

And tell me I'll do it, I'll not back out; I'll be strong, as strong as any vamibalombie could be. That's pretty damn strong, right?

Darkness closes in, the right kind. Thick, heavy, clouds covering/uncovering the moon. Perfect for Halloween. And see there, the first ghouls are out, the little ones, shepherded by parents as they go knocking. I know it's a new thing here in Britain, we absorbed this begging tradition from those pesky Yanks but let the kids enjoy it while they can. All too soon the realities of this most horrendous of nights will dawn on them, the night when the veil is thin, when the spirits walk and revenge is on the minds of those who have it in them to take it.

Time to move.

Mind, be quiet. This is my time now. I am complete. I am one.

Walk with me, Reaper. It's time. I can wait no longer. The hunger is tearing me apart, every particle of me aches with the need to kill, to drink, to eat. I cannot kill, eat or drink. The time is now. My revenge is now.

The pain is intense. Every step hurts. Every single one. Jars right through me. Food. Food. Food. A rhythm hard to ignore, impossible to ignore.

I'll see them, or one of them, shortly. Don't know if Joanna's still there.

Not Joanna. Mother.

Not Mother, Madam. Get it right. Get their names right before I get there.

St John's Hill, busy with cars, busy with people, busy with life.

The pavements are cold, the air carries a hint of the frost which might come if the clouds move themselves away and reveal the huge moon in all its unadorned glory.

And here we are in Quarry Road. I remember it so well. And there's the train in the station as I remembered it, lights in the carriages, lights on the station, lights on the road, traffic lights, headlights and all. The train is changing drivers and guard, clanging metal as the wheels grip the rails and begin their journey back to oh so distant Shanklin. Such a long way…

You with me, Reaper?

There're people out, people in strange costumes, older than the kids I saw before. These are the serious trick and treaters, ha! Call yourself a zombie, kid? You haven't got a clue. Not a single clue. Come see a real zombie… no, better not, you might freak out and call the police. Not that they'd do anything about me, but I don't want the attention.

Lights in houses, porch lights, people expecting the trick or treaters. Pumpkin lanterns, oh, what's this? Strange yellow/black tape on a gate.

BEWARE - HAUNTED HOUSE.

Oh very funny. Try looking at the house in Well Street later when I'm through with it. Then you'll see a haunted house for sure, haunted by memories of abuse and torment and hatred and outright evil.

And here's Well Street.

And there's the house. Here's where I decide what to do. Knock or smash the door in.

Simple choice.

Here's the path I walked a thousand times and never gave it a thought.

Here's the door I went through a thousand times. Looks like it needs paint. I can provide paint, but it may not stick to the door. It'll stick to walls, though.

Not a light on in the place.

Now that's one thing I didn't think of; what I would do if they were out.

But I know what to do. Find the key in its hiding place and go in.

Oh, socked in the face with memories.

Nothing's changed. Nothing.

Yes it has. It's older, scruffier, tattier; smellier. They had dogs in here or something? Or is that me I can smell? Am I beginning to disintegrate, not having eaten since yesterday? No way of knowing.

I can't see you, Reaper, it's so damn dark.

Lounge looks worn out. Curtains have holes; see the street light through them. Same old furniture, same old pictures, same old lamps. No books. Typical. Should I leave them my book? No, it's my book. Safe in my pocket. I want my book.

Kitchen looks – worn and weary. Like me. Left the washing up, so they did.

Garden looks – the same. From the window, anyway. Wonder if…

Do I want to go out there, knowing I'm walking on her grave?

No.

Tap's dripping. Not my problem. If the water meter clocks up usage, her problem, not mine.

Silly Jesse, it won't be her problem for much longer, either…

Can I manage the stairs?

Just. Not easy. I'm tiring fast.

Here we go. Bathroom's skuzzy. Yuk.

Oh. Our room. Just the same. Jay's bed, my bed. Jay's tat still here, she's not cleared it out. Keeping it as a shrine? My side looks as it did over nine years ago. Books, music, radio, clothes on the floor still, music posters…

Oh hell… I'd forgotten. A Foreigner poster.

Oh oh oh, explains so much, why the song hit me so hard. And still does, it's on a loop in my brain. What's left of it, that is.

How did I manage to forget I had that on the wall?

Because when you live with something for a long time, it disappears, I guess, becomes part of the wallpaper. Oh oh oh, that hurts.

Right, whilst I'm hurting… basement. Now. Before I lose my nerve.

Stairs. Slowly now, slowly. No falling, don't ruin it all now, Jesse boy, hold on.

Hall is skuzzy too, didn't see that when I came in. What's she been doing with this house while I've been gone, or more like, what hasn't she been doing with this house while I've been gone, and why am I talking like this… because I know where I'm heading and it hurts, it hurts, it hurts, just as it used to.

Oh oh oh oh oh.

Hell and damnation. Hell and double damnation.

Feels like yesterday, even though I've packed so much into the last nine days. It is nine days, isn't it?

Oh oh oh oh oh oh. Can't take this.

But I know what I'm going to do now. Oh yes.

Oh look, my bed, dented by my body still. Not cleared off, nothing's been cleared. Look, the chain's still there, that accursed hated chain. Look, the bucket's still there, the broom handle she dropped, still on the floor; the bars are still there, but the TV's off. That's the only difference. The only only difference.

It's like I could walk back in and attach myself to the pipe again, were I that stupid.

Oh oh oh ohohohohohohoh…

Sounds. Did I leave the door open?

Voices, two women. Joanna still lives here, then? Didn't check the other bedrooms.

Definitely in the hall.

Right, hurry! Up the stairs, out the door, the thing I could never ever do. Oh oh oh oh ohohohohohohoh…

There they are. Joanna and Madam. Side by side. They don't look any different. Oh yes they do, Madam looks much older.

"Jesse!" Both shouting at the same time, shouting, pure horror on their faces. Good. Nice start.

"Yes."

"God… Jesse…" Joanna's all but on her knees, sliding down the wall. See what we did, Reaper, by simply walking in here? "I didn't think… saw the picture, didn't believe it…"

Shocked, white, incapable. Not the smart businesswoman I once knew.

Good. I'm not the son she once knew, either.

"Get up, Mother! This is your son asking, trick or treat?"

"Oh Jesse… not Mother, please."

"Yes? You are, aren't you? I'm waiting on your answer, Mother. Trick or Treat?"

"I…"

"I've been waiting so long for this! Answer me!"

"Jesse, we…"

"Madam, shut up! Right now this is between my mother and me. Your turn comes later."

She's shut up. She'd better. I can forgo the formal taking out if I have to. She's shocked silent now, though.

"I…"

"Talk to me, Mother. I know you know you're looking at a dead man, I know you thought I was safely under the ground, out of your life, but I'm not, am I?"

"I…"

"Well? The question's the same on this night, trick or treat?"

"I…"

"Your choice but I know what I want."

"How did you… come back to life?"

"Easy." Watching her face, watching shock change to hatred, to loathing, to outright murderous intent. Thinking she doesn't know what I can see in her, thinking she can outwit a dead man. No, she can't. Been through too much; know too much. Reaper's helping, too.

Watching Madam, frozen to the spot. Never thought she would see me again, even though I was in the paper and all, did she? What fun…

Waiting on one of them to make a move. They won't let me live if they have their way. Cold-blooded killers, both of them.

"My need for revenge was stronger than death, Mother."

"Look, Jess…"

"The name's Jesse, dead or alive, it's Jesse, if you don't mind. Only Jasmine was allowed to call me Jess and Jasmine, thanks to all you both did, is deader than I was/am."

"We didn't…"

"Madam, you did. You won't shut up, will you? You allowed her into the basement with food in her arms, living food. You know it, I know it, Mother here knows it too. I hadn't been fed that day. Madam knows what happens when I've not fed. Be warned, both of you, I've not fed today – deliberately. Wanted to come and see you when I was good and hungry."

"Stop calling me Mother!"

"Why? Madam told me all about it, Joanna, if you prefer that. I know you're my natural mother, shame you had an unnatural child but there you go; accidents do happen. I don't know who you rutted with but something went wrong, didn't it? You brought a curse into this family, a curse called Jesse."

"Yes, and I hated you from the start!"

"I know. It's always been obvious. Right, no answer to my question, so the result is, I choose. I choose Trick!"

Snap.

She's dead.

Madam's screaming fit to wake the street. Only one thing to do if this isn't all going to go pear-shaped on me.

Grab the screaming yelling hysterical being that was once my keeper and drag her into the hated basement. Tempted to throw her down the steps but don't want her injured too much – yet.

Slam the door shut, just as she used to.

"Right. Now. Shut the fuck up, OK?"

I have the broom handle now, just as she did. Oh it feels good to be on the other end. She's shit scared, it's dripping out of her, shit and piss. Oh this feels so much better than I hoped and dreamed it would.

"Jesse…"

"I. Said. Shut. The. Fuck. Up!"

Cowering in the corner. Like I used to.

Processing pictures in my head.

Did I mean to kill Joanna like that?

Yes.

No need to lie, too late to lament. Joanna's dead and out of it. No blood, though, Madam's going to provide the blood. These blank hated walls need a pattern.

"Listen, You." No Madam anymore. She's no more than meat on feet. If I wanted to eat, I could. But I won't contaminate what's left of me with her tainted flesh.

“Jesse, let me…”

I want to know what love is. Come on, song, block out this hated despised loathed being who is no part of me, never has been, never will be.

Snap off her little fingers.

Screams. How easy they broke!

“Mine fell off, You. Fell off when they rotted, where not much else fell off. Wonder why? Because you damaged mine?”

“Yes, I… so sorry, Jesse…”

“Stop with the excuses, You. Cry all you like, there’s a long way to go yet. My dick fell off too. Because of your damned chain!” Rip her coat off, her thick padded coat, rip it off, throw it and her to one side. “You haven’t got one, so what can I take from you in its place… these?”

Fat ugly blobs of tit. Repulsive in my hands. Could I tear them off?

“Jesse…”

“I. Said. Shut. The. Fuck. Up.”

“Jesse, please…”

“You’re not listening, are you?”

Listen to the screams. Most satisfying.

“You tortured me for nine years, You! Deprived me of freedom, You! Tormented me with that accursed television which you knew I hated, You!”

And…

I feel -

“You made my life a living hell, You!”

She’s dead, Jesse. Stop now.

Reaper?

Yes. She's dead. You did it, Jesse, took your revenge just as you planned.

Look at her. Well, what's left of her. I flipped, didn't I?

Yes, you did.

Look at her, bitten everywhere. I did that, didn't I?

Yes, you did.

Are you pleased with me?

But of course. Would I have stood by and let you do it if I wasn't?

Blank walls. White walls. Hated walls. Splattered with blood - but not enough.

Do I have time to do one last thing?

Yes, of course.

Right.

Find that plastic bag. Dip it in the blood.

Write on the wall in big letters

JESSE

And a bit more blood for the curlicue.

There, immortalized, so I am.

Very artistic, Jesse, very artistic indeed.

I feel…

Empty?

Yes.

Usual feeling when revenge is taken. You did well, really.

Wrecked my new padded coat, though. All that blood. Ruined, for sure. Throw the bag on Her. It's all she's fit for. Rubbish. Garbage. Crap. Landfill. Would that I could do it. Stuff her in an unmarked grave forever.

It doesn't matter anymore.

Now where do I go, Reaper?
Who am I?
I don't know. Lucifer's disciple? God's agent?
Do you want to find out?
Yes.
Are you ready to go?
Oh yes. Yes, yes, yes.
Then we will go.
I want to know what love is.
You will.
Then let's -

Author's note

I want to acknowledge the many writers who have taken part and who still take part in the weekly Prediction Challenge. This is an online challenge started by horror writer and storyteller, Lily Childs, the aim being to write a one hundred word story around three words chosen at random from a dictionary. It proved to be of inestimable help to my writing, showing me how to truly write tight, but more than that, it's the friendship, comments and support shown by fellow Predictioneers that keeps all of us coming back week after week to test our writing skills and enjoy the work of the others.

Lily handed over the Challenge to Phil Ambler, horror writer and storyteller, who ran it capably until it began to interfere with work commitments, the same reason Lily gave it up. The Challenge passed to Colleen Foley, horror writer and storyteller, to host.

Skullface grew out of the Challenge: one week the words inspired me enough to create this offbeat zombie anomaly, as he calls himself. Fellow Predictioneers asked for more, so a serial developed and morphed into a book, with installments being posted on the Challenge each week.

Skullface outgrew his allocated one hundred word installments at much the same time as Phil Ambler handed over the Challenge to Colleen Foley, who kindly granted us a page of our own so Predictioneers could continue to read this story. It was she who called this The Skullface Chronicles; I had it titled merely as Skullface. Her title is so much better and acknowledges the work of my all-time favourite writer and major writing influence, Ray Bradbury, and echoes the title of his masterpiece, The Martian Chronicles. I have nothing but grateful thanks for Colleen for the inspired choice.

Many of the names listed here have read Skullface and encouraged the story onward: others, who have fallen away over time, were an integral part of my ongoing development as a horror writer and deserve a mention.

There are not enough words to say thank you to all of you, especially Colleen, for giving us the Skullface showcase. I will just do this:

Shaun Adams
Phil Ambler
Asuqi
Chris Allinotte
David Barber
Kevin G Bufton
Lily Childs
Andrew Clark (aka Keehar)
Anthony Cowin
Sandra Davies
William Davoll
Matt Farr
Zoe Farr
Colleen Foley
Aidan Fritz
Geraghty10598
Zaiure Grey
A J Hayes
Helen Howell
RR Kovar

Veronica Marie Lewis-Shaw
Marietta Miles
MuckieDuckie
Dex Raven
Paul Richardson.
Nick Robinson
Cindy Vaskova
Dion Winton-Polak
John Xero

Skullface is most grateful.
So am I.

www.ingramcontent.com/pod-product-compliance
Lightning Source LLC
LaVergne TN
LVHW030909080826
845145LV00010B/2823

* 9 7 8 1 7 8 6 9 5 5 2 8 9 *